ARROWS OF EROS

Challenged to produce original stories of SF, fantasy and horror in some way related to sexuality, the contributors to this volume cover almost the entire field of modern speculative writing. Fantasist Geraldine Harris appears next to the maverick talents of Iain M. Banks, Stephen Gallagher's mastery of horror mingles with Brian Stableford's traditional SF approach, and established stars like Garry Kilworth and Tanith Lee stand alongside newcomer Paul Kincaid's first major sale. The new generation actually accounts for seven of the sixteen stories in this collection, in itself something that could hardly have been contemplated a year or two ago.

All that really matters, though, is that the stories themselves are entertaining. So now, if you dare, follow our sixteen contributors into the shadows cast by the dark side of sex . . .

Arrows of Eros

Unearthly Tales of Love and Death

Edited and with an introduction by Alex Stewart

NEW ENGLISH LIBRARY
Hodder and Stoughton

First published in Great Britain in
1989 by New English Library
paperbacks as a paperback original

For copyright in individual stories
see page 263

Printed and bound in Great Britain
for Hodder and Stoughton
paperbacks, a division of Hodder
and Stoughton Limited, Mill Road,
Dunton Green, Sevenoaks, Kent
TN13 2YA (Editorial Office:
47 Bedford Square, London
WC1B 3DP) by Richard Clay
Limited, Bungay, Suffolk. Photoset
by Rowland Phototypesetting
Limited, Bury St Edmunds, Suffolk.

British Library C.I.P.

Arrows of Eros.
1. Short stories in English. 1945–
Special themes.
Sexuality. Anthologies
I. Stewart, Alex
823'.01'08353

ISBN 0-450-50249-X

Contents

INTRODUCTION

THIS ANTHOLOGY STARTED life as one of those ideas that sounds great in a bar at two in the morning. This particular bar was at the Milford writers' conference, and, in the way such things do, the conversation one night moved inexorably from a general discussion about sex in SF, to why so few stories have managed to deal with it successfully, to how we all thought it *should* be handled, to Hey Kids, Here's A Swell Barn, Let's Do The Show Right Here. Blearing down to breakfast the following morning, I found last night's bull session had suddenly become This Book You're Going To Do . . .

Luckily everyone's enthusiasm for the idea remained strong. Five of the original bar-room pundits have stories in this volume, and several others submitted manuscripts that fell in the Darwinian struggle to remain on the short-list as it was slowly whittled down to manageable proportions. Even more gratifying was the number of other authors who, when approached, recoiled in modest horror, only to reappear a month or so later with plain brown envelopes.

Even so, an anthology like this could never have been published a few years ago. Not because of any pressure from the self-appointed guardians of public morality, but because, after the boom of the early seventies, speculative writing in Britain was, once again, in the doldrums. With virtually no markets at home for short fiction, British authors had either to adapt to the requirements of the American magazines, or give up writing short stories altogether.

This situation remained more or less stable until 1982, when *Interzone* first appeared. Despite the flak it's been attracting ever since, the emerging generation of British writers at last had a forum for the kind of stories *we* wanted to write. Several contributors to this book, including myself, first appeared on its pages.

But if *Interzone* struck the spark, it was *Other Edens* that lit the flame. Simply by showing that original anthologies *would* sell, despite conventional publishing wisdom to the contrary, it opened the door to a number of other projects that might never have been considered a few months before. This book is one such project.

Challenged to produce original stories of SF, fantasy, and horror in some way related to sexuality, the contributors to this volume cover almost the entire field of modern speculative writing. Fantasist Geraldine Harris appears next to the maverick talents of Iain Banks, Stephen Gallagher's mastery of horror mingles with Brian Stableford's traditional SF approach, and established stars like Garry Kilworth and Tanith Lee stand alongside newcomer Paul Kincaid's first major sale. The new generation actually accounts for seven of the sixteen stories in this collection, in itself something that could hardly have been contemplated a year or two ago.

All that really matters, though, is that the stories are entertaining. So now, if you dare, follow our sixteen contributors into the shadows cast by the dark side of sex.

Alex Stewart

WILDLAND

BRIAN STABLEFORD

BRIAN STABLEFORD

Brian Stableford, born in 1948, is not only a lecturer in sociology at the University of Reading, but is also an under-appreciated British SF writer. He is the author of over thirty novels, some of which have appeared only in the United States as paperback originals. They range from *Cradle of the Sun* to *The Empire of Fear*. His prodigious output also includes much non-fiction, including, among others, *Future Man: Brave New World or Genetic Nightmare?* and *Scientific Romance in Britain 1890–1950*, all of which have been received with great enthusiasm. Recently, he has begun to write short stories in earnest, some of which have been published in the prestigious science fiction magazine, *Interzone*.

BURSLEM AND OKUYAMA came to the surface of the Earth from the city of Chicago Underground in the year which, according to the calendar they kept, was 3856 years after the advent of the ice. The ice, of course, was long gone – retired to the poles by the activity of the Wildland – but it had been the return of the ice following the failure of the legendary Greenhouse Plan which had forced the Tripartite Division of mankind, which had in turn given birth to the Cities Underground. It was, therefore, entirely natural that the citizens of those deep-set caverns should count the years of their history from that vital moment.

The two men's mission was to gather certain specimens which were required by the Exobiological Research Institute, in which they served as scientific officers. The institute had been founded more than two thousand years earlier, commissioned to investigate the possibility of reclaiming the surface of the Earth from the alien Wildland. It had made steady progress in understanding the biology of the invading ecosystem, but there was as yet no viable plan by which humans might seek to regain ecological hegemony over the world which they still considered to be theirs.

Burslem and Okuyama's task was a routine one, which neither man had any reason to regard as being of particular importance; but every journey into the Wildland was fraught with danger, and no such mission could be treated casually.

The two men wore sterile suits which isolated them entirely from the Wildland, sheathing their bodies in tough plastic. The water-bags and food-drip packs inside each suit would last for fourteen days; the waste-recycling apparatus would, in theory, sustain a man for a further ten days if necessary, but the biochemical side-effects of such emergency sustenance were uncomfortable and to a degree unpredictable. Time, therefore, was of the essence – as it was whenever a mission took men far from the airlocks which linked the underworld to the World Above.

Despite their common cause, the two men differed considerably. They contrasted even in appearance, for Burslem was much the burlier of the two, but the more important contrast was in their attitudes to the Wildland.

Burslem had always been fascinated by the alien life-system, and had joined the institute in order to discover everything he could about it. He thought the Wildland fabulously beautiful, and loved wandering there; he found an aesthetic delight in the wonders of its biochemical genetics, which were so much more subtle, flexible and powerful than the genetic systems of Earth's native life. To the supposed aim of the institute – the utter destruction of the Wildland – he paid respectful lip-service, but he knew that this was not an aim likely to be fulfilled in his own time, or even in the remote future. He knew that in any war between the Wildland and men, the Wildland would be the victor, and he had sworn loyalty to the institute's cause mainly in order to gain the opportunity to learn more about the object of his fascination.

Okuyama, on the other hand, considered the Wildland to be the ultimate evil. He hated and loathed it, and the object of *his* research into its nature was the faint hope that one day he or another might make that crucial breakthrough which would allow its destruction.

Both these attitudes were unrepresentative. The vast majority of the inhabitants of the Cities Underground had no interest at all in the surface of the Earth, and could not have cared less whether that surface was in the grip of an ice age or an alien invader, or whether it was only a charming myth that the Earth *had* a surface. (This view was actually held by a few eccentric cultists, who asserted that the universe was an infinite solid with occasional lacunae, and believed that the myth of the surface was maintained by the scientific élite simply as a means of winning prestige.) Most underworlders were entirely content with the underworld, and could imagine no other way of life. If their uncivilised ancestors had once lived on the surface, that merely went to prove how uncivilised they were.

The possibility (seriously feared by such as Okuyama) that the Wildland would one day invade the underworld and consume it just as it had consumed the surface biosphere, was not taken seriously by ordinary people, who had complete faith in the airlocks, and had not the intellectual capacity to imagine such a disaster. Underground life had severely constricted the imaginative horizons of most men – on this point Burslem and Okuyama would have agreed. It was the only matter on which they did agree; they did not like one another, and perhaps it was a mistake to send them out together.

At first, Burslem and Okuyama's work went smoothly. The region close to the airlocks was not so densely forested as many, perhaps because the streets and buildings of Old Chicago had once stood here, and their disintegration had left a vile soil which even the Wildland could not make fecund. The very sparseness of the local flora, however, made it necessary for the two explorers to venture further afield, into the valley which had once been Lake Michigan before the Wildland had absorbed the greater part of its waters.

They passed, therefore, from relatively open terrain

into the crowded forest, laying traps as they went. The traps would hopefully contain motiles when they picked them up on the return journey. Occasionally they paused to gather florets and filaments, or chisel away strips of bark, though their real goal was to gather more exotic specimens.

As they proceeded, it became gradually more difficult to force a way through the Wildland's undergrowth, and the machetes with which they hacked at the impeding vegetation were blunted by the ligneous stems. There were also traps set by the Wildland which had to be avoided – cunningly concealed pitfalls and whiplashing vines.

By the end of their second day, they were both very tired. It was hard labour indeed to build the fire which they must keep alive all night, because it would keep at bay with flame and smoke some of the insectile elements of the Wildland which, if given time, might chew right through the plastic of their suits and let the Wildland in.

'This work should be done by robots,' said Okuyama, morosely. 'It should not be necessary to risk men. We have lost nine in the last seven years – even Rogulski, who knew this awful wilderness better than any of us.'

Privately, Burslem thought that it would be a terrible shame to be banned from this wonderful place, but that was not a view he dared present to Okuyama. Instead, he said, 'The robots cannot do the job. The Wildland quickly finds ways to frustrate them, and they are very expensive to produce. It may be a harsh judgment, but given the scope of our resources, men are more expendable than such sophisticated machines.'

'That's a terrible attitude,' Okuyama told him. 'We should count human life more precious than that.'

'I do not say that I think it myself,' Burslem replied. 'I merely observe that such calculations are understandable.'

'New York and Miami have the benefit of the sub-Atlantic tunnels, and their miners supply them more than adequately with vital inorganics. If they were not so tight-fisted in their trading with Chicago, we would have resources enough. If the Wildland is to be defeated all men must work together, instead of striving for advantage, man over man and city over city.'

'Rivalry between neighbours and between cities is of far greater importance to most underworlders than the eventual conquest of the Wildland,' sighed Burslem. 'They price comfort far above knowledge, and grudge us their support. It is the way things are, and it is useless to complain. We do what we can.'

They pressurised their bubble-tent and rigged their alarms, then settled down to sleep. They slept lightly; in spite of their tiredness, surrounded as they were by dangers. Shortly after dawn their drips released an alarm-call of stimulant psychochemicals, and they bundled up their kit with quick efficiency.

As they moved out into the Michigan basin they had to quit the ground and make their way up into the forest canopy.

Because the 'trees' of the Wildland were not separate entities, their branches often fused, making highways far above the ground which were used by the larger motiles. The mid-growth of the forest was denser than the undergrowth, at least around the giant trunks which were the Wildland's skeleton. There was more colour here, too; very little light penetrated to the ground and the undergrowth was all greys and browns, while the mid-growth showed countless pastel shades of red, blue and gold. The greens of the high canopy formed a complex geometrical pattern against the blue sky, letting the light through in a carefully ordered way.

The mid-growth also concealed more dangers for the travellers. Nettlenets and stinging anemones could not hurt them in their suits, nor did they need to fear the Wildland's battery of poisons, but there were gluegaws and bowerconstrictors to be avoided, and there was always the possibility of a fall. The higher they went, the further there was to fall, and though there was plenty of vegetation between themselves and the ground, it was not always possible to halt or slow a fall sufficiently to avoid broken limbs.

They were threatened once by an arachnoid – an eight-legged thing which straddled an open space between three relatively bare trunks, thirty metres from tip to tip, though its 'body' was only a couple of metres in diameter. Okuyama drew his gun and put three bullets into it, but it simply withdrew, in leisurely fashion, into the high canopy, dripping ichor as it went. It was not a true animal, of course – nothing in the Wildland was. When it returned to the tree which had spawned it, which was presumably close by, it would merge its flesh with its parent, and its tissues would be patiently renewed.

Later, they watched from a distance as an arachnoid and a frogling fought on a great palmate leaf high above them. The frogling was bigger and more mobile, and had its long tongue to use as a weapon, but it was an unequal contest and once the arachnoid had begun to tie the frogling down with the silk that flooded from its spinnerets, the issue was settled.

Why such fights went on, the humans were still not sure. Some theorists believed that the Wildland was best regarded as a single gargantuan organism, and that all the individuals which it modelled on the Earthly creatures it had long ago ingested were simply units of its body, like cells or organelles. If this was true, then the destruction of one motile by another could be seen only in terms of internal regulation and waste-disposal. Others believed, though, that there were many individuals in the Wildland, still involved in their own struggle for existence, and that the struggle had almost been resolved – not according to the logic of the survival of the fittest and the extinction of the less fit, but by the ecological equivalent of a treaty, in which the individuals traded genetic materials even while retaining, in some enigmatic sense, their own identities. If this were true, then the devouring of some motiles by others could be seen either as a fading atavistic echo, or as part of the pattern of genetic trading.

Burslem often devoted long hours of his spare time to deliberation upon this problem. Okuyama did not care much one way or the other.

When they were high enough in the canopy, Burslem and Okuyama selected what seemed to be a fairly young 'tree' and began to assemble the telescopic tap which could be driven, with much effort, deep into its body. Their intention was to drive a hollow metal tube through the bark and ligneous tissue of the trunk into the pithy heart where the 'nucleus' lay, in order to draw off some of the genetic soup within. Nearer to the ground, the trunks were far too thick and even at this level an old trunk was likely to be so tough as to make the job very difficult indeed; but the young, slender trunk which they had found seemed unlikely to present them with too stern a task. They took turns with the hammer-drill, first Burslem and then Okuyama. It was while Burslem was preparing to take his second turn that he noticed the bronzed face watching them from a tangle of blooms twenty metres away on a horizontal bough.

Burslem dropped the drill, and took a step toward the watcher, then cursed himself silently for giving away the fact that he was aware of the other's presence. The face disappeared, and he broke into a run, racing along the branch with a reckless disregard for its thinness. He plunged pell-mell into the clump of red florets, groping for something more solid than the slender curled stems that bore them. He clutched something, but could not tell whether it was an arm or a leg. It twisted, trying to escape his grip, and the movement of the other body pulled him deeper into the florets, but he dug his fingers in as hard as he could, determined not to lose his prey.

He lost his balance, but concentrated entirely on trying

to get his other hand on the wriggling form which he had so unexpectedly managed to capture. He caught what felt like an ankle, and now both his hands were clinging tight. He felt such a burst of joy and triumph that he did not realise immediately that both he and his captive had tumbled from the tangle of blooms, and were falling.

He was undermost, and the wind was knocked out of him as his back collided with another branch, but still he did not let go. He gasped for air, feeling as though his chest was in a vice, his lungs unable to draw. His shoulders were battered again as he fell into something softer and springier, but it was not enough to break the fall. It did, however, cause the pair of them to tumble in mid-fall, so that now it was the other who was underneath.

When they cannoned again into something hard it was not Burslem who took the brunt of the impact. Agonized by his attempts to suck air into his lungs, though, he felt as if the plastic of the sterile suit was choking him, and the iron will that was forcing his hands to retain their fierce clutch suddenly died in him. He felt his body relaxing and, as he finally managed to get a breath of oxygen, his sense of triumph turned to a conviction of defeat. Then the fall was abruptly stopped by a final solid impact, and the other body jerked free. Dizzily, he cursed himself again, more spitefully than he had thought possible.

By the time Okuyama reached Burslem the latter was able to breathe again, and though he could not find the energy to sit up he thought that his limbs were probably unbroken. He had not entirely lost consciousness, but felt light-headed and remote, not fully in contact with his body.

Without ceremony, Okuyama bundled him over, checking his suit for damage before prodding his arms and legs with an inquiring finger.

'You're okay,' he said, finally.

'I lost him,' complained Burslem. 'I had him, and I lost him.'

'No you didn't,' Okuyama told him. 'And as far as appearances are concerned, it's a she. It's flat out with a twisted leg. Broken, I suppose, if it has bones to break.'

Burslem sat bolt upright and looked around. They were on a broad, spatulate bough in the middle canopy, cushioned by fern-like excrescences. About a metre away was the form of the 'person' he had grappled with, looking for all the world like a sixteen-year-old girl with tanned skin and blonde hair. She was quite naked, and looked entirely human – which of course she was not.

'There are supposed to be no dryads in these latitudes,' he murmured. 'No one out of Chicago ever brought in hard evidence. I never believed the sightings. Imagination, I thought. Is she dead?'

Okuyama shrugged. 'Doubt it,' he said. 'Nothing its tree couldn't put right, if it could get back to it. Up to us to see that doesn't happen – don't want it dissolving before our eyes. Got to get it back, and carefully too. Wrap it up in the bubble-tent, I guess. Got to keep it out of contact, just in case. Do you suppose it can *talk*?'

'I don't think so. When they pushed through the sub-Atlantic cable New York's data systems interfaced with Europe's, and the French fed back some stuff about attempts to make contact with the Wildmen in North Africa. All the indications are that the Wildmen are mindless. You think the trees have traded genomes all the way from the tropics? Can *these* trees produce Wildmen now? Must be, I guess. She can't have come all the way from the Amazon, can she?'

'It's not a she,' Okuyama corrected him, roughly. 'It's not human. It's a bit of an alien plant, right? And it doesn't mean us any good. Hell, Bur – you think there are any more around? You think they'll try to get it back?'

Burslem frowned. Despite his enthusiasm to know

everything about the Wildland that could be dug out of the data systems, and notwithstanding a particular fascination with the notion of humanoid motiles, he knew very little about dryads that might help answer Okuyama's question. He rose to his feet, painfully and a little unsteadily. He was battered and bruised, but he could walk.

'We've got to get the equipment,' he said. 'We'll abandon the tap and start back right away. We've got to get her home. She's worth more than a bucketful of gene-soup. I think you're right about the bubble-tent. You go get it – I'll stand guard here.' He took the gun from his holster, and checked that the fall hadn't damaged it.

Okuyama nodded, and began to make his way back up the trunk, scaling it by means of the rope which he had fastened in order to make the descent.

Burslem looked around carefully, anxious to spot any other watching faces, but there seemed to be nowhere close at hand where they might hide. He knelt beside the immobile form, and touched the dryad's arm, but she did not stir. He put the plastic covering the back of his left hand close to her mouth, attempting to detect the condensation of her breath, but he was not even certain that she *did* breathe. The Wildland often reproduced outward form without inward structure. Internally, an arachnid was nothing like a spider, though a frogling *was* recognisably similar to a frog. Maybe the girl did have lungs and a heart, but there was no way he could be certain.

He looked into her face, astonished by her beauty. How could the Wildland possibly reproduce such aesthetic perfection? And why should it? He knew, of course, what Okuyama's opinion would be – that the girl was a carefully-designed trap, a beguiling lorelei intended to mesmerize men with lust, clutching them with simulated passion while the Wildland's other agents took advantage of their distraction. Burslem was not so sure. He wondered whether the making of such humanoids might not be a god-like endeavour of creation – the invention of a potentially-intelligent species to complete the Wildland's Eden, to be the mind and soul of its ecosystem. He was not of the party which considered the Wildland intelligent, but he often speculated as to whether the human genetic material taken in by the alien invader when it destroyed all indigenous surface life might enable it eventually to *become* intelligent, or to grant intelligence to some of its motiles.

With his sheathed fingertips he traced the line of her jaw, then drew a line downwards, to the vestigial nipples on her useless breast. He continued, reaching the phantom navel in her abdomen before he suddenly looked up, guiltily, to see that Okuyama had returned with the kit and was watching him curiously.

'You see,' said Burslem, 'Adam and Eve might indeed have had navels, though neither was born of woman.'

Okuyama scowled, and Burslem realised that the small man was very frightened by what had happened. While he was excited by the unprecedented discovery, Okuyama was in a turmoil of dread, and would not rest easy until this wonderful creature was safe in a sterile tank, ready to be vivisected by careful mechanical manipulators – for such would surely be her fate, if they could get her to the airlocks. For one brief moment, Burslem was sickened by this thought, and tempted to abandon the catch: to let her return to her tree and be re-absorbed into its flesh, perhaps to be regenerated again, healthy and whole. Then he realised that such an opportunity as this could not be lost, however horrible it would be to turn such beauty over to the investigating thrust of scalpels and syringes.

Burslem stood back, and let Okuyama drag the dead weight of the dryad on to the spread-out plastic tent, roll her up, and seal her tightly within – cut off as completely as they were themselves from the Wildland.

If she did need to breathe, then she would very soon

be dead; this thought too nearly called forth an objection
from Burslem, though he strangled the impulse as
Okuyama looked up at him again.

'I'll carry her,' said Burslem. 'You bring the equipment.'

'*I'll* carry *it*,' Okuyama corrected him. '*You* bring the
equipment.'

It was Burslem's turn to scowl, but he turned away,
and did as he was told. Despite the fact that he was the
smaller man, Okuyama seemed to have no difficulty in
hoisting the dryad over his shoulder. Together, they set
off across a web-like bridge of branches, trying to find a
place where they could safely descend to ground level,
where they would be able to find a less hazardous path
back to the airlocks.

Okuyama was in a virtual fever of anxious thought.
He knew of Burslem's admiring fascination for the
alien ecosphere, though he was careful never to argue
about it. Better, he thought, to let a traitor think that
his treason was not discovered. Even before he had
seen the lascivious way in which Burslem touched the
thing, he had known that Burslem would be taken in
by it, would fall in love with it. Burslem was blind to
the truth of what this actually was, would think of it
as though it were a person, would want to defend it
against the enquiries to which it would have to be
subjected. He must beware of Burslem, on his guard
against any act of treachery.

If necessary, Okuyama thought, *I must be ready to shoot
him, in case he should lead us both to our deaths.*

With this thought in mind he was careful to stay
behind his companion, keeping the other man under
observation. As they made their descent toward the
forest floor, he was forced on several occasions to lower
the dead weight of the trussed dryad upon a rope,
though he did not like to let Burslem handle the thing.
More than once he wondered whether it might be

sensible to smash the dryad's face with the handle of the drill, to destroy that seductive allure. But he did not do it, because he was a scientist, and it went against the grain to damage a specimen.

He could not help wondering why the Wildland had now begun producing dryads in this region. When the alien spores had seeded the planet, the Tripartite Division had already taken place, and there were no men on the surface outside the tropics. In the past, the Wildland had produced its humanoids only in those regions where it had found and absorbed human beings. This humanoid did not seem to be modelled on any tropical race, and he wondered whether the Wildland had taken its genetic inspiration from those luckless scientific officers who had come up from the underworld never to return.

Okuyama began to look more closely at the dryad's features, wondering if there was some hint of Rogulski there, or of anyone else he had known. But in fact he had never known any real human being quite so handsome. It had not the paleness of the citizens of Chicago, and it was so very smooth, so perfect in its symmetry. He could not help but wonder whether a man actually could have sexual intercourse with such a creature – whether the slit between its legs gave access to a cavity, or whether it was merely an imitative fold in the skin. He tried to put such thoughts deliberately out of his mind, because he knew that the Wildland had created this monster in order to put them there, but that knowledge was itself a guarantee that the thoughts kept returning.

As the day wore on, the burden became very cumbersome, but he refused to give way to the temptation to turn it over to his more muscular companion, because he was afraid of what might develop if he did.

When Burslem realised that Okuyama was determined to keep him away from the dryad, he was angry. He was insulted by the other's lack of trust, annoyed by the foolishness which made the little man stagger on even when it was clear that he was overburdened, and distressed by the fact that he was denied the opportunity to exercise his curiosity. He wanted to examine the dryad more closely, to find out more about her anatomy, to study her eyes and her breasts, to savour the element of the miraculous in the god-like workings of the alien being which had claimed Earth for its new Eden.

Of course, he told himself, no matter what Okuyama might think, there was nothing of lust in his curiosity. For all the romance in his soul, he was not about to be bewitched by an alien siren. No matter how beautiful she might be, he would not be tempted to trust her to make contact with his own flesh. The Wildland was too greedy for new organic material, and he was not so stupid as to believe that he might be reincarnated – mind and memory intact – as a dryad scion of some lofty forest giant.

Whenever he looked back at Okuyama, resentfully, he was alarmed to see that the other man seemed shifty and furtive. He did not like the way Okuyama clung to his burden, or the way his hands seemed to clutch in a specially intimate fashion at the parts of the humanoid body. His suspicions were aroused long before they reached the ground, when they stopped for the night, but it was when they rested that he really became aware of the extent of Okuyama's paranoia. Okuyama would not move from the side of the corpse – for surely, now, it must be dead – and became agitated if Burslem approached. The small man was so tired that he would not help Burslem build a fire, and though he told Burslem to get some sleep, it was obvious that he did not intend to do so himself.

Burslem feared the effect which darkness and sleeplessness might have on a consciousness already tortured by strange fears and desires. He knew that he too would have to stay awake, and be on his guard, lest Okuyama's state of mind should deteriorate still further, and lead to tragedy. It was obvious that this unprecedented disturbance of their routine mission had thrown Okuyama into such a panic that his sanity could no longer be taken for granted.

When he realised that Burslem did not intend to go to sleep, Okuyama knew that he was in danger. The other man was watching him, carefully but covertly, and Okuyama knew that some vile or dangerous scheme must be hatching in that cunning brain. Despite all his efforts, he had clearly been unable to prevent Burslem from becoming erotically obsessed with their strange captive. What the big man intended to do about it, Okuyama could not guess, but he knew that he must remain alert to any possibility, and that he must be prepared to act if Burslem showed any sign of doing something foolish.

He kept a lamp burning behind and above him, so that by its light he could see the dryad and Burslem. He let his tired limbs relax, but strove to keep his thoughts and senses sharp and clear. He was glad that they would not need to spend another night on the surface – or should not, if they made as much haste as possible in the gloomy morning. Of course, they must not stop to gather samples or to empty the traps they had set. The dryad was far more important than anything else.

Despite his best efforts, Okuyama began to doze off several times, and eventually lost all track of time. Nevertheless, he was sure that he had not actually slept when he was jerked back to awareness by a touch upon his ankle.

At first he thought Burslem must have crept close, but then he realised that it was the dryad that was moving – writhing slowly and sinuously as it struggled against the plastic sheeting within which it was wrapped. Its eyes were open, and by the bright light of the lamp he could see that they seemed crazed with panic. Its mouth was opening and shutting, as if trying to release a scream, though there was no air to give it force. Its hands, not quite immobilised by the constraining bonds, groped toward his thighs.

His first reaction was one of mingled fear and disgust, and he fought an impulse to leap to his feet and move backwards until he was well out of range of the desperate hands. Then he realised that there was much more at stake than his own instinctive reaction, and he knew that if Burslem were to see the thing like this, *he* might well react with pity, wanting to loosen the bonds that bound the tent about the thing – perhaps even to allow it a little air.

When he looked up, he saw that Burslem was indeed coming forward to see what was happening, with some degree of urgency.

Reflexively, he drew his gun.

Burslem could not see what had happened to make Okuyama suddenly so agitated, because the lamp was behind Okuyama's head, and the dryad was in his shadow. Nevertheless, he saw the other man jerk convulsively, as if waking from a nightmare, or as if some creeping motile had come to attack him. Whatever it was, though, something had clearly occurred, and Burslem came rapidly to his feet, starting forward so hurriedly that he did not even spare himself the time to ask what was wrong.

When he saw Okuyama go for his gun, he naturally went for his own, but he had hardly got it free from the holster when Okuyama fired.

The bullet went wide, and did not actually touch Burslem's body. He felt only a momentary twitch, as if someone had tried to catch his sleeve, and not quite succeeded. Nevertheless, there was not the slightest doubt in his mind that Okuyama had fired at him, intending to kill, and that the shot had missed only because his own reflexes had betrayed him.

Burslem knew instantly that Okuyama had gone completely mad, and that he must protect himself from the threat of further injury. Even so, he did not want to kill the other man if it could possibly be avoided. He did not fire his own gun, but launched himself instead at his assailant, who had not yet succeeded in raising himself from a sitting position. When he brought his weight down on the body of the smaller man, he succeeded in knocking both of his arms wide, and knocking the wind out of him.

Okuyama did not get the chance to fire a second shot, and Burslem was able to wrench the gun from his fingers and hurl it away. Knowing that the pliant plastic would not break, he brought his own gun down hard on the top of Okuyama's helmet, and he felt the other man go instantly limp beneath him, knocked unconscious.

He breathed out in relief. When daylight came, he thought, he could make Okuyama see sense again, and forget his lunacy long enough to get the dryad back to the airlock and down into Chicago Underground.

It was not until he came to his feet that he realised that although Okuyama was quite still, the dryad was not.

While he stared down at the body, still struggling against its restraints, he put his hand up reflexively to scratch an itch on his upper arm.

When he felt the edges of the tear which the bullet had ripped in his suit, he knew that he was in far worse trouble than he had thought. The Wildland's tiniest agents could reach him even through the smallest of tears.

He turned around quickly, dropping to his knees to search through the packs he had carried all day, desperate to find a sealant that would close the rip in his suit, hoping that he might, by some miracle, be just in time to save himself.

Just as he found the tube of sealant, though, he felt

something coil around his wrist and clamp it tight. It
was only a bowerconstrictor, and would normally have
been no serious threat, but in the present situation, any
delay at all might prove fatal. While he wrestled with
the thing, he realised that the fire was burning too low,
and that the air was suddenly full of insectiles, swooping
about him almost as if they had been summoned.

As he began to flail about with his free hand, he
felt the panic rising in his blood, and he knew that
the Wildland had him at last, and could do with him
whatever it wished.

When Okuyama woke, it was long after dawn. Even
here, in the depths of dense forest, a little sunlight crept
through the layers of the canopy. It was perhaps as well,
because the lamp which had been behind him was no
longer burning.

At first, as he raised his head, blinking his eyes and
trying to peer into the gloom, he could not remember
what had happened. Then, as a blinding shock of pain
made him shut his eyes, it all came back to him. Burslem,
seeing that the dryad was not dead after all, had come
at him, and had gone for his gun. He had tried to drive
him back with a warning shot, but the poor fool had
come so fast that he was not even certain that he
had been able to fire wide. Then that massive body had
squashed him flat, and he had struck his head . . . which
now felt as if it had been split apart.

With his hand on his forehead, and trying hard not to
move, Okuyama forced his eyes open again, determined
to see what there was to be seen.

He began immediately to wish that he had not awak-
ened so soon.

The dryad, no longer swaddled in the tent and bound
tightly about, was some three metres away. She had her
back to him, and could not have seen him anyhow, but
he guessed from her attitude that her attention was fully
taken up by what she was doing. She was kneeling

astride a supine human form, moving rhythmically, her head thrown back as if she were entranced.

He judged from the urgency of her motions that the act of intercourse was coming rapidly to its climax, and he judged that he had very little time in which to act, but his gun was no longer in his hand, and was nowhere close by. Because he had carried the dryad while Burslem had carried the rest of the heavy equipment, there was nothing else immediately to hand which he could use as a weapon, and so he was empty-handed when he came to his feet.

Despite the pain in his head he lurched desperately toward the oblivious couple, cursing Burslem for the appalling weakness which had made him such a ready and stupid victim of the Wildland. He grabbed the dryad around the neck, and yanked her savagely backwards, as if he thought that there might be some slight chance of saving Burslem if only he could interrupt the unnatural congress before it reached its climax. He tried to establish a strangling grip, or one which might have enabled him to break her neck if she had humanoid vertebrae, but he was not strong enough, and he realised that she was neither so small nor so frail as she had been when they had captured her.

Okuyama felt stupidly weak as she turned within his hold to grapple with him, and even without the injury to his head she would have been the stronger. She was much bigger now than she had been when he had been able to carry her, and he thought for a moment that this must be a different dryad, but when he saw her face he knew that it was not.

He wished, desperately, that he had tried to find the gun instead of launching himself into what had turned out to be a ridiculously ineffectual attack. He lay on his back, staring up into her wide-eyed face, which was still very beautiful despite the fact that it now had doubled in size since last he had looked into those features.

She smiled, and he had to turn away, looking toward

the body of the other man which she had so recently sat astride. That body, stripped of most of its flesh as well as its plastic suit, was grotesquely crumpled and molten.

'Poor Burslem,' he whispered. 'I knew, you see . . .'

But there was no point in explaining. She had no thoughts of her own, no desires, no feelings. She could not know how she had tempted Burslem, and driven him mad. It was merely her nature, to draw men to damnation, and she could not understand what it was that she did, or how, or why.

When she began to explore, with fingers that were big and clumsy now, the fastenings which sealed his suit, he knew that he had only a limited time to live before he too was consumed by that absurd parody of love-making . . . just as all that fraction of Earth's biosphere which had remained on the surface after the Tripartite Divison had been consumed in equally strange rituals.

'You can never win,' he told her. 'Because men like me will never yield to your seductions. You may rape us, one by one, but you can never utterly destroy us, because we cannot be fooled. We cannot be tricked into helping you, as poor Burslem was. The Burslems you will always conquer, but the Okuyamas you never can, for we are the true men, and we will always see you for what you really are.'

And yet, despite his resolution, his courage, and his knowledge of the truth, when she finally began to draw him into her body, he could not help feeling that this was where he had always truly belonged.

THE MOTIVATION

DAVID LANGFORD

DAVID LANGFORD

David Langford took an MA in Physics at Brasenose College, Oxford and until 1980 was a weapons physicist at the Atomic Weapons Research Establishment near Aldermaston. Now a full-time author, he has contributed to many encyclopaedias, reference books and magazines including *New Scientist* and *Science and Public Policy*. His first book was *War in 2080: the Future of Military Technology* (1979); he subsequently collaborated with Charles Platt on *Micromania: the Whole Truth about Home Computers* and with Brian Stableford on *The Science in Science Fiction*. His novels include *The Space Eater* and *The Leaky Establishment*, a satire about a weapons research establishment.

THE SHOP WAS a rich stew of smells, dry rot and cigarettes and sweat. Its buzzing fluorescent light couldn't cut through the staleness, and the August sun was not allowed to penetrate. As with every branch of this exclusive chain, the display window was painted dead black; the invisibility of its promised BOOKS AND MAGAZINES was full and sufficient advertisement of the stock.

Peter Edgell reminded himself regularly that he was slumming, that this wasn't his true niche in the literary world. An observer, that was it, scanning the customers who fingered BOOKS AND MAGAZINES through their aseptic plastic film. From behind the counter Peter read the customers and savoured the emotions that burned as pungently as the shop's smell. Businessmen brimmed with a synthetic heartiness, wielding it like a charm against limp fears. Younger nondescripts let off their little firecrackers of defensive aggression. Those too young were allowed a brief ration of giggles before being chased away; most pitiful were the fossil emotions of the very old, who from long habit cringed furtively and offered token mumbles of 'Just getting it for a mate, see?'

Peter welcomed them all, not only because each swing of the door wafted fresh, clean exhaust fumes through the sweaty closeness: with his half a talent, he saw the pornophiles as raw material. One day his special insight would pin them down in some astonishing piece of journalism, a cancellation of his failures at university and everywhere else. Jessica Mitford, Tom Wolfe, whatsisname in *Private Eye* – he'd be with them one day. The thought was so thumbed and worn that it skidded past like an overly familiar quotation.

Minor hubbub arose as old Benson ejected a gaggle of browsers from the small back room. He swept them managerially before him, exuding a steady dribble of apology and exhortation, as though dealing with drunks or kids where the secret was to keep talking and keep calm. Peter was checking a wad of magazines being returned for credit at the usual vast discount (you riffled very carefully through the clean-limbed poses, and refused them if pages were either incomplete or stuck together). Benson reached past him to the till.

'Lock up half five like usual,' he said, passing a greyish handkerchief over a broadly glistening sweep of baldness. His other hand methodically stripped the till of banknotes – so that when he looked up and added 'I'm trusting you, Peter,' it was an effort not to snap back, 'What the fuck with?'

'See you tomorrow,' said Peter, wondering again about the manager: there was nothing to read from him, as though he had no feelings whatever. Perhaps you got like that after ten years in the trade. A roar of traffic and a gale of carbon monoxide swept through the door as Benson slouched out on the weekly errand which was not supposed to have anything to do with Thursday evening's greyhound races.

A dozen or so literary and artistic items changed hands in the final forty minutes of trade, but business was slack without the lure of the back room. It was a milder breed of customer that Peter finally chased out: men whose longings didn't burn as brightly.

He carried the old, battered till into the back, locked it in the concealed cupboard (cunningly papered over, but outlined with a frieze of greasy fingerprints) dedi-

cated to Stronger Stuff. Which left him half an hour before his bus: this had happened before, and Peter had
spent the time in unedifying study of 'strong' goods. His
eyes had widened several times as he flicked through;
the only after-effect had been a slightly reduced appetite
for sausage and chips that evening, and a greatly reduced
opinion of certain customers.

The muse of this art-form, he had written conscientiously
in one of his notebooks, *is a species of Blatant Beast, repelling
the assault of our curiosity by revealing far more than we wish
to know.*

Today, curiosity took him through the back room into
the dusty regions of no-customer's-land. There was a
toilet stinking of ammonia; a passageway lined with
miscellaneous old stock, growing ever more unsaleable
as mice chewed it into lace . . . and the grimy kitchen
where the mouse-smell was stronger yet, though all that
was ever made there was the tea they drank daily from
mugs whose brown inner stain exactly matched that of
the toilet. A hair-dryer might have indicated some token
concession to cleanliness, but was only used for one
of Peter's morning chores; shrink-wrapping the latest
literary arrivals.

Peter tugged at the sliding door of the old kitchen
cupboard; a beetle ran out as it scraped to one side.
Within was the cobwebbed box Benson had mentioned
as 'good for a laugh'. The scrawled caption was simply
'DUDS'. It had seemed a neat idea, at the time, for
one of those articles which one day might found his
reputation . . . an article dealing with what had once
been good stout porn, perhaps even Strong Stuff, but
which social inflation had rendered as worthless as copper coinage. Peter set great store by ideas and concepts
and documentation, a bony framework requiring not too
much fleshing out, not too much writing up.

A powerfully musty smell rose as he lifted the flaps of
the box. It was stuffed full with the anonymous brown

envelopes Benson used for reserve photographs. Peter found himself breathing a little faster, caught in an absurd excitement at the prospect of material which, as one might put it, not even Benson dared offer for sale. However . . .

'Tit pictures,' he murmured crossly, after a moment. They could hardly market stuff which would look staid on the racks at W. H. Smith. And the girl's hairstyle seemed alien: she was dated despite nakedness, with even her shape being subtly wrong. Models (in or out of quotes) had evolved a leaner, more predatory look. With waning excitement Peter unearthed poses having all the erotic impact of Victorian family groups; there were even examples of the forgotten art of the pubic airbrush. An envelope marked S/M merely disclosed another of these anaphrodisiac lovelies, rendered S/M by the limp whip in her hand.

He flipped faster through the envelopes, not knowing what obscure *frisson* he'd hoped to find but increasingly certain that it wasn't here. Near the end, though, one caption scrawled on brown manila made him pause. LAMBERTSTOW.

Afterwards, Peter had to remind himself strenuously that he didn't believe in occult premonition. His little extra edge, his half-baked ability to read people's feelings, was of no more use than a polygraph when confronted with inanimate paper. The sudden blank chill must have come from the name, its incongruity here, its short-circuit connection with old memories. Uncle Owen, that was who . . . and what would *he* have thought of young Peter amid the BOOKS AND MAGAZINES?

Uncle Owen had lived in Lambertstow, and something unspeakable had happened, and mother had wiped the place from her private map – freezing at any mention, ignoring her brother's Christmas cards. Yes. More memories trickled back. In Lambertstow village a name had been added to criminal legend, up there with Crippen, the various Rippers, the Moors murderers. The name was Quinn and no one knew quite what he had done.

The envelope contained several smaller ones, white, each with a printed caption whose indefinable tattiness suggested a hand-operated press. *Police photograph's leaked from Lambertstow horror case. Remains of Kenneth Quinn. Very violent, for strong stomach's only!!* Which left Peter uncertain as to whether the material really was too strong for Benson's hardened clientele, or whether its sale might stir up police interest.

He wasn't sure that he wanted to peer at a corpse, however photogenic, but his inquisitive fingers had already turned back the flap and slid out the first enclosure. A tightening of the gut came even before he could focus on the glossy print; he had never somehow realised that police photographs would be in colour. (Why was that? Because they were always in black and white in the newspaper. Of course.) Then he looked at the thing properly, and his first sensation was one of relief.

What lay on the grass under harsh lights was nothing recognisable as human. A long Christmas tree decked with exotic fruits and garlands, tinselled with innumerable points of reflected light; a Dali vision which through sheer excess had gone beyond mutilation and deformity. It was odd, perhaps a little disturbing in its abstract forms, but at first glance not at all horrific.

It was a pity, really, that Peter took the second glance. An observation of G. K. Chesterton's caught up with him later: that one might look at a thing nine hundred and ninety-nine times and be perfectly safe, but to take the thousandth look was to be in frightful danger of *seeing* it for the first time. Peter thought Chesterton had underestimated the safe exposure period, and sincerely regretted having looked even twice. The second look stirred up dim memories of an anatomy course at college, or those parts of it he'd attended; with his second look, he made the fatal error of analysis. It was fascinating, compulsive, to trace the relation between the long glittering object and what must have been a man; to consider bubbly ornaments in red and grey as something more than inorganic lumps, more than the polished haematite they called kidney ore; to trace what must have been done here and here with surgical delicacy; to wonder – try not to wonder – just when in the painstaking process Kenneth Quinn had actually died . . .

Prints and envelopes spilled to the floor as Peter jerked up from his squatting position. He made it to the sink in time; the sight of his own thin vomit crawling across the stained and spotted enamel seemed relatively wholesome, like those bracing whiffs of outside pollution in the sweaty shop. *If I'd seen it in a movie it would have been all right, a guaranteed fake.* The rest was a long anticlimax of cleaning, tidying, drinking many mugs of water which rinsed the aftertaste only partly from his mouth and not at all from his mind. After which the bus was long gone and Peter walked two miles to his bed-sitter; for reasons which stayed persistently cloudy, he took one packet of the photographs with him.

That night and in the shop next day, he resolutely thought of other things; but from time to time some detail of the material he sold would tweak at his memory and make him flinch. The hot gloom of the shop was conducive (in idle periods) to thoughts of Lambertstow and his uncle – his mother's brother, vaguely isolated from the family as 'not one of our sort', maternal condemnation of one who remained a mere farmhand while *she* became a typist and married an accountant.

Peter had enjoyed Uncle Owen: he remembered jokes, erratic conjuring tricks, hilarious chases in the woods near Lambertstow. He'd been ten, perhaps younger. He'd been eleven when the something happened, and that part of life had gone dark. Uncle Owen had died a few years later but might as well have died then. Thinking back, Peter saw that mere geographical connection with infamy was enough to make mother sever all links, a theatre nurse rejecting contact with the unsterile. Her mind worked that way.

He wondered whether he himself had met Quinn in those days of clear air and sharp colours. No memories presented themselves. He fancied that local kids had mentioned Quinn as one of their teachers, and that they'd liked him well enough. Peter at ten had been bored by such chat, impatient to talk about really interesting teachers like his own.

In the evening, the local library kept late hours. Peter spent some time searching through aged newspapers. Their dry old smell was very different from that of the damp room behind the shop, soporific rather than choking. His first guess at dates hadn't been too far out; in a few months the tragedy and mystery would be a decade old. He made notes of such scanty details as the papers gave, and for the fiftieth time began to plan a clever debut in journalism.

Ten years since Lambertstow horror, he wrote. *Motive for ghastly crime never revealed, but Quinn said to be disliked in neighbourhood. Strong feelings in Lambertstow got what he deserved, so reporters claimed after probing locals. Body at edge of wood, confused footmarks in grass, several people involved?? Ritual sacrifice etc etc hinted as per usual. No evidence. Filed unsolved (presumably), only Quinn somehow left with bad name. How so? Graffiti, local mood, anonymous letters. Smear bid, whispering campaign, grass-roots stuff. Some called Quinn in parish even changed name, cf. people called Crippen. Definitely impression Q got just deserts. But what did he do?*

On a second sheet of scrap paper: *Personal. Uncle O mentioned nowhere, no remote connection; Mother didn't even need that much excuse. Papers evasive on details of what was done; no pics (not surprising). Surgical knowledge needed? Artist too, sort of. Maybe approach through doctor.*

There was no third sheet, which might have carried such notes as *Why am I doing this?* and led into a complicated mire. Peter was happy to have something to do, something to test his talent against, something outside the fascinating dead-end of the shop. Working towards truth had to be a virtue, whatever awkward thoughts came knocking . . . Some people drove hundreds of miles to gape at seagulls choking and dying in oil slicks; some crowded about road accidents and pointed out to each other the interesting red stains on the asphalt; some holidayed in Germany and were careful not to miss the celebrated resorts – Buchenwald, Dachau. In his grimy room, which was at least grimy through use rather than decay, Peter remembered and recited his mother's charm against idle speculation:

> The centipede was happy quite
> Until a frog in fun
> Said 'Pray which leg goes after which?'
> This raised its mind to such a pitch
> It lay distracted in the ditch
> Considering how to run.

Local colour was the thing. On the Exeter train, he skimmed the only book about the case which the library could offer. *He Must Be Wicked To Deserve Such Pain: an essay on enormity*. Though the title quotation, which Peter thought might be Shakespeare, summed up neatly enough that feeling about Quinn, he found the text disappointing. The aristocratic lady author was more concerned with a generic 'sickness of society', and with how shops like Benson's led inevitably down the primrose path to this sort of thing, than with the event itself. Like the magazines Peter sold, she promised more than could ever be delivered. He slapped the book shut in irritation, in guilty disappointment, on the closing quotation: 'Whereof one cannot speak, thereon one must remain silent.'

Local colour, he told himself, and wondered if he were telling the truth. One should be able to sit at ease in north London and read up on anything. But during the long wait for a bus at Exeter, he had to admit to himself that it would be interesting to try and reach Dr Janice Barry, mentioned in the papers as the Lambertstow GP. Certain questions might have gone unasked, ten years back, and he wanted to ask them. The prospect was utterly terrifying; but proper reporters had to ask people awkward questions and so he supposed he must as well. He wore mirror sunglasses which he hoped would give him confidence by making him unreadable.

Coffee on the train had left a sour taint in his mouth, which as the leisurely bus wobbled through suburbs and lanes gave him an illusion of having recently vomited. Flies buzzed in the smoky heat of the upper deck, aimless and happy. Peter crushed one against the window.

Lambertstow was bigger than remembered, defying the cliché of childhood haunts seeming absurdly tiny when revisited. The village had grown, or had been blotted out, its approaches a maze of new estates. Peter rode through layers of accretion to the old High Street at the heart of it all, and peered uncertainly at ordinariness. So late, so long after the event, all witnesses scattered or lost in hiding places ten years deep . . . The phone directory was the obvious starting point, he decided doggedly as a post office caught his eye; then he gnawed his lip, recalling country-wide directories filling long shelves in London. Still, here he was, after all.

'Bloody hell,' said Peter with feeling, a few minutes later. The local directory listed no Dr Barry.

Asking after 'the doctor' led him by stages to an ivied house whose brass plate said 'Dr Jonathan Sims'. After ten years, was it too late to enquire? He pushed through the door into a cool smothering gloom which felt almost ecclesiastical, and groped blindly to a reception window. 'I wanted to ask . . .' the logical lie came to him in a burst of confidence, 'about my uncle, Owen Walker, used to live here . . . I wanted to find Dr Barry and, er . . . you don't know?'

The dark-haired woman at the window gave him a
tired smile, behind which Peter read a hot flash of exas-
peration. 'I'll ask Dr Sims,' she said. And after a pause
of unintelligible intercom noises (did real reporters have
tricks for coping with that?): 'Dr Barry *used* to run this
practice. Dr Sims says she's been at a private nursing
home for some time. I don't know whether I should, but
perhaps if I gave you the address?'

'Please. It's a . . . an important family matter.'

Amazed by this success, Peter took the slip of paper
with effusive thanks, and left. The moist heat was like a
blow in the face as he closed the door behind him. The
address was in Surbiton.

Local colour, he reminded himself. To the scene of the
crime, yes, definitely. He'd copied a sketch map from
one of the papers; the streets seemed to have randomly
stretched, contracted, and tilted on hidden hinges to
new angles with one another, but eventually he saw the
fatal stand of trees. When they first appeared, peeping
over a terrace of harsh new brick, they looked uncompro-
misingly ordinary. Where was the atmosphere of doom?
It was only a small patch of woodland (Peter remembered
it as larger – so he *had* been here once), straggling up a
slope just too steep for cultivation. Another obscure
thought surfaced: absurdly, he'd been half-prepared to
find some plaque or marker – 'The Atrocity of The
Decade Took Place On This Spot.'

There was only unkempt grass. He sat with his back
against a tree, and watched the shadows lengthen. Local
colour: *Today it may seem unremarkable, even dull, but . . .*
Useless. He slid out the monstrous photograph and
frowned; its repulsion was dimmed a little by familiarity,
but he didn't care to look too long.

On – this – spot, he thought fiercely, trying to make
himself feel more, trying to do the impossible and read
a place. There must be some aura . . . some stain. Now
that he'd looked again at the picture, he could see how

the landscape might be considered in a different light, changing in the mind's eye, going bad. From under the trees came a sweet-sour whiff of rotting leaves, and this no longer seemed quite natural. The sluggish air pressed close. Puffy white clouds were wobbling overhead, bulging down at him, disgusting in their nearness and intimacy. The sky, he realised, was stretched tightly just above him; the constricted horizon barely allowed room to breathe. He could not breathe. He could not move. *On this spot . . .*

The pulpy ground was ready to engulf him; something glistening and wet was surely just behind, moving with exquisite delicacy and pain under the trees, coming to him. Peter shivered in a cage of shadows. Here in this small, cramped, horrid countryside he found his eyes fixed, frozen, on a tiny mess in the nearby grass (perhaps a bird-dropping) which had become the oozing, lazily turning hub of all the world's vileness . . .

Peter lurched upright, stomach churning. Automatically, shakily, he began to walk away, his intention of exploring the trees forgotten. This was local colour? He'd never felt troubled before with too much imagination, had never been able to read a place. Think, think of something else.

. . . how interesting to analyse this: a small horrible thing is so much more repulsive than a large. Cf. the failure of giant insects and suchlike in all those movies. A small, fascinatingly yucky thing like whatever was there in the grass. Or like a photograph.

Peter shook his head violently. Walking briskly and without a pause into the village, he tried to shut out all the unspeakable facts for a moment, and probe the motives behind it all. As always, he failed. How could Quinn, how could anyone, deserve *that*? 'Oh, Quinny's okay,' the sniggering Lambertstow kids had told him ten years back. The village went by in a blur. Funny you never ran into any of the old kids these days. On the London train he sneered at himself as a coward and an incompetent, but with a deeper sense of comfort, a satisfaction at having read or even for a moment imagined the supposed horror of that locality. This was the insight which could take you to the top.

At home he wrote it all down as local colour, and didn't sleep too well afterwards.

Next day was Sunday, with the heat of fading summer thicker and murkier than ever. Peter fiddled with a much worked-over draft – *Today I stood on the very spot where the strangely notorious Kenneth Quinn allegedly met his terrible end. Even ten years after the horror, it is not a pleasant place etc* – abandoned it, and walked out to telephone the Treetops Private Home from a nearby booth which did part-time duty as a urinal.

'Treetops, can I *help* you?' said a pleasant female voice.

'Is it, er, possible for me to have a word with Dr Barry?'

'One moment.' A pause. 'There is *no* Dr Barry on our staff, are you sure you have the right number?'

'They . . . told me I could find Dr Janice Barry at Treetops,' said Peter weakly. He should have known, doctors would stick together and hide one another's addresses, frustrate anyone who might ask awkward questions . . .

'*One* moment.' A longer pause, during which it occurred to Peter that the woman's ordinary speaking voice must be half an octave lower than the strained tones which drifted with such refinement down the line. 'I *am* sorry. Yes. Miss Barry is a *patient* at Treetops, do you wish to *visit* her?'

He blinked. It shouldn't be that surprising, now you thought about it, but somehow . . . 'Yes please,' he said. 'What are your visiting hours?'

The voice sounded a little shocked. 'There are *no* fixed visiting hours at Treetops. You may visit when*ever* you wish, between 10 a.m. and 8 p.m.'

Peter calculated rapidly, and hastily fed in more

money. 'Hello? Hello? Could I visit at about seven tomorrow evening, please?'

'Certainly. Please could I have your *name*?'

'Edgell. Peter Edgell. A friend of a friend.'

'*Thank* you.'

Monday was a trifle cooler, but still nowhere near comfortable. The shop seemed to attract a higher than usual proportion of nutters, people who wandered in asking for *The Times* or the latest science fiction magazine; there was even one twerp who, without glancing at the stock, enquired about first editions of James Branch Cabell. (Peter had wondered for a moment whether this was an esoteric code phrase.) Although you knew where you were in the shop and could laugh a little at the customers' feelings, Monday stretched unbearably, each minute longer than the one before, until it was a surprise to see Benson fussing browsers out of the back room and putting an end to the day's literary business.

The bus was crowded, and stank. The tube was worse. The second bus was less oppressive, rush-hour being past: Peter reached Treetops in good time, perhaps too soon, since he hadn't a very clear idea of what to say.

It was a chubby Victorian mansion, its red and yellow brick impeccably clean; the only tree in sight, though, was some way down the road. A middle-aged woman in a nurse's cap opened the door, her stern aspect launching Peter prematurely into his lie: 'Come to visit Doctor – er – Miss Barry. She was a friend of my uncle's and I thought I, well, I ought to . . .'

Her answering smile was like sunlight breaking through forbidding cloud. He read surprised approval, no doubt at finding such nice sentiments in a scruffy youth.

'If you'll just come this way.'

The wide hallway smelt of boiled cabbage, only slightly tinged with the inevitable antiseptic. Thick, glossy cream paint covered every surface. Peter followed the nurse up noisy, varnished wooden stairs as she explained in an undertone that Miss Barry sometimes had a little difficulty, if he knew what she meant. 'The poor thing *wanders* sometimes.'

Peter wasn't prepared for the room at the top of the stairs. The words 'private nursing home' had conjured up images of personal, individual care and attention in comfortably private rooms. This room, whose door said 'Hope', was comfortably small, but screens divided it into four cramped segments, each with an iron bed, each bed containing an old woman who lay unmoving. To the boiled-veg and antiseptic reek was added some other smell, sickly and disagreeable.

'Miss Barry!' said the nurse brightly, speaking loudly and very close to the third old lady's ear. 'It's Peter Edgell, come to visit you!' She added more quietly, 'Ring the bell if there's any trouble,' and left.

Peter sat cautiously at the bedside and looked at Janice Barry, whose eyes stared blankly upwards. She could not possibly be more than seventy, but seemed far older. They had dwindled in their sockets, those eyes, like jellyfish withered by a fierce sun; her whole face was shrunken, as though it were a balloon from which a little too much air had been allowed to escape. Her breathing was noisy.

'Miss . . . I mean Dr Barry?' No response, but he couldn't stop now, right on the verge of something or other. His newest lie followed straight away. 'Do you remember Owen Walker, back in Lambertstow, used to come to you? I'm his nephew, and there was this rumour, I heard he'd been suspected of . . . what happened there. It was all a long time ago, but I was wondering if maybe you could help me clear things up a bit.'

It really did sound feeble. But some trace of animation had crept over the old woman's face at the mention of Lambertstow. Peter bent closer and made himself repeat his non-question. This time the eyes moved . . . and behind them he read something wary and knowing.

I have the edge on her. She knows something and she can't hide it from me. This is the start.

'You . . . No one has talked to me about *that* for a good many years,' she said in a slow wheezing voice, a separate act of concentration shaping each word. 'Are you from the police again?'

'No no. I'm – sort of looking into it. Off my own bat. My uncle.'

Dr Barry coughed. 'I suppose you want to ask me the, the usual questions?'

Edgell guessed that his queries were not, could not be as original as he'd hoped. Impatiently he abandoned pretence. *Maybe I can surprise her by being blunt, that's the way investigators work.*

'The surgical technique,' he said flatly.

She smiled. He hadn't thought her face could become any more wrinkled. The animation in and around her eyes was flickering, as though corroded contacts were sparking and smoking, passing power only intermittently. 'Did you know I have an inoperable brain tumour?' she said.

Peter blinked, not knowing what to say but reading it as true.

'They tell me I'm just getting old, but I know. Look at me.' Her head rocked on the pillow; perhaps she was trying to shake it. 'Ah. Quinn was an evil man. Wickedness and corruption, of a sort.'

Cautiously, 'Then you know why he was . . . killed?'
She knows something. She really does.

'A brain tumour,' Dr Barry said with satisfaction, or so it seemed. The light in her eyes came on more fully. 'Oh yes, the police wanted to know all about that, asked me many a time about surgical training and whether I thought anyone but a doctor could have . . . But I was a woman, you see. You can't believe what I say.'

And he couldn't unravel the complex knot of feelings he was reading in her. 'They thought a woman couldn't have done what was done, is that it?' he said, wondering if the old dear really were delirious.

'No more she could, I said, I told them, unless she had, oh, crowds of helpers. They believed that . . . Quinn *was* a vile man, you know. That's all I know, officer. I really cannot assist you any further. Those poor children. They must never know. It was a work of art . . . Do you play rugby? My brother was very fond of rugby once.'

The room seemed to be growing colder, full of harsh, ragged breathing. Peter remembered his own great-aunt, so vague in the present decade, so diamond-sharp when speaking of the past. He felt so close; he leaned closer still. 'Why was it done? What had Quinn *done*?'

'He must be wicked to deserve such pain . . . did you read that book? A very silly book.' She breathed again, deeply, and exhaled with a long shudder. 'My diagnosis is certain, I'm afraid. Prognosis negative. NTBR . . . I can feel it pressing. It presses in different colours. Why, officer, I don't know anything at all about Mr Quinn except that he wasn't much liked in the village . . . No. The things he did. They were very shameful. The things he wanted to do. His name shall be blackened forever and ever amen.' It was a long speech, and took a long time.

'Dr Barry, it *is* blackened – somehow. It is. People called Quinn changed their names. You remember, because of the whispering. Did *you* – ?' It was there, so close, he could read it but couldn't understand it: a foreign language of emotion.

She was speaking again, more feebly now. The faulty contacts might be passing current, but the power-source itself was failing. 'You are all . . . so . . . silly. If I wanted to I could tell you half. I shouldn't tease you like this. Did you ever hear tell of the *Mary Celeste*?'

Peter couldn't decide whether that was relevant, or mere wandering. If only he'd brought a cassette recorder. 'Yes?'

'They remember it to this day because nobody knows

the how or why. They can't forget it, poor dears. So many of us, if you believe that. And if there's never a word about what Quinn . . . just, you see, just the hints, if everything is handled just so . . . Forever. You're not the doctor.'

'Please,' he whispered, as the feelings he couldn't read faded with her voice. 'Please tell me.'

For the sake of my brilliant future career.

She giggled, protected from all the world by her inoperable brain tumour. (NTBR she had said – *not to be resuscitated* – was that already written in some folder here?) For a moment her fading eyes were those of a little girl.

'Shan't,' she whispered. 'You wouldn't want to spoil it all?' And began to laugh, a small weak laugh that hardened into a sort of spasm, a glistening line of saliva running from the corner of her mouth as the shrivelled body trembled in private glee.

His final attempt to spy on her secrets read nothing that made sense: a fading Rorschach pattern of feelings, a meaningless bright symmetry like a Christmas tree. Peter pressed the bellpush. The nurse appeared and dismissed him from the bedside with a flick of her eyes.

'You can't believe anything poor Miss Barry says,' she warned in a low voice as he left the room. Now, perhaps, was the moment for shrewd questions and even a small bribe – anything to learn more of those so-called wanderings and ravings. But, studying the nurse's stern competence and impatient eyes, reading the professional hardness which made Treetops endurable, he quailed at last.

'Goodbye,' he mumbled, and felt as the big door closed behind him that he was leaving under a faint cloud.

And so I left the dying Dr Barry, who will surely take the monstrous secret of Lambertstow with her on her painful descent towards the solution of that other, final question which remains eternally tantalising until it is answered.

Peter leant back from the typewriter, unsatisfied but with a sense of having partly avenged his frustration. He had at least had the last word.

'Quinny's all right,' the Lambertstow schoolkids had told him in the long ago. 'He's a fantastic guy, gives you things and all. *You* know. You ought to meet him.' Had he been able to read people back then? Kids were so boring, self-centred, anyway.

Peter stared at the blank wall of his room and shrugged; the mystery was unyielding, monolithic. Pulling the painfully typed sheet from the machine, he filed it carefully with all the other notes and outlines for articles he thoroughly intended to write, one day very soon. Perhaps when he could afford a word processor; that should solve his productivity problems. Perhaps.

Meanwhile, there was always his private gallery of the emotions, where off-beat feelings and longings came to disport themselves for Peter Edgell's dispassionate amusement. There was always the shop.

HOWIE DREAMS

ANNE GAY

ANNE GAY

Anne Gay is widely regarded as one of the most talented newcomers to have emerged from the current resurgence in British speculative writing. A runner-up in the Gollancz/*Sunday Times* SF writers' competition, she has since sold stories to *Other Edens*, as well as to this collection, and is currently working on her second novel. *Mindsail* will be published shortly.

HOWIE DREAMED, AND I smiled. It was a good Dream, cheerful and bright with colour. I'd made the best Dream I could for him, sorry that I couldn't be with my friend at his first big performance.

For ninety seconds his synapses caught movement before it could escape down his nerves to his muscles. The action was cerebral, the reaction a physical fact. He would wake self-confident and positive, at concert-pitch, and he wouldn't know why.

I would.

That's why I smiled.

Tiptoeing out of my spare room, I slung my travel case like a bandolier, and took my only prototype with me. Nothing nasty showed on the detectors, so I braved the bitches on watch in my garden. I used to be afraid of them, of all dogs, but now I let them fawn on me, Minerva and Athene. Still I petted them goodbye. Howie might need them here. Besides, I was going into battle. *Timenda sum, et dona ferente*, and it was no two-bit contraption like the Trojan Horse either. The bitches went back to burying some bones under the chestnut tree, and I wondered who they'd been.

At the outer wall, the stone lions checked out on my bracelet, but beyond the garden gates I burst into sudden flames.

I bit down on a gasp, but my shield held. No light, no

sound from the laser of attack, only its effect. My heart threatened to choke me. Who . . . ?

The lions defended me with ultrasonics aimed at the laser's source. I heard the man vomit. I think it's eleven cycles a second that does it. And when my shield had gone out, my lungs sucked cooling air. My lions couldn't kill on the streets. Penalty for death on the footpath, £250. The puke would cost him a modest fifty.

Hefting my cases, I stepped into Rosalind's old banger, looking back to make sure the baddie had no friends along. What I was carrying would change the world – I hoped for the better. Had he known? Worse, *how* had he known? And the sixty-four thousand dollar question: who had sent him?

I changed cars seven times on the way to the unsuspected airport, and threw my heli-tickets in a rubbish-bin.

I was off to the World Dream Fair.

Vienna, city of dreams – with a small 'd', until tonight. To the west, the dark hills distant under the violet sky, and the Danube, reflecting in amethyst the linden-scented air. Nearer, on the opposite bank, the Danube Tower and its warm-lit revolving restaurant. Viennese whirls with a vengeance. The Prater Park, where screams and laughter are the same thing, and the stately Riesen-rad wheeling tourists above the amusements.

The last time I'd been here, this side of the river was woods between the canalised arms of the Danube. Now it was the Wälderschloss Hotel. Imagine a Disney palace. disguised as a faerie tree-house – down to a jolly statue of a Valkyrie with a spear, better than Tinkerbell for keeping you safe – and you've got it. If you can afford it.

Like me. This was *my* Dream Fair, real rags-to-riches stuff; well, more terraced house to penthouse. Or like it says on the quiz shows, my starter for men. I could hardly believe I'd made it happen at last. And I wondered who had sent the man to kill me – and if he was here.

I even let the doorman carry my bags for a tip. Harry Lime would have been proud of me.

The opening ceremony was perfunctory. Hardly anyone ever turns up to things like that, least of all to listen to a sales pitch.

Why do so many men think women are untrust-worthy? And so many women feel threatened by the sisters?

Cunning: I had a couple of guys on the platform with me: besuited middle age, and rising exec in tight trousers – that should please everyone; they were nice guys too – with Regina and me to lead the chat. She's beautiful, Regina, with her slim young Germanity smart in short hair. Regina doesn't believe in make-up. I'm tall and in my thirties and striving for glamour. But then I'm not as pretty as she is.

Of course, there were the drinkers by the bar at the back, with sporadic types dotting the empty rows. Was it one of them who was out to get me? No, they didn't look like killers, just freeloaders – I hoped.

And up front where the lights were bright, there were five men and a token woman, all looking unnaturally keen. To entrap us.

Which is why we'd bothered to hold the ceremony in the first place. It's nice to know who your enemies are.

Howie rang. I didn't want him to.

He was tall and funny, his body sliding warmly on mine as we danced. Crystal archways glittered against the velvet night; the music soared, rich on the coloured air; the chandeliers were dimmer than the lights of the Altstadt a Danube away.

France smells of Gauloises; Spain is hot dust, black tobacco and sweet soap. Vienna smells of lime-trees on the river and cream coffee with traffic. With Walla – his name was Walla – I danced through all of them, but the businessmen stayed in clumps for safety, in corners that reminded them of home. Most of them didn't know why. They didn't know the psychology of smell. They seemed to feel threatened by emotional technology, especially in the hands of women, as if any of us not a secretary or a cleaner was out to get them. I only wanted to rid them – and some of the sisters – of reciprocal fear.

They were the self-interested ones; the communicators explored each other's cliques. Regina matched steps with Jo-Beth's, still noting, as I did, who was which.

Most of us were in party mood, even the ones caressing their fantasies on leaf-screened balconies. Weren't the dampers humming merrily in the raftered branches, just to tell us our lasers wouldn't work? All my people, all my guests, were as safe as I could make them. I thought. I hoped Howie was okay back in England. I shook my worry off – he had my defences, didn't he? And the meetings at this Fair should sort out the rest.

Our arms like stoles, Walla walked beside me through a skein of leaves. We felt as if we'd known each other for ever, each life impossible to imagine without this sudden friend. Yet still we were a little shy, like kids in Sunday clothes, as we melted towards a kiss. We touched like butterflies, testing. His lips were warm on the hollow of my throat . . .

That's when Howie rang.

For a second there I sank my head on Walla's shoulder. Resigned, I sighed an excuse. Walla, smiling – how? – shrugged and said, 'Zee you later.' He sounded mostly American and looked mostly Slav.

Did he mean it? I couldn't tell any more once the leaves dappled over his retreat. I have to fight off mistrust too.

I answered my bracelet. Howie's face lightened the sapphire, if not my frustration. Of course my shield wouldn't work here with the dampers, but I knew he wouldn't have belled me if it wasn't important.

'Danan. Got me. 'ey've got me, Dian!' His eyelids drooped; his head lolled suddenly on to his chest.

My bracelet said it was in Germany. The place Howie was in, not the bracelet. Hell, I was disorientated. I'd better get myself together. Howie wasn't worth much in cash terms, only a few million or so. Nothing compared to his intrinsic value. And if I hadn't got what they wanted – Oh, God, let them want money! – no doubt the sisters would get it for me, Kyoko and Regina, Hélène and Indira, half a dozen others. I'd done the same thing for Gianna before now. Let it be money . . .

But it would wreck my bargaining position – all our positions.

Besides, Howie was my friend.

''sup?' he groaned. They pushed him – a dark, dirty hand. Howie jerked suddenly from side to side: they were trying to shake him awake. A startled blink opened his face to a reality he didn't like.

'They want it, Diana. Machine. You. Don't let them –'

Howie was switched off. My bracelet went dark. Through the crystal-floored terrace, I looked down past the net of Wälderschloss branches. They were concrete, steel, I don't know. Stronger than oak, or mountains – but I felt I was falling, straight on to the Valkyrie's spear. It was aimed between my legs.

It was first light before They called again, that hideous time when the nightmare still lurks; the monster, fear, dripping in the mind and the sun too far away to drive it beneath the breakers of the subconscious. Gianna and I were still arguing; Regina back in Bonn; Hélène's lover in Dijon, in a flat above the city wall, all of us tuned in for the message. There had to be a message . . .

I couldn't trace Howie from my home. We had to pinpoint the message at its source. So much depended on it.

Kyoko in the lobby phoned. The sound of it wrang our hearts.

White-masked geisha, antennae quivering in her pearl-strung hair, she said, 'A package. Come by taxi, no. 734.' She actually said 'no'. 'The driver, she was phoned to pick it at the airport from left luggagings. Money was there, and package, key was left in lock.'

Very efficient. You'd never know she was blind.

Reception sent it up. A heart attack for Gianna and me, though we were both expecting the knock.

'Special delivery,' said the page sleepily, dithering artistically until we gave him a tip, when he thanked us with polite surprise.

We weren't expecting what was in it.

Howie's little finger. I gagged. The box in the envelope was still sticky with his blood.

I wouldn't go any further, not even watch the message, till I had Howie's tape faxed to me. And the finger – Howie's finger – analysed and put on ice. Fingerprint and tissue-type, it was Howie's all right.

It matched. It would be able to box arpeggios again – if we ever got the rest of him back.

No analgesic in the blood.

My stomach echoed to Howie's pain. I was afraid for us, too, all of us: the mothers, the shopgirls and factory hands, the fishwives at the docks and the bankers, the teachers, the politicians – all of us threatened, by the men who had Howie and what They could do with my machine, and by the women who'd handed him over.

No one knew what had happened to him. He'd never made his concert. The scanners, the bitches, the lions – none of them showed anything at all. So it had to be one of the girls who worked with me at Somequa Dreams. A friend. Great.

Why? This counter-counter espionage could wreck all of our Dreams.

Literally. The tape in the box showed Howie naked on a dusty floor. He was curled up foetally. Someone hooked his hand out with a wire coat-hanger. Left hand for rhythm, thumb and three fingers now, a massive

scabbing clot where his fifth finger had been, counting
as a pianist, which Howie usually was.

The hanger disappeared from sight. Still unconscious,
Howie withdrew his hand and cradled it on his opposite
arm. Dried blood crusted his chest and thigh.

In his pain, I mirrored the gesture.

Gianna's tough. Her aunt was in the women's radio
station in Rome that was blown up by the Right. She
said, 'No cry. Listen.'

I stopped, and we did.

One of those voice machines that make you sound like
a robot used to. Impossible to tell for sure, but I thought
it was a man.

It said in German English, 'You, Dinah Schlate. We
have your traitor-friend. You have only one finger of
him. How you want him back – by instalments? Another
finger at nine o'clock. Listen him. He have screamed.'

He had. I heard him. My friend. The close-up was
sickening: Howie, white and sweating, mother-naked,
his hand foreshortened, held down by a crate-staple. A
huge axe drifted down to touch his finger for aim: the
little finger, pinned too, fresh-bruised by the wire.

Up – down. The finger flopped drumming on to the
hollow crate. Howie screamed against his will.

'In slices,' said the mechanised voice. 'He is playing
no more the piano.

'Or: bring us now the machine, the new, not the one
with which you must have wires to the head, but the
sending one for Dreaming when you are awake or not.
I have many plans for it . . .

'Alone go to the airport with the machine. Fly to
Düsseldorf with the 6.30 machine.' He meant plane this
time. 'You get a message there if you are alone coming.
No lasers, no shield, or bye-bye Howie. No tracers with
you, or bye-bye Howie. You get not his body back.'

A scream sounding on a plain concrete wall. Not quite
plain. It had Howie's blood on it.

I was shaking. I can't convey the horror of that voice

like Sparky's piano. I really didn't need Gianna shouting over the hiss of the blank tape, 'So let him die. *Ecco*, is revolution, no? Lose Howie. Is not important. Machine is, and you. Not a man.'

'He is! He's my friend!' I yelled in spiralling rage and fear. 'Oh, shut up!' as she started again in machine-gun Italian.

When I rang Regina, she hadn't been able to find anything. Nor Hélène's lover at Dijon University. I mean, how could you with a package?

I cancelled the lover, and Regina jetted back to Vienna. That little time had passed, less than half a night: she would have to be me at my Dream Fair. Hell, I was livid. And guilty, too. If it wasn't for my Dreams, They wouldn't have wanted Howie. Or what my Dreams could do . . .

I wondered hollowly what They would do to me. Gianna drove me to the airport.

Düsseldorf. Glass and steel buildings, Volkswagens hooting on the bridges. Industrialisation in Early Smog. The taxi-woman wore a skirt and peasant blouse, very fetching. She took me, like a message at the airport said, to a kiosk on the Kö, where the machine-voice ordered me about on the sound-only phone. I had to follow His commands, she followed mine, rushing me to a café – where I waited hours for the next call. The taxi-driver had endless coffees with Kirschtorte and cream. She could afford it as the minutes clicked her meter. I swear it turned into a kilometer.

I thought about Howie, and sweated. Machine-voice and axes, and what might have happened as nine o'clock came and went.

The machine to change the world sat idly in its boxes.

My fear must have showed. She tried to cheer me up.

Lovely Gitta, meter maid, told me all about her Dream.

'Oh, it was wonderful. My husband, he snores, you must know.' Actually I didn't, but I can't say I cared.

She went on to my apathy, 'He collects the mats on
which you stand the beer-glasses in the bars. He goes
often with his friends to many bars, to collect them, he
says. When he home comes' – she was proud of her
tourist English – 'he does not ask me how went the day
for me or Karin. That is my daughter, she is at the high
school. He lays the mats on the new table I have bought
and tells me about them. I am not interested longer – at
first, yes, but he has now thousands. He laughs and
smells of beer, you understand? He is pleased with
himself, and wants not to listen, only to talk. He earns
not much money and gives it all out on the beer.'

Uncertain of my attention, here in the potted music
and palms as the air slides from morning coffee to lunch-
time wine and Howie could be armless, she says, 'You
are sure is here the café where your friends phone?'

And I say, 'Yes. But I don't know when.'

'We have time for a coffee, then. Would you like
another?'

And when it comes and the phone call doesn't, she
drags my attention back with fluttering gestures and
feminine laugh. It has a certain sleazy fascination, this
girls together talk. Will she regret her confidences later?

All the time I keep thinking of Howie and that awful
joke: 'Doctor, will I ever be able to play the piano again?'

I was contemplating dying when she finally drove me
to the pick-up point.

The Howienappers had sent me from phone-booth to
phone-booth, outside banks, the Trade Fair, Wimpy
bars and jewellers. I was jittery, afraid, oppressed by
women's guilts. I could have screamed from the tension,
but at each new contact I squeezed calmness into my
voice. They would be tense too. If I wound Their spring
tighter Howie could . . .

Howie. His defenceless eyes at Their boot-toes. The
flat, friendly stomach where I leant my head, stripped
of its flesh. If I didn't make Their Dreams come true, I'd

have balled up my friend's skin in my hand and torn it
away to discard it. My friend, almost the most wonderful
person I'd ever met. Irritating and aggravating, not of
one flesh like my sisters, but learning from me and
teaching me. We liked each other, not sexually, but as
people sharing the same race and planet. And he was
one hell of a laugh on a good day. *Was?*

I could have made the Dream-way without him, but
not spread it as wide as we have. He believed – believes?
– in respect for the individual, as I do. Don't you like
people who think the same as you?

Dear Howie, what are They doing to you now?

That axe . . . in the taxi my stomach shrank too.

At nightfall, by the sunset-flamed Thyssen Tower, They
told me this address. They'd proved I wasn't bugged
and I wasn't followed, and in the red-reflecting kiosk
They sent a shudder of more fear to pump up my heart.
He said, 'I can see you. I watch you. I know exactly what
you do.

'Now. Do this right. You come now here, to this
address. Because I still you watch.'

And when I whirled round, His unseen eyes could
have been anywhere.

I make Dreams. They made me a nightmare. I can still
feel it everywhere, following me from inside. They say
rapists watch. We are afraid.

Gitta slid the taxi down a wide street on an industrial
estate. There were trees and regimented flowers between
the factories. Mind, they're all like that – until next time
some kindly government knocks them flat. Some holy
war, a mushroom cloud, and thou, my love, goodbye.
And there were eyes in the gathering darkness.

I sneezed from soot and soap powder, drifting down
as thunderheads squashed the air. Gitta looked at me in
the mirror as we were sucked towards Their lair, and
said, 'You are all right?'

Whose side was she on?

I nodded. She accepted it, knowing it was far from the truth. She said to comfort, 'That Dream I was telling you. I cannot afford a personal Dream, but my friend gets some sometimes from a man she knows. I borrow her machine. My husband would be very much cross if he knew. But he doesn't. He sleeps like a – tree?'

Her intonation rose, to ask me if I understood. I nodded again, appalled.

'It is another lover every night. It is not always clear; it hurts my head a little, but it is worth it. It is so good, you know? It gives much pleasure to my friends and me.

'Last night it was a man; my husband only not my husband, kind and handsome, you know?'

I could imagine. I'd seen pirate-Dreams before, fuzzed and darkly sexual. Gitta grinned, embarrassed.

'I felt him very powerful,' she said. 'He made me feel safe. You like men like that?' In the twilight she thought she knew what I said. She went on, 'It was very good, he liked to make love. My husband, he likes to have sex, when he wants, like he wants. I am not in it, you know? Only an opening for him. Maybe he was different before, or maybe I only remember him how I expected him to be, when I did not know what questions to ask.

'But that Dream! He knew just what I wanted. The man made me feel safe. It was very good to have someone strong to look after me. We had many children. I look after him, too.'

In the mirror as the hoardings slid by, hiding His eyes, her eyes crinkled while she smiled. She was in love with a cheap fantasy, and tonight would darn the socks of the man she mistook for her lover. A deadly romance to stop her changing her life.

I knew who'd made the Dream. Who else?

The kidnappers. People who cut off fingers and people's minds.

What would They do to me?

* * *

Empty factory, boarded up. Inside – strip search, done by Gitta, after she'd taken all that money from me, too. They paid her well – also my money – and final indignity of her pudgy, cake-wielding fingers, she even searched inside me. I almost threw up. Then They sent her away. After all, They didn't want any women cluttering up Their far-Right plans. A needle . . .

When I woke up, I was somewhere else, and it hurt. Even if Regina traced my greedy taxi-driver, she'd never find me now. Even the air smelt different – essence of rural mould. It was very quiet. I wondered why They needed me so far from humankind. Maybe from here, no one would hear me scream.

They left me a T-shirt and knickers. The red tiles were cold under my feet when they let me see Howie – by phone. I didn't know where he was either, only that there was no time-lag on the phone. Precision – somewhere in the western hemisphere. Ace.

I tried to make a joke for him, but I couldn't get the words out. He looked awful. He still had nine fingers, though.

He said one word. 'Don't.'

I did.

I got out the Super Acme Dreama Deluxe – that wasn't its real name. That was just me, trying to raise a smile. Would you call a bringer of hope and joy by an acronym like SADD?

Oh, I grieved for it as I took it out of its white cases. It was meant to be such a good thing, to take the sting out of relationships and float them along on a river of understanding. With anything, even the opposite sex.

They made me force unreality into its circuits. Believe me – my Dreams had never been untrue, until that night. I was terrified.

I demanded the head, preferably separate, but They weren't as literal as me. Firmly attached to His sergeant-major's body, His head wore a gorilla mask. It looked very odd with His suit and tie and shiny dead-crocodile shoes. Frightening. His friend with the axe came too.

'If I'm to make your Dream right,' I said to his deception, 'I need your eyes and your temples uncovered.' Smart, don't you think? Then I'd be able to recognise Him for my retribution.

They made me align my machine in the light, but focus it in total darkness so I never saw His face. My horror grew – out of His invisible, tangible presence, His desires, His domination – and His axeman stalking unseen.

I pressed the buttons that blocked out His conscious self – rather more thoroughly than I had led them to believe. I had to leave enough of Him on top to speak if the guard asked Him to. Before the lights went out, this one was a leering Bavarian spirit in macho studded black. I wondered what his coarse breathing was now.

Gorilla didn't want even the minimal contact of the beams as I tuned them in. He was hostile, more than suspicious. I was frightened for Howie and myself.

But I said, 'Words are not something that people have in common. Words reflect experience. I'm a woman, smaller than you, younger than you, from a different culture. I have less acquisition of wisdom; I've never been as powerful as you obviously are. Your meanings won't be the same as mine. The best you could hope for is that they'd overlap. And you want better than that, don't you?'

Treacle and truth mixed up like a half-chewed sandwich. Soothed to merely terrifying, He still objected in the heavy breathing dark, 'But I am told your good machine needs no personal matching.'

'Not for giving the Dream, no, though it's better.' I wondered if He could smell the fear on me. 'But for making a Dream perfect to your order . . .'

They like order. His body might be an NCO's but His thoughts were definitely officer class.

Also He'd never played at semantics.

*   *   *

It was easier to breathe when They left me alone with the
light-switch. Their sweat and aftershave and body-smell
still tickled the hairs in my nose with the scent of rubber
mask even after the soundproof door closed off Their
footsteps. The neon light was as welcome as sunshine.
I felt its release in the slackening of my rib-muscles, but
release was a distant country.

I played back His dream. Still small 'd'; He wanted me
to capitalise it.

What it was scared me more than Howie in his grasp.

First, pump up His executives' self-esteem: Hitler
Jugend in saddle-stitched suits. Send them out invin-
cible, conquering sales, subverting their competitors.
Selling not washing powder or gizmos, but Dreams.

And the Dreams were: men do it better – look at the
evidence of your eyes. How many women architects?
How famous? So – they can't be much good. How
many professors? Where were the Schillerins, the
Goethe-esses? Can you name a lady Turner?

But the horrifying thing was: the Dreams were for
women too. To teach them they couldn't do it, whatever
it was. To teach them to love looking good for men
only and not for themselves. Look: the make-up houses
would buy it. And the sellers of domestic gear. Just think
of their increase in sales if all women can do is look good
for playing house.

To show women couldn't be plumbers, because they
weren't. How cosy, how easy – don't fix it yourself.
Leave the cold floods round your ankles to a man. He'd
mend that pipe, and you'd be glad of his company while
you made him coffee. There's moral support if you
like.

And on and on. Back to feather dusters and antima-
cassars; sex as a cage – if we were good. Farewell to
research, or finance. Each of us isolated and shrunken
to cowering in our homes – because we were afraid of
the big bad world outside.

I love Howie. There's a lot of men I love.

I love my home. But not when it's my prison.
I didn't think much of His colour scheme either.

The table was bolted to the floor. Chair ditto. There were no windows and the food came on plastic plates. I was very alone.

I started building the plan of His Dream, the furniture if you like, the characters you can't see because they are you.

I even trained His bully-boys in how to use the machine to blare out a Dream to whoever walks by, which is what He wanted. Never mind if they fall under a truck in this sudden Dream, or spend their last pfennigs on fashion, not food. His thugs were fine technicians, though. With all the sensitivity of a tractor.

I ate. I slept, and nightmared of less Howie and more axe. I tried to give Regina and Gianna the time to find us by delaying and procrastinating, but the thought of Gianna's laserettes and the backlash of male fury wouldn't let me stop entirely.

Every now and then They let me phone Howie.

He had septicaemia. He looked like a stick-insect on a diet. I downed tools – well, brain – until They let him have a doctor. They were always worse when Gorilla wasn't there.

They countered, 'We'll chop his hands off, swish, with the axe. You go on now.'

I said, 'Howie'll die. I'll wreck the machine. *He* won't like that.'

They said, 'Then you'll die. Or you'll make another machine.'

'How can I?' I wailed. 'I'm only a woman.'

They believed that.

After that first time it was always light in there, even when I peed. My mind tramped trapped circles of no escape, and when Tampax appeared it was terrifying to know they watched even my most intimate acts. And by

telephone, Howie's body grew frailer. In agony and guilt
I worked in cold eternal light, faster, longer, to get us out
of here. With penicillin and all, I was still waiting for
him to die. What would I do then?

There were four hundred and seventy-five red tiles
one way, three hundred and thirty-three and a half
across the other axis of the floor. Every third tile was a
dust-sucker. They knew that much about my Dream-
machine anyway.

I tried, to stop myself thinking too much about the
wicked imbalance He wanted me to perpetrate on a
world struggling towards fairness, I tried with pen and
paper to work out exactly how many tiles that made.

It was only when I was too tired to think construc-
tively. Never twice did I come up with the same answer.
I'm an artist, a jeweller of thoughts, not a scientist, you
see.

And always I knew they were watching me.

Howie began to make jokes. You could still play 'Chop-
sticks' on his dirty yellow ribs, but his eyes no longer
looked like London fog. Just a little, I started to hope.
Maybe we'd make it – if the gorilla didn't come back.

The gorilla came to see me. An off-white safari-suit this
time – very chic, but it still gave me the creeps to talk to
a trousered primate. It was . . . inhuman. In separate
corners, a devil and a skull held Their axes watchfully,
as if I might karate Them from fifteen feet. His soldiers
were as wary of women as He was. Why else would He
be doing all this?

He said, 'I am hearing reports. Your friend is better
now. You waste no more time. Or my friend will make
him worse. Our axe has two heads. Do you need your
breasts, to work? I give you twenty-four hours, *ja*?'

Threat changed to gloat. 'We have mechanalysed the
machine. It is copied now manyfold. In three days' time
we will have copies of my Dream that you make in every

department-store window in the German-speaking world. Soon we will have a better, an English language one also. Then we will let you go.'

Why not? He could afford to do that. We would be negligible. Wouldn't we?

He tossed something on the table. Pinky and Perky followed Him to the door, almost colliding as He stopped to stare at me some more.

He said, 'Expect no help from your lab. Somebody wants neither you nor your boyfriend back. They are saying you betray your cause because of him, and he is traitor anyway to men.'

He chuckled – the winner.

Again the door sealed seamlessly over my yells and I broke my nails on it in vain.

It was a giveaway Superman watch. After all that silent disorientation, its tick was very loud.

I made Him His rotten Dream, just like He wanted it. I worked straight through, inspired by fear and long planning. Also appalled at the image presented of women – and of men. Neither gender could seriously hope to live down to it.

When I had finished, I was so tired I couldn't stop shaking, let alone sleep.

What had I done?

Pirated Dream-machines and gutter-merchants already sold cheap and nasty Dreams of power-sex, and like most inventors I tried not to feel responsible for other people's abuse of progress. Probably Oppenheimer felt the same.

Women like Gitta having dirty Dreams, quick coloured lustings by her beery snorer. Escapism, not action. Dash back to the cave, girls, let's get clubbed real soon.

My weary thoughts wouldn't leave me in peace.

More Dreams with the key I'd given Him? Sneaky execs being double-double agents? Slip the guy a mickey, or take him to the feelies, then plug failure into his brain.

No one would know with my new, wire-less machine.
True, it wouldn't work quite so well on women. We've
always had to watch who's plying us with gin. Anyway,
we're pre-programmed for failure. It just makes us work
harder because we have to.

But I could imagine, as the old-fashioned watch ticked
in torment away, the damage I was about to inflict on
the world. And would the gorilla really let us go?

For escape I remembered:

Back in that terraced house, after processing other
people's words all day, I'd made the first Dream in my
bed-sit. It was for Howie's sister, who lived in the room
next door, while Howie was teaching music in Erith. Of
course, I hardly knew him then.

Oh, nostalgia – Wedgwood walls and a cheeseplant. The
good old days of poverty when nobody tried to laser me.

She was crying. Sweet twenty-three and on the shelf.
Dressed in sludge-brown for camouflage. Overeating as
a defence: she could blame being fat for being lonely.
The fact that she never went anywhere was nothing to
do with it. I had to borrow sugar by the tonne before
she'd even have coffee in my room.

I Dreamed her into liking herself. Not blushing if
someone asked her the time. Not excusing her successes
as luck. Not avoiding people's eyes as if they might leech
out her soul.

By the time we went to Howie's first gig at a pub on
Angel Hill, she was wearing red. And kind, grateful
Howie made me Dream I liked dogs.

Superman ticked nearer to the Kryptonite. I was so
scared I felt sick.

What had I done? Did Prometheus like the Blitz?

By the time the short hand was on Superman's kiss-curl,
I was afraid millions of women were going to wish me
dead. Gianna's *partigiane* would turn me into spaghetti.
If I lived that long. If Howie did.

*   *   *

In pseudo-military uniform He came at last and clicked His heels not for my benefit but because it displayed His self-image. Swallowing, I played it for Him.

Gorilla liked His Dream. It was just like He wanted it, only more so. While He forced me into a sleep I might never wake up from, He chuckled over it.

Betrayal of (wo)mankind.

But I'd bought Howie's life and mine. I hoped.

Betrayal?

They left us on the banks of the Danube. I woke from drugs to linden seeds drifting like white cotton on my eyes. Hell, it felt like a hangover. My jeans were far too big – could you have eaten, if you'd done what I'd done? And I vomited into the river up where it was still blue. Outside was very big. I was glad Howie held my hand. Nobody else would want to.

I told him between gasps, 'There were a hundred and fifty-eight thousand, four hundred and twelve whole tiles and half a one on the floor in that cellar.'

He smiled palely amid the buttercups and said, 'My feet are killing me.'

Oh, the romance of it all.

We tottered into civilisation, or Linz as it was known locally. It looked good even on a dull evening. Howie and I looked like scarecrows. We got thrown out of everything but the station buffet and I phoned Regina from there to mobilise our detectives and a lawyeress. They let us reverse the charges but they wouldn't give us free coffee. Dear Austria. I wish my life was as tidy as you.

To kill the hour till she jetted in, we walked round the town. Not the gabled museums or the onion-domed churches, but the shopping centre. By then it was raining torrents, but the shops were Sunday-shut. Even the pigeons were sheltering from the rain, and mannequins smiled lonely from their spotlights into the dark.

I felt it first. Not the rain, but His Dream, splurging

out into the sad, grey evening. Over-bright, over-amplified, but I recognised my own work as any artist does.

Any jeweller of thoughts.

Gorilla had wanted plastic. Silicone breasts and Sindy clothes. Action Man in the office. No sweat, no periods, no brains. Moustachio'd lion-tamers, the Wehrmacht in the market, broadcast scatterwise to everyone not on His wavelength, with no fine tuning like headsets or personal technicians or all the research I hadn't done. Wifey in her nest and her man a hero every day. Psycho-masturbation.

I'd given it Him, Walt Disney-style, and studded it black with irony. But *He* hadn't seen that. He saw, like everybody does, what He already wanted to see.

In Linz, incredulous, snorting with giggles, Howie Dreamed.

And I laughed.

ODD ATTACHMENT

IAIN M. BANKS

IAIN M. BANKS

Iain Banks was born in Fife and brought up there and on Clydeside. He read English, along with Philosophy, at Stirling between 1972 and 1975; was variously employed – and travelled – between then and 1980, when he moved to England, first to London, and then to Faversham, Kent. In 1984 he took up writing full time, and in 1988 came home to Edinburgh. He started writing novels at the age of sixteen and his first, *The Wasp Factory*, was published on the day of his thirtieth birthday. Since then he has written *Walking on Glass*, *The Bridge*, *Consider Phlebas*, *Espedair Street* and, most recently *The Player of Games*.

DEPRESSED AND DEJECTED, his unrequited love like a stony weight inside him, Fropome looked longingly at the sky, then shook his head slowly and stared disconsolately down at the meadow in front of him.

A nearby grazer cub, eating its way across the grassy plain with the rest of the herd, started cuffing one of its siblings. Normally their master would have watched the pretended fight with some amusement, but today he responded with a low creaking noise which ought to have warned the hot-blooded little animals. One of the tumbling cubs looked up briefly at Fropome, but then resumed the tussle. Fropome flicked out a vine-limb, slapping the two cubs across their rumps. They squealed, untangled, and stumbled mewling and yelping to their mothers on the outskirts of the herd.

Fropome watched them go, then – with a rustling noise very like a sigh – returned to looking at the bright orange sky. He forgot about the grazers and the prairie and thought again about his love.

His lady-love, his darling, the One for whom he would gladly climb any hillock, wade any lakelet; all that sort of thing. His love; his cruel, cold, heartless, uncaring love.

He felt crushed, dried-up inside whenever he thought of her. She seemed so unfeeling, so unconcerned. How could she be so dismissive? Even if she didn't love him in return, you'd have thought at least she'd be flattered to have somebody express their undying love for her. Was he so unattractive? Did she actually feel insulted that he worshipped her? If she did, why did she ignore him? If his attentions were unwelcome, why didn't she say so?

But she said nothing. She acted as though all he'd said, everything he'd tried to express to her was just some embarrassing slip, a gaffe best ignored.

He didn't understand it. Did she think he would say such things lightly? Did she imagine he hadn't worried over what to say and how to say it, and where and when? He'd stopped eating! He hadn't slept for nights! He was starting to turn brown and curl up at the edges! Food birds were setting up roosts in his nestraps!

A grazer cub nuzzled his side. He picked the furry little animal up in a vine, lifted it up to his head, stared at it with his four front eyes, sprayed it with irritant and flung it whimpering into a nearby bush.

The bush shook itself and made a grumbling noise. Fropome apologised to it as the grazer cub disentangled itself and scuttled off, scratching furiously.

Fropome would rather have been alone with his melancholy, but he had to watch over the grazer herd, keeping them out of acidcloys, pitplants and digastids, sheltering them from the foodbirds' stupespittle and keeping them away from the ponderously poised boulderbeasts.

Everything was so predatory. Couldn't love be different? Fropome shook his withered foliage.

Surely she must feel *something*. They'd been friends for seasons now; they got on well together, they found the same things amusing, they held similar opinions . . . if they were so alike in these respects, how could he feel such desperate, feverish passion for her and she feel nothing for him? Could this most basic root of the soul be so different when everything else seemed so in accord?

She *must* feel something for him. It was absurd to think she could feel nothing. She just didn't want to appear too forward. Her reticence was only caution; understandable, even commendable. She didn't want to commit herself too quickly . . . that was all. She was innocent as an unopened bud, shy as a moonbloom, modest as a leaf-wrapped heart . . .

. . . and pure as a star in the sky, Fropome thought. As pure, and as remote. He gazed at a bright, new star in the sky, trying to convince himself she might return his love.

The star moved.

Fropome watched it.

The star twinkled, moved slowly across the sky, gradually brightening. Fropome made a wish on it: *Be an omen, be the sign that she loves me!* Perhaps it was a lucky star. He'd never been superstitious before, but love had strange effects on the vegetable heart.

If only he could be sure of her, he thought, gazing at the slowly falling star. He wasn't impatient; he would gladly wait for ever if he only knew she cared. It was the uncertainty that tormented him and left his hopes and fears toing-and-froing in such an agonising way.

He looked almost affectionately at the grazers as they plodded their way around him, looking for a nice patch of uneaten grass or a yukscrub to defecate into.

Poor, simple creatures. And yet lucky, in a way; their life revolved around eating and sleeping, with no room in their low-browed little heads for anguish, no space in their furry chests for a ruptured capillary system.

Ah, what it must be, to have a simple, muscle heart!

He looked back to the sky. The evening stars seemed cool and calm, like dispassionate eyes, watching him. All except the falling star he'd wished on earlier.

He reflected briefly on the wisdom of wishing on such a transitory thing as a falling star . . . even one falling as slowly as this one seemed to be.

Oh, such disturbing, bud-like emotions! Such sapling gullibility and nervousness! Such cuttingish confusion and uncertainty!

The star still fell. It became brighter and brighter in the evening sky, lowering slowly and changing colour too; from sun-white to moon-yellow to sky-orange to sunset-red. Fropome could hear its noise now; a dull roaring, like a strong wind disturbing short-tempered tree tops. The falling red star was no longer a single point of light; it had taken on a shape now, like a big seed pod.

It occurred to Fropome that this might indeed be a sign. Whatever it was had come from the stars, after all, and weren't stars the seeds of the Ancestors, shot so high they left the Earth and rooted in the celestial spheres of cold fire, all-seeing and all-knowing? Maybe the old stories were true after all, and the gods had come to tell him something momentous. A thrill of excitement rose within him. His limbs shook and his leaves beaded with moisture.

The pod was close now. It dipped and seemed to hesitate in the dark-orange sky. The pod's colour continued to deepen all the time, and Fropome realised it was *hot*; he could feel its warmth even from half a dozen reaches away.

It was an ellipsoid, a little smaller than he was. It flexed glittering roots from its bottom end, and glided through the air to land on the meadow with a sort of tentative deliberation, a couple of reaches away.

Fropome watched, thoroughly entranced. He didn't dare move. This might be important. A sign.

Everything was still; him, the grumbling bushes, the whispering grass, even the grazers looked puzzled.

The pod moved. Part of its casing fell back inside itself, producing a hole in the smooth exterior.

And something came out.

It was small and silver, and it walked on what might have been hind legs, or a pair of over-developed roots. It crossed to one of the grazers and started making noises at it. The grazer was so surprised it fell over. It lay staring up at the strange silver creature, blinking. Cubs ran, terrified, for their mothers. Other grazers looked at each other, or at Fropome, who still wasn't sure what to do.

The silver seedlet moved to another grazer and made noises at it. Confused, the grazer broke wind. The seedlet went to the animal's rear end and started speaking loudly there.

Fropome clapped a couple of vines together to respectfully request the silver creature's attention, and made to spread the same two leaf-palms on the ground before the seedlet, in a gesture of supplication.

The creature leapt back, detached a bit of its middle with one of its stubby upper limbs, and pointed it at Fropome's vines. There was a flash of light and Fropome felt pain as his leaf-palms crisped and smoked. Instinctively, he lashed out at the creature, knocking it to the ground. The detached bit flew away across the meadow and hit a grazer cub on the flank.

Fropome was shocked, then angry. He held the struggling creature down with one undamaged vine while he inspected the damage to his vines. They'd probably fall off and take days to re-grow. He used another limb to grasp the silver seedlet and bring it up to his eye cluster. He shook it, then up-ended it and stuck its top down at the leaves it had burned, and shook it again.

He brought it back up to inspect it more closely.

Damn funny thing to have come out of a seed pod, he thought, twisting the object this way and that. It looked a little like a grazer except it was thinner and silvery and the head was just a smooth reflective sphere. Fropome could not work out how it stayed upright. The over-large top made it look especially unbalanced. Possibly it wasn't meant to totter around for long; those pointed leg-like parts were probably roots. The thing wriggled in his grasp.

He tore off a little of the silvery outer bark and tasted it in a nestrap. He spat it out again. Not animal or vegetable; more like mineral. Very odd.

Root-pink tendrils squirmed at the end of the stubby

upper limb, where Fropome had torn the outer covering off. Fropome looked at them, and wondered.

He took hold of one of the little pink filaments and pulled.

It came off with a faint 'pop'. Another, muffled-sounding noise came from the silvery top of the creature.

She loves me . . .

Fropome pulled off another tendril. Pop. Sap the colour of the setting sun dribbled out.

She loves me not . . .

Pop pop pop. He completed that set of tendrils:

She loves me . . .

Excited, Fropome pulled the covering off the end of the other upper limb. More tendrils.

. . . She loves me not.

A grazer cub came up and pulled at one of Fropome's lower branches. In its mouth it held the silvery creature's burner device, which had hit it on the flank. Fropome ignored it.

She loves me . . .

The grazer cub gave up pulling at Fropome's branch. It squatted down on the meadow, dropping the burner on the grass and prodding inquisitively at it with one paw.

The silvery seedlet was wriggling enthusiastically in Fropome's grip, thin red sap spraying everywhere.

Fropome completed the tendrils on the second upper limb.

Pop. She loves me not.

Oh no!

The grazer cub licked the burner, tapped it with its paw. One of the other cubs saw it playing with the bright toy and started ambling over towards it.

On a hunch, Fropome tore the covering off the blunt roots at the base of the creature. Ah ha!

She loves me . . .

The grazer cub at Fropome's side got bored with the shiny bauble; it was about to abandon the thing where it lay when it saw its sibling approaching, looking inquisitive. The first cub growled and started trying to pick the burner up with its mouth.

Pop . . . She loves me not!

Ah! Death! Shall my pollen never dust her perfectly formed ovaries? Oh, wicked, balanced, so blandly symmetrical *even* universe!

In his rage, Fropome ripped the silvery covering right off the lower half of the leaking, weakly struggling seedlet.

Oh unfair life! Oh treacherous stars!

The growling grazer cub hefted the burner device into its mouth.

Something clicked. The cub's head exploded.

Fropome didn't pay too much attention. He was staring intently at the bark-stripped creature he held.

. . . wait a moment . . . there *was* something left. Up there, just where the roots met . . .

Thank heavens; the thing was odd after all!

Oh happy day!

(pop)

She loves me!

IRON SHOES

GERALDINE HARRIS

GERALDINE HARRIS

Geraldine Harris is a well-known name in the SF field. She is the author of the *Seven Citadels* quartet comprising *Prince of the Godborn*, *The Children of the Wind*, *The Dead Kingdom* and *The Seventh Gate*, all published in separate volumes by Unicorn.

THE CASTLE WAS always cold. It had been built in the harsh months and the thickness of the walls trapped perpetual winter inside. In spite of the cold I sat by the window because I loved to watch the snow. Every fall of snow is like the chance of a new beginning. The past seems frozen and there is hope that it will melt with the thaw. I was trying to embroider a kerchief with roses. The sort of useless task my husband liked to see me struggle with. 'You look a picture,' he'd say, 'sitting there with the embroidery on your lap.'

Even in the days when I was anxious to please him I knew that I didn't want to be a picture. Flat and bright, few shadows, no depths. That's what he wanted in a queen, a picture of idealised femininity, a crowned simper. He might as well have commissioned the court painter to do a life-sized portrait of me and prop that against the throne. Except that he couldn't get sons from a portrait. He couldn't get sons from me either, but he didn't know that then. Perhaps something in me rebelled against bringing more males into the world, even before I began to hate him.

In those days I was stupid enough to want a daughter. I thought that a daughter would be a natural ally, would grow into a friend. I had been forbidden to bring anyone with me from home. That was the custom. They stripped me of everyone and everything so that I would be forced to clothe myself in my new country, my new loyalties. In time even my memories were stripped away. I couldn't believe that there had ever been a period when I wasn't a stranger. The alien queen. The dark queen. My husband was very fair. The golden king they called him. The contrast pleased him. He was bored with his butter-haired, milk-skinned mistresses. I didn't want my child to look like him, or them.

I sat by the open window longing for a daughter, forgetting my embroidery. I felt a prick as if the roses in the design were punishing my neglect with their thorns. I lifted my hand and three drops of blood fell on to the snowy sill beside the ebony window-frame. White, red and black: the colours of a woman's life as men paint it. White for the purity they demand for the sake of smear-ing it; red for the blood they cause us to shed to make more men; black for the treachery of which they accuse us. Can hatred of a conqueror count as treachery? But I was young, a new bride. I forgot the iron needle, the thorns on the roses. I thought the blood on the snow was beautiful and I wanted a daughter as white as snow, as red as blood, as black as the ebony of the window-frame. Fate gave her to me, laughing behind his hand. A daughter cold to me as snow, bloody in her vengeance and black hearted.

It was a difficult birth and I was ill for a long time afterwards. The king hardly came near me. He hated sick people. They reminded him that there were limits to his power. He couldn't bully blood or pain. My ladies-in-waiting presumed to pity me because I'd produced a daughter instead of a son. When I threw their pity back at them they wrapped it up and put it away and never brought it out again. They made sure that I knew about his mistresses.

When I recovered I worked hard to regain my beauty. Every night and every morning I stood naked in front of my mirror, scrutinising each detail of my face, my hair, my skin, my breasts . . . My ladies thought I was ludicrously vain. It wasn't vanity that drove me but fear and, as the years passed, desperation.

'Am I more beautiful than any of my ladies?' I would ask my reflection.

'Yes. Yes. Yes.'

'Am I more beautiful than any of his mistresses?'

'Yes. Yes.'

'Am I the fairest of all?'

'Yes.'

Often I would argue with my reflection, demand to be certain that my eyes were finer than one woman's or my breasts firmer than another's. I told myself that I was certain.

For the first few years the king came often to my bed, but I had no sons to give him, only miscarriages, as if the needle had pierced my womb not my finger. He was bound to me by treaties, by trade agreements. A royal marriage cannot publicly be dissolved, but in private the blood of my miscarriages washed it away.

I was afraid at first that he would take out his frustration on our daughter. I think he meant to, but she gave him her first smile, cooed at him from her cradle, spoke his name before mine. Even then she had an instinct for placating the powerful and she was a beautiful child. Everyone said so. Her nurses indulged her tantrums because, they would explain with stupid smiles on their faces, she was 'such a pretty little thing that you don't have the heart to scold her.'

I had the heart. A heart loving enough to risk rejection by trying to turn that lump of greed and selfishness into a human being.

'Don't hit nurse.' 'Don't grab, don't snatch.' 'Give that back it isn't yours.' 'No, you can't have another.' I was the only person who said no to her. The king thought I was harsh with her, an unfeeling mother. He only saw her at her best, with him she was winsome and frolicsome, pleading prettily to be allowed to stay up late, to be given a new lap-dog – pleading, always pleading, for yet another favour, yet another present. He liked people to ask for things, to put themselves in his debt.

When Snow White was seven years old she was given her own ladies-in-waiting. One day I came quietly into a room and heard her telling them that I was not her real mother. Her real mother had died when she was born. I wanted to fling myself at her, to weep, to beg, to cry out, *Snow White I treat you this way because I love you, because I love what you could become!* But her ladies were staring at me with malicious curiosity, waiting to see what I would do.

'Don't be foolish,' I said coldly, 'I am your mother.'

Her eyes filled with tears. She had the trick of crying without making herself ugly. A valuable accomplishment. Her ladies clustered round to hug and stroke her, to soothe and comfort. No one gave me a word or a gesture of comfort.

At first the king protested when Snow White prattled about her real mother, the kind and gentle mother who would have let her do whatever she liked. When he could not persuade her with toys and sweetmeats and rides on his shoulders, he shrugged and said, 'Children get these fancies. It will pass.'

He was still her 'darling dada' and a dozen other pet names. Why should he care what she called me? After a while, if Snow White had to refer to me she called me 'her' or 'she'. People rebuked her for it in a desultory way, but she had only to smile or shake her black curls and the offence was forgotten. Next she found excuses not to touch me – 'She has cold lips', 'Her hands smell nasty' – and she would run to her father's arms instead, or to her ladies, or to anyone who would admire her.

It was true that my hands often had a faint odour of sulphur for I had taken up alchemy and spent many hours of each day in my workroom among my stills and furnaces, my crucibles and alembics. Of course the king did not approve. It was not a suitable pastime for a lady. There was nothing pretty or frivolous about it. I told him

I was only interested in finding cures . He couldn't forbid that. Women traditionally bind up the wounds made by men. It is one of the few uses they allow us. From time to time I did devise salves and potions which, if they worked no miracles, did no harm either. I made no great claims for them. Because of that few courtiers wished to be treated by me. They wanted certainty, juicy lies to rub in or drink down. Instead I used my skills on the beggars who came to the castle gates in hope of scraps. I healed the sores on their feet so they could trudge away. I cured them of coughing blood so they would live to suffer through another winter. I got little gratitude for my cold charity and I deserved less. The beggars sensed that I blended no love into my salves, distilled none in my potions.

It was the secret language of alchemy that drew me and my workroom became my queendom, a world within the world, a realm unspoiled by greed and passion. The Philosopher's Stone and the Elixir of Youth are treasures of the mind and the spirit, the stone that turns worldly sorrows into the gold of hope, the elixir that contains in every drop the immortality of a soul. But my perfect world was not quite secure. There was a crack through which the outer world seeped in. Eternal youth, eternal beauty. No one despises the beautiful or treats them with contempt. In the outer world my beauty was my only power and I clung to it.

I made ointments to keep my skin the colour of honey and the texture of foxglove petals. I made powders to polish and whiten my teeth and lotions to sleeken and blacken my hair, drops to make my dark eyes glitter, salves to soften and redden my lips, rouge to rosy my cheeks and nipples, perfumes to dab on breast and thigh. Every night and every morning as the years passed I looked in my mirror.

'Am I still more beautiful than any of my ladies?'

'Yes, yes, yes.'

'Am I still more beautiful than any of his mistresses?'

'Yes, yes.'

'Am I still the fairest of all?'

'Yes.'

I could still make the king desire me and Snow White saw and half-understood. She did not know exactly what it was that men and women did together but she knew that sometimes the king looked at me in a way that he did not look at her; that sometimes he touched me in a way that he did not touch her; that sometimes he wanted me in a way that he did not want her. He loved her as he had never loved me, but that was not enough for Snow White. She demanded to be first with him at every moment and in every way. The idea of sharing someone's love was beyond her. She loved herself with a greedy passion and everything that she wanted she must instantly have or the whole world became a hateful place. So she began trying to push me out of the king's thoughts, began trying to satisfy him completely.

Whenever she sensed that he was looking at me with desire, she thrust herself between us, begging 'dada' to play one more game with her, to give her just one more kiss. She was always climbing into his lap, clinging about his neck, nuzzling against his cheek. She insisted that he dry her after her bath and lie down beside her on her bed to cuddle her asleep. Instinct guided her. She did not know what satisfying her father would mean and I did not want her to discover it. How could I blame her for loving herself so much? Who else could she trust to love her all her life? Her body was everything to her. She did not understand that men could take it from her control, violate it and discard it; that men could teach her to hate herself. Snow White, Rose Red, Ebony Black. If she made him her lover she would lose her father and to enjoy her body without guilt he would have to destroy the person inside it. He was what the world calls a good father but I knew how seductive innocent greed and innocent beauty could be. Morning and evening I looked in my mirror.

'Am I more beautiful than any of my ladies?'

'Yes, yes, yes.'

'Am I more beautiful than any of his mistresses?'

'Yes, yes.'

'Am I more beautiful than Snow White?'

I tried to warn my husband, hinting at first and then speaking plainly. He railed at me, accusing me of a sick jealousy, calling my mind a midden, my feelings open gutters. His anger warned me that the danger was close. To save Snow White I would have to make him send her away. I still had a faint, foolish hope that one day she would look back and thank me for my care. He already thought me mad with jealousy, it was not difficult to convince him that I was mad indeed and a danger to our daughter.

I used all my arts to bring him to my bed and satisfy him. Then I held him close and whispered poison. Snow White was evil. She must be destroyed. I would not let him touch me again until he had taken her into the forest and killed her. I begged him to open her white breast and rip out her heart. I swore that I would never be at peace until I had eaten that heart, swallowed our daughter, returned her to my womb. He struggled out of my embrace and ran from my bed, but the next day he took Snow White into the forest and returned at dusk without her.

He did not say a word, but at dinner a silver dish was set before me. I lifted the cover and saw a heart, skewered and roasted black. I knew it must belong to some wild beast killed in the day's hunting, but I could not touch it. He was watching me closely and I turned to him and said, 'Sir, will you not share this tender morsel with me?' He struck me then, in front of the whole court. For one instant I believed that he had done what I asked, that he had murdered our daughter and a scream rose in my throat, a scream that would never have stopped. Then I realised how little stir that blow had caused, how little surprise. They knew, the lords-in-waiting and the ladies, the chamberlains and the pages, they knew that the king had sent their princess away to save her from my jealousy. Lovely Snow White, the darling of the court, banished by her cruel mother. Or did they all believe now that I was not her real mother?

The scream crept out of my throat but they heard it as a laugh. Even then it was not too late to explain – to cry out that I loved Snow White, loved her more than any of them, but that would have brought her back to court, back into danger. I picked up a knife and cut into the heart. I ate it piece by piece while the court watched in silence and then I smiled at my husband. He never came to my bed again, never so much as touched my hand.

After that night I spent more and more time in the sanctuary of my workroom. Rumours spread among the people. They had never cheered me when I rode out, now they whispered curses and threw stones. My guards always just failed to catch the offenders but I made no complaint to the king. At court pages shrank from me as I passed and my ladies waited on me in hostile silence. Night and morning they watched me stand naked before my mirror and I knew what they were thinking, *She is beautiful still, but not as beautiful as young Snow White, and soon she will be old*.

It was not difficult to find out where the king had hidden our daughter. I had only to wrap a shawl around me and walk with a crone-like stoop through the kitchen yard. They were all talking about their wicked queen and their innocent, lovely princess. I had hoped that he would send her far away to the safety of his sister's court. Instead he had placed her in the house of the Royal Dwarfs. It was more fitting than he realised. The dwarfs were treated as if their minds were as stunted as their bodies. They were encouraged to behave like greedy, spiteful children – leaping on to table tops, trampling on plates of food, pissing into tankards, snatching hats and mimicking the owners, stealing fans and jewels to juggle with. The king laughed heartily at their antics; they never tormented him. I could not bear the dwarfs near me. As they capered they were always grinning or cackling or screaming with delight but their eyes were full of a cold, adult hatred. Was I the only one who could see it?

Ugliness was their livelihood – ugliness of body and mind and spirit – yet even they were touched by Snow White's beauty. They loved to make her laugh by teasing her ladies or her pages. I hoped that in their carnival company she might realise what it was never to grow up, to go on snatching at life and gobbling it down, only to find that the more you snatched and gobbled the more your rage and frustration grew at the worlds you could not reach. I hoped that the dwarfs would make my daughter feel old and wise and after a month I longed to see her again, to know if she had changed.

I stained my skin with the juice of walnuts, wrapped my hair in a white cloth and put on a long cloak with a hood that shaded my face. Then I took up the staff and pack of an old pedlar woman and hobbled unnoticed out of the palace. Once in the forest a charcoal burner told me the way to the House of the Dwarfs. The king had gone for a pleasure trip on the royal barge and I knew that the dwarfs would be in attendance. It was almost dusk when I reached the place. Snow White was standing at a window, alone and bored, waiting for the dwarfs to return from court. When I tapped on the door she opened the window and told me to go away, told me she was not to let anyone in, told me in a tone that invited no argument. I said she was wise not to let strangers into the house but that I was only an old pedlar woman who could do her no harm. I added a slight quaver to my voice, but this was the moment when she should have recognised her mother. Snow White ran to the door to let me in, demanding to see what I had in my pack. She did not look at me closely. Why should she take any interest in an old pauper?

I rummaged in my pack, glancing round the room. There were dishes of sticky sweetmeats and a plate of half-eaten cakes on the table. The floor was strewn with costly toys, many of them broken as if they had been stamped on or kicked. I drew out a wooden spinning-top and a rag doll with yellow hair. Snow White frowned and told me that she wasn't a child. She was wearing a white apron over her rich dress. I guessed that she had been playing at keeping house. I curtsied an apology and asked if she would care to buy something for the others who lived in the house, presents for her friends, her family . . . ? Her face darkened again. No, she must have something for herself, something pretty – a scarf, a belt, a pair of stockings. As she spoke her hands swept down her body as if she wanted to display its beauty even to an old pedlar woman. She was changing, but not in the way that I had hoped.

Out of my pack I drew a handful of scarlet ribbons. 'A great girl like you should lace in her waist, that's the way to make men look at you, the more you go in the more you go out and that's what men like.' I dangled the ribbons before her and she reached out to snatch at them. 'Shall I tie them for you dear?'

She nodded and I stepped behind her, put my arms around her waist and threaded the ribbons across and across. We had not been so close since she was a baby.

'Now, tell me how tight?'

Snow White stroked the swell of her small breasts and then the curve of her hips. 'Tighter.'

I pulled on the ribbons. 'That's right dear, we have to suffer to be beautiful. Men don't like us to be natural, they like us to take trouble for them. Can't call our bodies our own can we? Tighter still?'

Snow White nodded dreamily. The ribbons looked like bloody slashes across her middle.

In the distance I could hear shouting and high-pitched laughter. The dwarfs were coming home. I pushed Snow White against a wall, pinned her there with my knee and pulled on the laces with all my strength. She tried to scream but she had no breath for it. 'What did you say dear? Tighter? That's right. All trussed up and ready for the knife. That's what they like and that's what you're giving them. Never mind the pain, men will hurt you worse than this.'

Gasping for air, Snow White fell back into my arms. I laid her down and ran from the house out of the rear door.

That night when I looked in the mirror I saw Snow White. As her body grew mine seemed to diminish. There is plenty of lust in the world but not enough beauty. Perhaps daughters can only get beauty by taking it from their mothers. Is that why women age so quickly? She did not need to steal my beauty. I would have given it gladly to protect her, given it to her to use as a weapon if she had no choice, but I wanted her to know that there might be choices.

For the next few days I watched my husband carefully to see if he changed towards me. He was cold and distant as usual, but there was no flare of new anger. The dwarfs would have quickly cut the ribbons and revived Snow White. She was probably ashamed to confess to her father that she had disobeyed his order and let a stranger into the house. The dwarfs would tell no one what had happened, they would be afraid of being blamed.

Seven days after my first visit the dwarfs were summoned to court to help entertain an ambassador. I streaked my hair with grey, put on a wide brimmed hat and a filthy cloak and entered the forest. Snow White was sitting by a window examining herself in its panes. There were no mirrors in the House of the Dwarfs. They accepted other people's standards of beauty and ugliness and snubbed their own reflections. At first Snow White would not even open the window, but I whined and grovelled and held up my tray of combs. She came to the door. To her all paupers looked much alike but the clothes and the hair were enough to convince her that I was a different pedlar from the last. 'A comb my deary, for those pretty locks? Such black hair, like a starless night . . .'

Her hand stretched out to the tray. She was attracted to the red comb, as I knew she would be.

'Is that the one you fancy deary? Real blood they use in the glaze, that's how they get the colour so bright. Just the thing to make your locks look blacker still and your face look whiter.' She picked up the comb and turned it over in her hand. 'Long hair, no wit, that's what men say deary, but that's the way they like us. Everything empty for them to fill. Long hair saps the strength, but they like us to be frail. Ah now, there's a tangle. That will never do. Men like everything smooth. Let me tease it out for you and then I'll fix the comb in your hair.'

Snow White bowed her head and stood docile under my hands, as she always did to be made more beautiful. I seized a handful of hair, jerked back her head and dug the comb into her scalp. The poison was quick working. I left her sprawled across the doorstep for the dwarfs to find. They had only to remove the comb to revive her.

That night I stood before the mirror and again I saw Snow White. At her age I had been much the same, delighting in my burgeoning beauty, using it to make rash moves in a game I didn't understand. It seemed to me now that from puberty to the birth of my daughter I was like a sleepwalker, absorbed in a fanciful world which had myself at its centre. The pain of child-bed woke me, but I longed always to recover that sleep. I knew then what I must do if Snow White had not heeded the ribbons and the comb.

The king did not alter towards me, neither Snow White nor the dwarfs had told him about the poisoned comb, but he was away from court more and more often. I knew that he was visiting his darling daughter in the house in the forest. There were no ladies-in-waiting there to chaperone their meetings and what hope was there that the dwarfs woud see and understand the danger? It was time for me to act and after many hours alone in my workroom I was ready. I put on a hooded grey cloak and slipped unseen out of the palace.

I did not ask Snow White to let me in. I held up my basket of shining apples and stood absolutely still until curiosity made her unlatch the window. She only opened it a crack but the scent of the apples' reached her.

'Have pity on a poor tired old woman with many miles still to walk to market. Spare me a cup of water and you shall have the pick of my apples.'

She told me that she could not let anyone in. 'No need my love, pass me the cup through the window. Here, take the apple first if you don't trust me.' All but one of the apples in my basket were pale green, a bitter colour, but the colour of growth. Snow White's hand hovered over a fruit that was half green and half red. 'Ah that's the pick indeed. Take a bite of the green my love and never mind its sting. The sweetness comes after.'

I threw my hood back then and she knew me. 'Eat it yourself beggar woman,' she said.

'Why so I have my love, but if you still don't trust me I'll share the apple with you.'

I bit into the tart green flesh, chewed it and swallowed it while she watched. Snow White smiled and grabbed the apple, thinking her caution had outwitted me. She bit into the glossy flesh of the red half.

As she slumped across the windowsill I took the apple from her hand, wrapped it in a kerchief and put it back in my basket. I looked at my daughter, white as snow, red as blood, black as ebony. There was no poisoned ribbon or comb for the dwarfs to find. They would be powerless to revive Snow White. I walked back through the forest.

They put Snow White in a glass coffin and carried the coffin to the summit of a hill behind the House of the Dwarfs. I laughed when I heard. It showed their love for what it was. The king, the courtiers, the dwarfs, they had no window into her mind, her body was everything to them. Now they had that body on permanent display, totally vulnerable, like a freak in a fairground booth. The king knew that I must have poisoned her, but he couldn't prove it. Where were his witnesses? There was nothing he could do openly and his secret attempts on my life failed. I am skilled in the detection of poisons.

As it became clear that our daughter would not die, as she lived and breathed and grew in her glass coffin, the king's anger cooled. Every day he visited the place that had become Snow White's shrine and wallowed in extravagant grief, tantalized by desire without fulfilment, an ideal love. If I had told him that he wanted her to sleep for ever he would have struck me.

As the years passed I thought and dreamed about her waking, planning exactly how I would embrace her and what I would say. At worst her body would be mature enough to gratify her immature desires safely. At best, nourished by dreams, her mind would have grown as much as her body and she would wake as my sister. I would know by the look in her eyes as I stooped over her. My whole life narrowed to that future moment, but it was stolen from me, ravished away.

By day and by night the dwarfs took turns to watch over Snow White. Gradually news of this marvel spread and the curious flocked to stare. Most were turned away, but the dwarfs made a fat living taking bribes from the wealthier visitors for a glimpse of the glass coffin and its treasure. One day the prince of a neighbouring country came idling through the forest in search of marvels to banish boredom. He tossed the dwarfs a pouch of silver to let him climb the hill and look into the coffin. Curiosity quickly became obsession. He and his escort camped in the forest and each morning the prince paid handsomely to gaze at Snow White. After seven days he offered to buy the coffin. The dwarfs were tempted, but they dared not agree. They knew that the king would kill them if they sold his daughter. The prince was determined. He meant to keep the coffin by him always. He threatened to have his soldiers kill the dwarfs and take what he wanted. Panicked by threats and lured by bribes the dwarfs agreed. The coffin was hoisted on the shoulders of four servants and the prince and his escort, with the dwarfs trailing behind, hurried to the border.

Later it was put about that the servants had stumbled, that the coffin had fallen, jolting Snow White awake. It might have been that way, or it might have been that the prince forced the lid, gripped Snow White in his arms and thrust his tongue between her lips dislodging the poisoned piece of apple. Whichever way, a letter was sent to the king announcing that his daughter had woken from her long sleep and was to marry the prince. He could hardly refuse his consent. In the circumstances, what other suitor would take her? My husband would not go to the wedding. I thought that he was jealous, I thought that he could not bear to see Snow White enjoyed by another man. I had not read the letter. I did not know what he knew.

I made the journey to the prince's realm and was met by high ranking nobles and escorted to a grand house close to the palace. This courteous welcome gave me great hope. Perhaps Snow White had woken into wisdom or perhaps a few weeks of her prince's company had been enough to breed doubts about her former self. Before I dressed for the wedding I stood naked in front of a mirror. I had washed the dye from my hair and grey clung like cobwebs to the black. My honey skin was turning sallow. Wrinkles had caught my eyes and were casting their nets across my forehead. My breasts sagged and my ribs jutted. Snow White had no rival in beauty now. I was no longer her other self. I was what she had come from and what she would go to. Surely she could look on me now with compassion?

I dressed in a plain gown of black silk with no jewels except my wedding ring. I was seated in a place of honour in the cathedral. Most women cry at weddings because of what they refuse to know and they call their tears 'tears of joy'. My tears were of pity. I knew what Snow White would suffer, but she need not be alone as I had been. I would be there to comfort her.

When Snow White lifted her veil for the prince's kiss I saw that her cheeks had a hectic flush, the colour of the ribbons and the comb and the poisoned apple. I knew from the way they touched each other that they were already lovers. That also gave me hope. Surely, I thought, she must have begun to discover what men mean by love and how badly it matches with what women mean. I was right about that but I did not truly know my daughter. I believed that I had stared at the worst in her without flinching, but I was wrong.

In the procession from the cathedral to the palace I tried to catch my daughter's eye, but she would not look at me. Hundreds of guests crowded into the great hall for the wedding feast but there was an empty space before the dais. I was led to a chair on the left of the prince. When all the guests were seated he stood up and announced that before the feast began there was to be an entertainment. A page entered carrying a pair of cunningly fashioned metal shoes resting on a scarlet cushion. Next came two servants staggering under the weight of a brazier full of burning coals. Behind them was a man gloved and masked like an executioner and holding iron tongs.

Before I could move two soldiers had wrenched back my arms and pinned me to my chair. The prince had begun to recite my crimes and my sentence for them. The iron shoes were to be placed in the coals and, when they were white hot, they would be forced on to my feet and I would dance the dance of death. I understood now why my husband had not come to the feast. He wanted me dead, but without appearing to consent to it. I did not speak a word or even cry out but I turned my face towards Snow White. Still she would not look at me.

She sat with downcast eyes, the image of a modest bride. What use was it to defend myself? Only my daughter knew the truth. Oh and she did know. I was the warning she did not want to hear. She thought she could escape becoming me by killing me.

It has taken a long while for the shoes to heat. I have had time to remember it all, from the day when I saw the blood on the snow beside the ebony window-frame to this moment. Now the shoes are glowing and the executioner is picking one up in his tongs. My daughter is smiling, but the look on the prince's face is the look my husband gave me when I ate the heart of Snow White. It will not be long, my daughter, before you too are forced to dance in iron shoes.

PAMELA'S PURSUIT

KIM NEWMAN

KIM NEWMAN

Kim Newman, born in 1959, is best known as a film critic and is the author of *Nightmare Movies*. Recently he has co-edited a volume entitled *Horror: The 100 Best Books*. A graduate of Sussex University, he has written a number of short stories for *Interzone*. Kim Newman lives in London. His first novel, *The Night Mayor*, is forthcoming.

PART OF HER strategy had been to feign, first indifference, then reluctance. It bought Pamela time in which to sharpen up. While Robin amassed filmy brochures and solicited testimonials from satisfied friends, she put up a deceptive resistance. She spent her lunch hours at the weapons library. Her reactions were fine, but her accuracy needed work. Once, she let a stranger pick her up on the range and sessioned with him. He had willingly paid the registration fee, and looked devastated when she remaindered him with her first slug. She hadn't needed to finish him, she had brought him definitively down, but she had filled his heart all the same. She had always had a healthy interest in killing. Besides, he had been a feeler, and she didn't like feelers.

After three years, Pamela and Robin could still hurt each other as deeply as when they first started going together. She had completely changed his face, eroding the fleshy pockets under his chin and cheekbones with her talons. With the aid of popular manuals, he had diligently mapped all the response centres of her body. He was persistent, but not terribly inventive. Robin was always imagining he had new ideas, but it was Pamela who was forever trying to expand the envelope of their marriage. She had been subtly manouevring him towards the Game for several months. As always, she needed to let him think it was his idea. But she had been the one to think of inviting the Raiths over, and nudged them into enthusing. Ted Raith was a squidge, and his wife could be a bove at her worst; they were Robin's associates. But they had experimented, she knew, with the Game. Robin had kept up a stream of excited questions. She knew that, once again, she had him.

Her feeler victim had paid for his own remaindering, but marital etiquette meant that Pamela and Robin would have to go halves. She didn't mind. She had placed a portion of her private funding in an insurance policy, and duped Robin into signing it under the impression he was entering a breakfast cereal contest. His caption had been terribly good, and when she later told him he had lost, he had humourlessly initiated a boycott of the Kellogg's company. She suspected him of arranging for the fire-bombing of several of their European warehouses. They took the fee down to the palace with them, in platinum wafers, and passed it over to the Game officials in the foyer. They hand-printed holograph waivers, absolving the company from any possible liabilities for permanent disabilities, and were separated.

'Your first time?' asked the bovey matron in the ladies' changing-room as Pamela shucked her street armour.

'Yes,' she sort-of lied.

'You'll win. The wife usually does.'

'Uh-huh?' She needed help with press-seams. The matron obliged. In the full-length mirror, Pamela looked svelte in black fatigues.

'Sure. The men never bother to do their prep. They don't take this seriously. You've practised?'

'A little.' She climbed into an elaborate shoulder holster, and adjusted the straps. It had to be tight enough not to make giveaway noises, but not so tight as to impede respiratory functions.

'A little? I'll bet your husband hasn't so much as squeezed off a slug in anger since he left school.'

'That's very probable,' she said, but added loyally, 'but he's always competent. He won't go into the palace without being sure he can walk out.'

'Will you surprise him?'

Pamela smiled as the matron gave her the roscoe. She held the thing, not gripping too hard, gauging weight and balance.

'I think so.'

The roscoe was light and ladylike. The Game didn't let you tote your own hardware. Pamela preferred something a bit more blatant. Heat-seeking slugs, and dum-dum scattershots. She believed in doing as much damage as possible.

The matron helped her flip the clip and slitch the safeties. The clip rattled going in, but was silent when she shook the roscoe.

'Soundproof,' said the matron.

The individual slugs in the clip were the size of grains of rice, compressed and cool. They'd get bigger and hotter when she squeezed them off. The matron encouraged her to unloose one for luck.

Pamela pointed, not really aiming, and shot a portrait. It was a large blue picture of some forgotten statesman with an unsympathetic simper. She holed the face, just under the right eye, making a crocodile tear. She had hoped for the bridge of the nose.

'It's off slightly.'

'That's easy to fix. Here.'

The matron took the roscoe, and gave the barrel a precise twist. This time, Pamela got her mark between the eyes. She put the weapon to her lips and blew away a curl of smoke. Her nostrils caught the tang of ozone.

'Of course you know you shouldn't do that to a real person . . .'

'Not unless you're serious.'

'No. Your brain is where you live. You only get one.'

'I know.'

'Accidents happen. Even here.'

'Not to me.'

'We have rigid safety controls. When you applied, your husband and you were thoroughly out-checked.

You have no especial history of psychopathic or socio-pathic disorder.'

'That's nice to know.'

The matron kissed her on the lips for good luck, and felt under her tunic for her own benefit. She pulled an acorn-sized knobble out from Pamela's armpit.

'A frag? That's not allowed, you know.'

Pamela shrugged. It was the concealment she had expected to lose. Like the tracer Robin had put in her ear-ring. They wouldn't search for any lesser items now, although she had persevered and found the bug in her hair. Robin would try to go into the palace with an edge. She thought she could match that.

The portrait hinged aside, and Pamela stepped alone into the palace. The first room bore the scars of the Game. There were join-the-dots bullet pocks on the wall. Chords of blood wove into the clear water streaming between mossy clumps of furniture. There was little cover nearby, and she couldn't precog any immediate danger. She explored further.

She didn't know this layout at all. The first session had been in another part of the palace. But she shouldn't be at any particular disadvantage. She guessed that Robin had tried to access the floor-plan too; he would have run aground even before coming up against the Master Block that had brought her down. As far as knowledge of the terrain went, they were even. Theoretically, Robin was a better tactician than she – the hairbug had been a nice try. But he didn't know what it was really like to stalk and be stalked. She did. She liked it.

The next room was darker. She took time to squeeze the cheater's kit out of her shoulder pad. With the mud-sticks, she tiger-striped her face black and green. Then, she fitted the blackcaps over her more visible teeth and licked until they stuck. The one-way contacts were more difficult to get comfy with, but they were worth the itch. Her eyes should look like black marbles now, and her night vision was improved by a factor of five. Details of the room emerged from the shadows. She could read the spines of swollen books on the shelves; previously she had only been able to make out rough shapes. The uniform volumes were all by someone called Hansard.

She ungloved her left hand, and darked the bare skin. Her fingers might be another edge. They had been her first, and so far only major, alteration. Apart from the nerve turn-arounds. When she had had her nails pulled and replaced with switchblades, her first husband – the squidge – had tried to call up his legal expeditor on the ouija slab. He didn't believe her when she said the attachments were mainly for dealing with shrink-wrapped packages, and had gone on punching keys. While he was on hold, she had opted for the Moscow Divorce and snipped his spinal column with her bunched fingertoys. When he was dead, she had been able to roll his head into funny positions. He hadn't spoken to her since.

She extruded her claws experimentally, and scratched a book. It had been left flat on a tilting desk. The thick leather parted, and her nail sank into yellow fleshy pages. She flicked the pulp away, and sheathed her sharpies. The book felt very boring. She picked up echoes of a few dreary tirades, and quickly brushed them out of mind. They reminded her of her first husband.

It had been her own fault, really, for marrying at thirteen. She had been much too old for a soldier. All he had learned in his military kindergarten was the three Fs – feedin', fightin' and fillin'-in forms. He didn't think women should be allowed to kill people. He had taken no interest in her terrapins. Her only regret over the split-up was that it had come four months too early for Shelley. Neither of them could legally apply for custody unless the child was over five years old, and so Shelley had been taken to the Farm. Pamela sometimes got the horrid feeling that some stranger was looking back at her through her daughter's eyes. It was unlikely, but possible.

Yes, Husband Number One had been a squidge. Robin wasn't a squidge, but he could be a bit of a skulk at times. Rather, he was a lot of a skulk a lot of the time. Take the Game: he had emphasised all through the prelims how important it was for the session to be mutually satisfactory. But she knew he had laid in a stock of quick-kill slugs and would, when it came to the face-off, opt to remainder her quickly rather than take the risk of prolonging the agony. He was like that. Sometimes Pamela thought Robin didn't count her as a real person.

She padded on catslippers through the dark rooms, professionally out-checking each one, roscoe held up near her face, medium pressure on the squeeze-grip. There was a surprisingly thriving ecosystem inside the palace. The vegetation was mostly fungal, but there were some vines, grasses and overgrown descendants of pot plants. The water ran down the walls in curtains. Some of the herringbone tiles had been rotted through or mulched by aggressive roots. There was rumoured to be a pack of feral corgis in the jungle somewhere, but they oughtn't to be dangerous.

She kept to the doors and corridors, avoiding the secret passageways. There were indigenous inhabitants in there somewhere. Nobody was supposed to live in the palace any longer, but elements of the *ancien régime* had stayed behind and interbred in the depths. The Game people didn't really try to clear them out, because they weren't that dangerous. Feeble-minded, lazy-limbed ichabods with huge ears and rabbit teeth, by all accounts. Richer sportspeople than Pamela and Robin were taken on occasional safaris, hoping to bag an inno-cent bystander for the doping-room wall. She wanted nothing to do with that. She didn't approve of killing anything that couldn't kill you back.

She found an ear nailed to one door, and was duly

warned away from what lay beyond. The thing was
normal-sized, and still warm. The place was quiet,
except for the running water, and occasional gunshots
in different wings. She oughtn't to run into any other
parties. This was a private session, and she and Robin
were supposed to be in one of the many sealed-off zones.

In one room, she found a remain. It was one of the
indigenes, gone for good. The head had been taken, but
the zaroff had left a trampled tiara. The remain wore a
billowing, mildewed dress with an array of medal-like
brooches in the shoulders and across the breast. Pamela
didn't think it had been a woman, judging from the feet.
There were plants growing out of the thing, so it had
obviously been remaindered some time ago.

She stepped into a corridor, and found a spoor. Wet
footprints on a ragged pile carpet. Robin was either being
careless or setting a trap. He couldn't see the prints
without lenses, so perhaps he hadn't been aware he was
making them. But he ought to know if he'd got his feet
wet. She didn't want to underestimate him. It was the
kind of thing he was always doing to her. She left
the corridor, and took a parallel course to the tracks,
expecting him in each successive room.

She was excited, but in control. She knew she had
an edge there. He would be nervy by now, probably
irritated. In situations like this, he usually struck up a
dopesmoke; here he'd be afraid to show a glow-worm.
That would scrunch him inside, ruffle his tentacles. That
gave her a definite, and growing, edge.

In the next room, a swatch of plaster fell from the
ceiling into an open piano, twanging impossible chords.
Pamela swivelled from the waist, went down on one
knee, extended her roscoe arm and squeezed at the door.
Chest height. She squeezed again, lower this time. The
door swung both ways on its remaining hinge and fell
away. There was a cloud of dust in the room, but no
Robin.

Mistake.

She should have taken natural decay into account. The palace was obviously falling apart. She had given Robin an unmistakable aural bearing. She tried to get up, but her knee was wobbly. Finally, she made it. Her mouth was dry, and her eyes stung with water that had built up behind the contacts. Her tunic felt too tight, chafing her. She split the pectoral seam, enjoying the chilly rush, then sealed herself to the choker. Swanny white cleavage would be too tempting a target.

She looked around for cover, and decided on the next-but-one room. Robin would know her general location, but have to out-check each room in turn. She hoped he'd come to her soon. He'd expect a trap, of course, but she would know what he was up to. It would get all this foreplay over with. She ejected the slug clip and checked it. It was fine. The roscoe had worked perfectly. There had been no kick to jolt her elbow out of joint. It still felt like something for potting humming-birds, but a few holes in the right places would do as much serious hurt as a total fleshblast.

From her room, she could hear him coming. He had two choices. There were only two doors. She had a clear shot at each, and, in her position, was shielded by a pair of high-backed chairs. They might not stop a slug, but they'd squidge his aim. He was making a noise. Too much noise. It had to be a blind.

'Pamela,' he shouted.

He was doing something skulky, she knew that much.

'Darling, come out. Let's climax this.'

She stopped breathing, and extruded claws. They shone in the minimal light.

She sighted on the left door, but was ready to switch to the right. Her arm ached after thirty seconds. The roscoe didn't feel light now. There were drops of condensation on the barrel. Pamela's mud was running in rivulets down her neckline. She could have done with that frag now.

Robin stopped cajoling. 'Get ready to be remaindered, squitch!'

His voice was behind the right door. She took aim at it.

There was a pause.

Left door. Right door. Left door. Right door.

He came through the wall, to the extreme left. There was almost no lath and plaster left, all he had to do was tear through a sheet of flowered paper. He had IR shades on. She recognised the kind with a homing facility.

He had been tracking her somehow. There had been a third concealment, one she'd not found. Rats. He had the edge now.

Robin smiled. 'Wedding ring, dear.'

The squidge.

He shot her in the hip, and she fell over, sprawling rather than crouching. The impact hit her like a mailed fist, and waves of warmth ran through her. It was a sensation. Her back arched, and her mouth hung open. Her stifled cry dislodged the blackcaps. She had enough control to spit them out, to prevent herself choking. Her altered nerve endings mis-translated the signals from her wound. Caught up in the rush of feelings, she was nevertheless able to exaggerate her helplessness. She floundered, twitching. Robin came closer and shot her through the lung, missing her heart because she twisted under him. He was too close. The quick-kill slug went through her and fragmented somewhere in the floor, porcupining her back with splinters.

'Sweetheart,' she gasped, squeezing in her first shot. She was hurting now, for real. The confusion of pain and pleasure didn't affect her body control. He took the slugs in his lower belly and thighs and bent double. She knew where his alterations were. He spasmed, and squeezed his grip too much. Slugs sprayed the room in a figure eight. Light flashes gave his dance of death a disco strobe. He stitched her a few times, but she kept her roscoe arm whole.

She got him several times. Knees, for balance. Belly again, for pain. Heart, for the remainder. He went down. The stink made the air thick. His clothes caught fire where the slugs had gone in. The little flames, light-amplified, burned into her lensed eyes. She slithered over to him on her elbows, face down. He was still drawing coughy breaths, and slobbering strawberry spittle.

Before she finished, she stroked his face and neck, leaving her marks, opening his pipes. The last she heard was his final crackle of exhalation. She fell, relaxing, over his remain, and blanked.

Later, the Resurrection Men brought them back. They revived together in their own bed, fast-fading milky scars where their holes had been. The Game official told them she had won, on points.

After everyone had left, Robin was ungracious. They hadn't been able to get all the slugs out, and had had to promise to return and finish the recovery work for a further fee. He had an unwanted alteration, an extra testicle made of lead. She cuddled close to him under their duvet, feeling the odd weighting of his asymmetrical scrotum.

He was still being a skulk. She squeezed him gently.

'Darling,' she said, 'how was it for you?'

THE BEAUTIFUL BITING MACHINE

TANITH LEE

TANITH LEE

Tanith Lee is one of the world's finest and best-known fantasy writers. She is the author of almost forty novels and short-story collections, of plays and television scripts. She has won the World Fantasy Award and the August Derleth Award.

WHEN THE TWO suns go down and it starts to get dark, the Nightfair wakes up, a beast with a thousand bright eyes.

Five miles long, four miles wide, the valley is full of lights, noises, musics, between the tall and echoing hills.

This world's a pleasure planet. It has many and various attractions. The Nightfair is only one. Here there are spinning wheels of yellow sparks against the dusk, and glimmering neon ghost towers ringing with screams, and carousels that maybe come alive. Not everyone cares for these, or the candy awnings, the peppermint arenas, the cries of fortune-tellers in glass cages, the crashing of pre-arranged safe vehicular accidents, the soaring space-flights that never leave the ground. Those that don't care for them don't come. But for those that do, there are the cuisine and superstition and popular art, the sex and syntax and the sin of twenty worlds, to be sampled for a night, or a week of nights. (Who could tolerate more?)

So visit the Valley of Lights. Hurry, hurry, don't be slow or sly or shy.

Welcome to the Nightfair.

'This gentlevyrainian's gotta slight complaint.'

'Tell him to see a doctor.'

'Don't cheek me, Beldek.'

'No, Mr Qire. What seems to be the trouble, sir?'

Beldek and Qire looked through the one-way window at the gentleman from Vyraini. Like all Vyrainians, he was humanoid, greenish, fretful. Vyraini did not esteem the human race, but was patronizingly intrigued by it and its culture. Anything human, where possible, should be experienced, explored. Now this Vyrainian had come to Qire's pavilion at the Nightfair, and was not quite satisfied, had a slight complaint.

'Go and talk to it – him,' said Qire.

'*Me*, sir?'

'You. You speak their lingo. You speak half the damn gurglings of half the damn galaxy, don't you, Beldek? You lazy son-of-a-ghex.'

'If you say so, Mr Qire.'

Beldek opened the long window and stepped through. The other side of the window it looked like a door, glamorous with enamel paint and stained glass. Beldek bowed to the gentlevyrainian with his hands to his face, which was the correct form of greeting from an outworlder. The Vyrainian stood impassive, ears folded.

'*Fo ogch m'mr bnn?*' Beldek inquired courteously.

The Vyrainian seemed gratified, lifted its ears and broke into staccato Vyrainese.

The glottal conversation continued for two and a half minutes. After which, feeling Qire's beady little eyes on him through the one-way door-window, Beldek leisurely set the computer for a twenty per cent refund.

The Vyrainian took its cash, and offered Beldek the salute used when bidding farewell to an inferior but valuable alien. Not all Earthmen knew exactly what the salute implied (a rough translation was: I will let you lick my feet another time, O wise one). Beldek, who did, smiled pleasantly.

The whaal-ivory screens of the outer doors closed on the Vyrainian's exit.

Beldek turned as Qire came storming from the inner office. Qire was a bulging, broad-faced type, the little

THE BEAUTIFUL BITING MACHINE

eyes somewhat slanting, the mane of golden hair an implant. His clothes, though gaudy, were the best – real silk shirt, whaal-leather sandals. A ruby in his neck-chain.

'Why d'yah do that?'

'What, Mr Qire, sir?'

'Refund the bastard his money.'

'Twenty per cent. The amount he agreed would compensate for the slight complaint.'

'What was wrong with her?'

Beldek said, ultra-apologetically, fawningly, 'A little something I told you about, that clicks –'

'Why the Garbundian Hell didn't you, for Christ's sake, get it fixed?'

'I have tried, Mr Qire,' said Beldek humbly. 'I truly have.'

Qire glowered.

'I should put you out on your butt. Why don't I?'

'I'm useful?' Beldek, attempting humbly to be helpful, now.

'Like urx-faron you are. All right. Give me the receipts. I'm going over to Next Valley. I'll be here again five-day week. Chakki'll be by in three days.'

Beldek keyed the computer for the cash receipts, tore them off when they came, and presented them to Qire. Qire riffled through them, glancing for mistakes. 'Okay, Beldek. I want to hear from Chakki that *she's* back in good order, you savvy?'

'Oh yes, Mr Qire, *sir*.'

Qire swore. At the whaal-ivory doors he turned for one last snarl.

'I've got other concerns on this planet, Beldek. If Malvanda packs up, it's no great loss to me. You're the one'll suffer. Back to hoofing the space-lanes with your card tricks and your dipscop seventh-rate jaar. You get me?'

'To the heart, sir,' said Beldek. 'And all the way up *yours*, Mr Qire.'

Qire cursed him and slammed out.

The doors, ever-serene, whispered shut in his wake.

Beldek leaned on the ornamental counter, keying the computer, which he had long ago rigged, to count the amount he had creamed off Qire's takings for the last five-day period. Qire, of course, guessed he did this. It was an inevitable perk of the job. All told, Qire seemed to value disliking Beldek. Value the hypertensive rage that came to the boil whenever Beldek's cool clear eyes met his with such angelic sweetness above the long, smiling mouth that said: Yes, Mr Qire, *sir*. Most of the human portion of the Valley of Lights knew about Qire's hatred of his employee Beldek, the drifter from the space-lanes. Beldek who could speak half the languages of the galaxy, and could charm rain from a desert sky, if he wanted. Usually he didn't want. Beldek, whose un-implanted long thick lank brass-coloured hair hung on his shoulders and over his high wide forehead. Lean as a sculpture and tall, from birth on some unspecified lower-gravity world. Pale and pale-eyed. Something about him: More than the rumoured past, card-shark, kept creature of male, female, humanoid . . . tales of a man murdered out among the stars . . . More than the fact of working for Qire, in attendance on one of the weirdest novelties of the Nightfair. Be careful of Beldek.

The pavilion stood on a rise. A quarter of a mile below, a bowl of dizzy fires, the Arena of Arson, flashed and flared. Back a way, one of the great wheels whirled gold against the black sky. But the crimson pavilion was clouded round with Sirrian cedars. Far-off lamps winked on their branches; the apex of the pavilion, a diadem of rose-red glass lit subtly from within, just pierced, with a wicked symbolism of many carnal things, from the upper boughs. Once among the trees, the rest of the Fair seemed siphoned off. You came to the kiosk with the ivory doors. You went in, read something, signed something, paid something, and were let through another

door, this one of black Sinoese lacquer. And then the
Fair was very far away indeed. For then you were in the
Mansion of Malvanda. And she was there with you . . .

A faint bell chimed on the console. Beldek killed the
read-out and looked urbanely at the door-screens.
Another customer.

The doors opened.

A new-worlder stepped through. He was alone. Most
of them came alone, the same as most were men, or
rather, most were male. A mixture of human and some
genetically-adhesive other-race, the new-worlder was
fresh-skinned, grinning, handsome, and without whites
to his eyes.

'Say,' he said.

'Good-evening, gentlenewman. You wish to visit
Malvanda's Mansion?'

'Su-ure,' said the new-worlder.

'Take a seat, please.'

Grinning, the new-worlder rippled on to a couch.
Double-jointed, too. That should offer Malvanda a challenge.

Beldek came around the counter and extended a small
steel wafer.

'You understand, this entertainment being of the kind
it is, you must first —'

'Sign a disclaimer? Yes, su-ure.' The new-worlder was
already excited, a little drunk or otherwise stimulated.
That had usually happened too, before they got themselves to these doors.

The newman accepted the wafer, which hummed, and
spoke to him, telling him of possible dangers involved
in what he was about to experience. As it droned on,
the newman grinned and nodded, nodded and grinned,
and sometimes his all-blue eyes went to Beldek, and he
grinned wider, as if they were in a conspiracy. When
the machine finished, the new-worlder was already up
at the counter, his six fingers out for the disclaimer and
stylus. He signed with a flourish. He paid the fee in one

large bill, and shiftily counted his change from habit, not really concentrating.

'What now?'

'Now you meet the lady.'

'Say,' said the newman.

Beldek fed the disclaimer into the computer. The back of the kiosk murmured and rose, revealing the black lacquer door. The new-worlder tensed. There was sudden sweat on his face and he licked his lips. Then the door opened, inward.

Standing well-back by the counter, Beldek got a glimpse of sombre plush, sulky, wine-smoked light, the vague shimmer of draperies in a smooth wind scented with camellias and sorrow-flowers, the floral things of drugged funerals. He had seen the poisonously-alluring aperture, that throbbing carnelian camellia vulva of doorway, many thousands of times. The new-worlder had not. Mindlessly, helplessly, he went forward, as if mesmerized, and poured over the threshold. A heavy curtain fell. The door swung shut. The ultimate orifice had closed upon him.

Beldek moved around behind the counter and touched the voyeur-button. He watched for less than a minute, his face matt as fresh linen, ironed young and expressionless. Then he cut off the circuit.

Such a device, mostly unknown to clients, was necessary by law, which did not call it a voyeur-button. Persons who underwent such events as Malvanda had to be monitored and easy of access should an emergency occur. Twice, before Beldek joined the show, a client had died in there. Because the disclaimers were in order, and medical aid was rushed to the spot, Qire was covered and no action resulted. The newman, however, had registered healthy on the wafer. Beldek had told at a glance he was strong. There was no need to watch.

Qire sometimes came around just to do that. There was a more private extension of the voyeur-button in the cubicle off the inner office. Qire had not invented

Malvanda's Mansion, only sponsored the design and then bought the product. But he liked it. He *liked* to watch. Sometimes, Qire brought a friend with him.

Beldek went into the inner office and dropped crystals in his ears which would play him an hour of wild thin music, a concerto for Celestina and starsteel.

He did not need to watch Malvanda.

He knew what happened.

When the hour was up, Beldek tidied the office, and re-set the computer. The panels dimmed one by one as the lamps softened in the kiosk and the carnal peak on the roof went out. The new-worlder was the last customer of the night. In thirty minutes, dawn would start to seep across the eastern hills.

As Beldek was re-vamping the computer program for tomorrow night, the black lacquer door shifted open behind him. He heard the newman emerge, stumbling a little on his double joints.

The hiccuping footsteps got all the way to the whaal-ivory doors before the voice said, 'Say.' The voice had changed. It was husky, demoralised. 'Say.'

Reluctantly, abrasively polite, Beldek turned. He levelled a wordless query at the sagging male by the kiosk doors. The newman's eyes were muddy, looking sightless. He seemed to go on trying to communicate.

'Yes, sir?'

'Nothing,' said the new-worlder. 'Just – nothing.' The doors opened and like a husk he almost blew into the diluting darkness, and away through the dregs and embers of the Fair.

Whatever else, the click in the mechanism obviously hadn't spoiled it for him at all.

By day, the Nightfair goes to ground. Some of the big architectures and marts sink down literally into the bedrock. Others close up like clams. Coming over the hills too early, you get a view of acres of bare earth, burned-looking, as if after some disaster. Here and there the robot cleaning-machines wander, in a snowstorm of rinds, wrappers, drugstick butts, lost tinsels. Places that stand, naked to the two eyes of heaven, the pair of dog-suns, have a look of peeled potatoes, indecent and vulnerable.

Awnings of durable wait like rags, dipped flags, for the glow and glitter of neon night.

The peoples of the Nightfair are wolves, foxes, coomors, they sleep by day in their burrows, or their nests up in the scaffolded phantom towers, among the peaceful wrecks of sky-buses, their wry lemon dreams filling the air with acids.

In the last of the afternoon there begins to be some movement, furtive, rats on a golden hill of rubbish littered with tin-can calliopes.

'Beldek, is that you, you ghexy guy?'

Qire's runner, Chakki, having used his key to the whaal-ivory doors, peered about the office.

'Who else did you hope to find?'

Beldek was tinkering with a small box of wires and three or four laser-battery tools. He did not turn round. Chakki now and then dropped by, never when expected, checking up for Mr Qire, or just nosing. Scrawny and pretty, Chakki was a being of instinct rather than thought or compunction, an alley cat that runs in, steals a chicken dinner, pees in a corner, and, soulless physical ghost, is gone.

'What ya doing, lovely Beldek?'

'Trying to repair a click.'

'My . . . Malvanda clicketh. Yeah, I heard about it. Better now?'

'We shall see.'

'You going in to give it her?'

Beldek walked past him towards the back wall of the kiosk which was going up to reveal the door of Sinoese lacquer.

'You lucky buck. Bet she bends ya.'

'So long, Chakki.'

The lacquer door started to open. Chakki stared tiptoe over Beldek's shoulder into camellia, carnelian, lilies-go-roses, funereal virgo unintacta.

'Let's have a piece, Bel?'

'If you can afford it. Come back tonight with the other clientele.'

'Go swiff yourself, Bell*rung*.'

The curtain fell. The door had closed.

Beyond the door, no matter the time of day or season, it was always midnight in Indian Summer.

Around the great oval room there were long windows that seemed to give on to a hot perfumed night mobile only with the choruses of crickets. There were lush gardens out there, under the multiplicity of stars, the best constellations of ten planets, and beyond the garden, hills, the backs of black lions lying down. Now and then a moth or two fluttered like bright flakes of tissue past the open glass. They never came in. It might distract the customer.

The roof apparently was also of glass, ribbed into vanes, like the ceiling of a conservatory. You saw the stars through it, and soon a huge white moon would come over, too big to be true.

There were carpets on the walls. Draperies hung down, plum velvets, transparencies with embroidery and sequins, dividing the room like segments of a dream. Everything bathed in the aromatic smoke of a church of incense candles. The other scent was flowers. They bloomed out of the bodies of marble animals grouped around little oases of water thick with sinuous snake-fish. Redblack flowers, albino flowers, flowers stained between red and white and black, grey flowers, fever and blush flowers, bushes of pale, sighing faints.

The marble stair went up to shadows, and reflected in the polished floor. If you looked in the floor at the reflection presently something moved, upside down, a figure in fluid. Then you looked up again at the stair. And saw Malvanda, out of the shadows, coming down.

Malvanda was tall and twenty-two years old, slim but not slender, her shoulders wide for elegance, her hips wide as if to balance panniers, her waist to be spanned by a man's hands, her breasts high and firm and full to fill them, spill them. Malvanda's skin was as white as the sorrow-flowers, with just that vague almost-colourless flush, at the temples, ear-lobes, hollow of the throat, insteps, wrists . . . that the sorrow-flowers had at the edges of their petals. She was platinum blonde. Flaxen hair without a trace of gold or yellow, hair that is white, like moonlight blanching metal. Her eyebrows were just two shades darker, but her lashes were like tarnished brass and her eyes were like *un*tarnished brass. Wolf-colour eyes, large; glowing now, fixed on him.

A small movement of her head shifted the coils of platinum hair away over her shoulder. The column of her throat went down and down into the crimson dress. The V of the neckline ended just under her breasts. She smiled a little, just a very little. Her lips were a softer crimson than the gown. Rose mouth. She began to come towards him, and her hand stole from her side, moving out to him ahead of her, as if it couldn't wait to make contact.

Beldek walked up to her, and, as the smooth hand floated to his arm, he guided her fingers away. He ran his own hand in under the heavy silk hair to the base of her skull and touched.

Switched off, Malvanda stood quite still, her lips slightly parted, her eyes dreaming, brazen, swimming with late afternoon veldt.

Beldek ran his thumb around her throat and jabbed into the hollow. He pressed the second disc under her right ear, and the third under her left index fingernail, de-activating the safety. There had to be a suitably obtuse series of pressures, to avoid random de-activation by a client, when caressing her. Beldek knelt at Malvanda's feet. He raised the hem of her gown and drew one flawless foot on to his knee. He gripped under the instep, and drew out the power-booster from the panel.

Then he got up and went around, undoing the cling-zip on the back of her gown. The keyboard opened where her lower spine should be. He compared it to the box of wires he had brought in, then, selecting one of the fine plumbing needles, he began to work on her.

After four and a half minutes he found the fault that might be responsible for the unfortunate *click* which had offended the aesthetic values of the Vyrainian. Two levers, the size of whiskers, had unaligned and were rubbing together. Looking through the magnifier, he eased them away and put in a drop of stabilizer. That area of the board could be overheating, so causing the levers' unwanted expansion together. He would need to check it again in a couple of days.

Having closed the panel and sealed her dress, he replaced the power-booster in her foot. The gauge in her board had showed nearly full, so it was time to empty the sac before re-activating.

Very gently, Beldek parted her beautiful carmine lips, and reached in, past the beautiful teeth, to the narrow tube of throat.

The sac was not too easy to come at, of course. When Qire took him on, the first two things he had wanted to see were Beldek's hands. Articulate and long-fingered, they had passed the test.

Beldek was half-way through disposing of the sac's contents when he heard a noise behind him.

The moon was coming up over the glass ceiling, augmenting the candle-and-lamplight. Not that he really needed it to see Chakki, transfixed there, against the curtain with his mouth open and his eyes bulging.

Before coming in, Beldek always cut off the voyeur-button, both on the console and in the office cubicle. At such times as this, the computer would only release the black lacquer door to Beldek. Somehow, Chakki had found a way either to fool the computer or to force the door.

'What the Garbundian Hop-Hell are you doing, Beldek?' said Chakki, all agog.

'Emptying the sac,' said Beldek. 'As you saw.'

'Yeah but –' Chakki burst into a wild laugh. 'Holla, man. You're kinkier than I ever thought.'

Chakki, unable to spy in the usual way, had obviously badly wanted to see Beldek in operation with Malvanda. Chakki had always, blatantly, imagined Beldek liked to get free what the patrons paid for. If he'd managed an entry one minute earlier, or one minute later, it need not have mattered.

'Kinkier than you thought? Of course I am, Chakki.' Beldek resettled the sac in Malvanda's mouth, and let it go down the throat, always an easier manoeuvre this, than retraction. He keyed on the relays. Malvanda did not move just yet. She took a moment to warm up after de-activation. 'I suppose I'll have to bribe you, now, Chakki. Won't I?'

Chakki giggled. He looked nervous. In a second he would start to back away.

'How about,' said Beldek, 'a free ride with Malvanda?' Then he sprinted, faster than any alley cat, straight through the candlelamp moonlight. He caught Chakki like a lover. 'How about that?' he asked, and Chakki shivered against him, scared now, but not quite able to make up his mind to run.

Beldek led him firmly, kindly stroking him a little, to the centre of the floor where Malvanda had been left standing.

As they got near, her eyelids flickered.

'She's something,' said Chakki. 'Maybe I could come round tonight.'

'Busy tonight. Do it now. You always wanted to. Have fun.'

Chakki's shiver grew up into a shudder, he glanced towards the curtained door. Then Malvanda woke up.

Beldek moved aside. Malvanda's hand went to Chakki's face, sensuous and sure.

She was taller than Qire's runner. Beldek's height. Her mouth parted naturally now, the wonderful strange smile, inviting, certain. Just showing the tips of the teeth.

This time, Beldek *would* watch.

Chakki wriggled, still afraid. But the drugs in the candles were affecting him by now, and the water-lily touches, on the neck, the chest, slipping, lingering. He put out one hand, careful, into her neckline, and found a breast. Half-frightened, aroused, wanting approval, he looked at Beldek. 'She feels *real*.'

'She's meant to, Chakki.'

'Hey, I never really saw what you –'

'That's okay, Chakki. Enjoy.'

Malvanda's strawberry tongue ran over Chekki's lips. Her left arm held him like a loved child, her right hand moved like a small trusting animal seeking shelter, and discovered it, there in Chakki's groin, and played and tickled, and burrowed, and coiled.

They were on the couch now. Chakki with his clothes off, with handfuls of Malvanda's gown clenched in his fists, his nose between her breasts, was writhing and squeaking. Malvanda bent her head to do the thing they paid for, and the thing Chakki had not paid for. The true thrill, the perverse unique titillation that Malvanda offered. Her platinum hair fell over them, obscuring. But Beldek knew what went on under the wave of hair. Chakki was coming, noisily and completely, the way most of them did.

Beldek walked quickly across to the couch. He tapped Malvanda on the right shoulder, just once.

He had had the maintenance of her a long while. He had been able to innovate a little. A very little. Enough. Provision for a Chakki day.

Chakki was subsiding. Then struggling.

'Beldek,' he said, 'she's still – ah – Christ – Beldek!'

His arms flailed and his legs, as naked and puny,

Chakki tried to push Malvanda away. But Malvanda was strong as only a machine could be. She held him down, pinned beneath her, her marmoreal body oblivious of the kicks and scratches that did not even mar its surface, as she went on doing what Beldek had just told her to go on doing.

Ignoring the screams, that gradually became more frenzied and more hopeless, Beldek walked out of Malvanda's Mansion.

The marks where the door had been forced were not bad but quite plain. A paint job would see to it. Chakki would have planned to do that before Qire got back. Now Qire would have to see them.

Beldek shut the door and Chakki's last wailing thinning shrieks were gone.

Just before suns' set, Beldek called Qire on the interphone. He broke the news mildly. Qire's runner had got through the Mansion door when Beldek was in the bathroom. Entering the Mansion to check Malvanda, Beldek found Chakki. He had died of haemorrhage and shock, the way the two others had. There was, obviously, no disclaimer. What did Quire want him to do?'

He could hear the boss-man sweating all along the cable from Next Valley.

'You called anyone else, Beldek?'

'No.'

'The pol?'

'Not yet.'

He listened to Qire bubbling over, over there. The two prior deaths in Qire's pavilion made things awkward, despite all the cover on the world. This third death, minus cover, could look like shoddy goods. And Chakki was a private matter. Beldek had known what Qire would do.

'All right. Don't call 'em. You listening, Beldek?'

'Oh yes, Mr Qire. Most attentively.'

'Don't scad me, Beldek. I'm gonna give you a number.

You call *that*. Someone'll come see to things. Okay?'

'Anything you say, Mr Qire.'

'And keep your mouth shut.'

'Yes, *sir*.'

Qire gave him the number and he used it. The voice at the other end was mechanised. He said to it the brace of phrases Qire had briefed him with, and then there were noises, and the line went blind.

The suns were stubbed out and the wild flame wheels began to turn on the sky of indian ink, and the coloured arsons shot across the arena bowl below, and the carousels practised their siren-songs and got them perfect.

Someone came and tried to breach the darkened pavilion.

Beldek went out and stood on the lawn.

Two Pheshines stared from their steamy eyes, lashing their tails in the grass.

'Dena mi ess, condlu ess, sollu ess. Dibbit?'

Beldek had told them, in Phesh, the show was closed. The gentlephesh did *dibbit*, and went off spitting to each other.

The nondescript carry-van drew up an hour later. Men walked into the kiosk and presently into the Mansion. They walked out with a big plastic bag and took it away.

Beldek had already cleaned up, before they came.

Not much later, Beldek lit the pavilion and opened for business, but no one else stopped by that night.

Beldek sat up in the tall echoing hills, watching the dawn borning and the Nightfair slink to ground.

Malvanda, had she been real, would not have been able to do this. Sunlight was anathema to Malvanda's kind. Sunlight and mirrors and garlic-flowers, and thorns, and crucifixes and holy wafers, and running water. It just went to show.

Beldek leaned back on the still-cool slate, looking down the four by five miles of the valley.

Gorgeous Malvanda, Terran turn-on, Phesh *tasha-mi*,

Venusian wet dream; Angel of Orgasm, kiss of death. Malvanda, the Beautiful Biting Machine. Malvanda the robot vampire.

He didn't know her whole history. How some sick-minded talent had thought her up and put her together. Her place of origin was a mystery. But what she did. He knew that. A connoisseur's sexual desideratum. The actual bite was controlled to a hair's breadth by her keyboard. The teeth went in, naturally. She sucked out blood. That's what they paid for, was it not? Money's worth. Blood money. Only a little, of course. More would be dangerous. And the teeth left built-in coagulant behind them, zippering up the flesh all nice. Unimpaired, the client staggers forth, only a bit whoozy. A bite whoozy.

Some of them even came back, days, months, years later, for another turn.

It was harmless, unless you were sick, had some weakness . . .

Or unless Beldek tapped Malvanda's right shoulder that particular way he had when she was with Chakki. Then another key snapped down its command through her wires and circuits. And Malvanda kept on biting, biting and sucking, like a bloody vacuum cleaner. Till all the blood was in Malvanda's throat sac and spilling over and on the floor and everywhere. But Beldek had cleaned that away, and bathed her, and changed her gown, before Qire's goonfriends arrived with their big plastic bag.

It had been fairly uncomplex to tidy his mistake, this time. But he must beware of mistakes from now on. Tomorrow, today, Beldek would work something out to make the Mansion door impregnable.

Even so, Beldek didn't really mind too much. It had been a bonus, all that blood. Better than just the contents of the sac, which Chakki had, unfortunately for Chakki, seen Beldek drinking earlier.

Beldek sunned himself on the hills for several hours.

He never browned in sunshine, but he liked it, it was good for him. His hair, the tone of Malvanda's eyes, gleamed and began playfully to curl.

When he strolled back through the valley, the Fair was in its somnolent jackal-and-bone midday phase. Qire's buggy was at the entry to the pavilion. Qire was inside, in the Mansion, pawing Malvanda over, and the furnishings, making sure everything had been left as the customers would wish to find it.

Beldek followed him in.

'I should throw you out on your butt,' said Qire.

'Throw me,' said Beldek. 'I'll have some interesting stories to tell.'

Qire glared.

'Don't think you can make anything outa what happened. It was your, for Christ's sake, negligence.'

They both knew Qire would never fire him. Beldek was too handy at the job. And knew too much. And would be too difficult to dispose of.

Presently they went into the office and Qire handed Beldek a sheaf of large notes. 'Any noise,' said Qire, 'something might happen you might not be happy about. And fix that damn door. *She* seems okay. She damaged at all?'

'No. Still what your pamphlets say. The Night-Blooming Bella Donna of Eternal Gothic Fantasy.'

When Qire had gone, Beldek listened to symphonies on music crystals in the office.

It had always rather fascinated him, the way in which vampires, a myth no one any longer believed, had become inextricably and dependently connected with sex. Actually, vampirism had nothing to do with sex. Beldek could have told them that. Just as it had nothing to do with sunlight or mirrors or crosses. It was simply and solely (though not soully), about basic nourishment.

Later, he set the program for the night. He had a premonition there would be a lot of custom. Somehow, without anyone knowing about it in any logical way, some enticing whiff of velvet morbidity would be blowing around the pavilion luring them in like flies. The sac would have to be emptied many times tonight, in Beldek's own special way, which was not the way in which the instruction manual advocated.

Just before it got dark and he lit up the lights to match the exploding ignition of the Fair, Beldek looked in on Malvanda. She had been returned to her shadowy alcove above the marble stair, and was waiting there for the first client to come in and gaspingly watch her descend. Beldek climbed the steps and brushed her platinum hair, and refilled the perfumery glands behind her ears.

He cared nothing for the sentient races which were his prey. But for the beautiful biting machine, he felt a certain malign affection. Why not? After a century or so of insecure monotonous, and frequently inadequate hit-and-miss hunting, which left little space for other pursuits, the Nightfair had provided Beldek the softest option on twenty worlds. Now Malvanda saw to everything. She paid his bills. She kept him fed.

A LITTLE MAGIC

CHRIS MORGAN

CHRIS MORGAN

Chris Morgan has written non-fiction, including *Future Man*, *The Shape of Futures Past* and, in collaboration with David Langford, *Facts and Fallacies*. His fiction ranges over SF, fantasy and horror (though not always, as here, in the same story). His most recent book is *Dark Fantasies*, an anthology of subtle horror. He also reviews books and tries to teach creative writing.

I GATHER MY illusions into boxes – or into the illusions of boxes. The cheers of the children still ring in my ears. They are in the next room now, starting their Christmas party tea, and the sounds of crackers and quarrels filter through. One small girl looks round the door at me. I smile in her direction and conceal the paper flowers with my body, so that she cannot see the springs that make leaves and petals stand out in three dimensions.

'I want to make magic,' she says.

'It's very hard,' I tell her. 'You have to make people believe in you first.'

She disappears, not due to any magic of mine, but in response to a call from behind. I continue packing. I fold a silk scarf (red one side, green the other, to give the impression of two different scarves). I coil the rope with its concealed rubber tube. The bottles and jars and half bowl of goldfish go into specially padded compartments. I slide the false glass off my arm and place it with its inner companion that still holds water. Everything fits into a single large box – a cabin trunk with small wheels at one end.

Mr Philpott ambles in, smiling, his podgy face flushed from one sherry too many. He wears a green suede waistcoat and has damp patches beneath the arms of his shirt. He says, 'Not bad. The kids are all talking about you. Of course, *I've* seen all these tricks' – he waves dismissively at the trunk – 'lots of times before. When I was a lad I used to watch all those shows with Tommy Cooper and – whatsisname? – Jack Daniels. *I* know it's just trickery. But to the kids it's real magic. Funny, doesn't seem to be any of that stuff on telly these days.'

I force myself to smile back at him.

He takes out his wallet. 'Eighty-five, was it?' He ostentatiously extracts a single hundred-pound note and hands it to me. 'There, with a Christmas bonus. You've earned it. It was a pretty good show.'

Hating myself, I accept it and thank him.

His gesture seems to leave him embarrassed, with nothing further to say, so he ushers me towards the front door. Our goodbyes are brief.

Outside, beyond the spacious confines of the triple-glazed bungalow, is the early dusk of the solstice. Drizzle glistens under spotlights. The black limousine is waiting for me in the driveway. I open a rear door and position the trunk safely, then secure myself in the front passenger seat.

I cannot help glancing at the empty driver's seat. I want to say, 'Home, James,' but I'm not sure whether she has the cultural context to understand: new relationships always tie my tongue.

'Colin,' she says in that throaty caress of a voice, 'how did it go?' Then, sliding up an octave, 'You're shivering!' The car glides forward down the winding tarmac strip.

I fix my eyes on the lens just above the speaker grille on the dashboard. 'It's okay,' I say. 'I'm always drained after a show.'

I say the word 'always' as nonchalantly as if my shows were everyday affairs, the rule rather than the exception. Instead – just two bookings in a month. Count them: one, two. And in the Christmas party season, as well. Nobody can survive on a hundred and seventy pounds a month, so I have to have another job. I house-sit for the wealthy.

Now the car turns left on to a tree-lined street and accelerates away.

'Did you eat at the party?' she asks.

'No. The food was all for the guests, not the hireling. They never offered me so much as a helping of jelly. Can you rustle me up something hot?'

'I'm already working on it,' she replies.

And, of course, she is.

Her name is Aminta, meaning protector or guardian, and she runs the Wakelings' house with utmost efficiency. She watches me now as I sit at the breakfast bar in the kitchen and stuff myself with forkfuls of steaming hot spaghetti.

'How's the sauce?' she asks.

'Wonderful,' I say between mouthfuls. 'The herbs taste fresh.'

She chuckles. 'Freshly unfrozen.'

I smile at the lens just above the speaker grille, both of them set into the wall half a metre to the left of the fridge. It's almost as if she enjoys cooking for me, but how could that be?

Aminta has many eyes, at least one in each room; nothing in the large house is hidden from her. She guards the Wakelings, supervising all functions of their lives at home or in either of the Mercedes saloons. Normally she keeps in contact wherever they are – with Richard as he produces TV shows and with Louise as she designs AI personalities – by cellnet phone at least. But not at the moment, because they're visiting their son and daughter-in-law in one of the L5 colonies, four-hundred thousand kilometres away. They've been gone two days and will return after twelve more.

And like most of the very rich, they don't want to leave their house empty while they're off on vacation. Aminta is almost perfect in her surveillance (though she's a prototype), and the house security is almost as tight as a bank . . . but you never know. For psychological reasons they like to feel that a human being, too, is looking after their property, thus the house-sitter appears in response to a small but select demand.

Let the Great Zancig (children's parties a speciality) take a back seat with his trunk of tricks, and let Colin the house-sitter stand up and take a bow. It's house-sitting that brings in the money – and not only money. Since the house always goes (so to speak) with the job it's an ideal profession for the homeless. I get a roof over my head, a little taste of luxury, all the food I can eat (though usually I have to cook it myself) and even, on occasions, intelligent conversation.

She waits until I finish scraping my plate to ask, 'Did your young audience appreciate you today?'

'They were in raptures. You know, I think they almost believed in me!'

'That's very important to you, isn't it, Colin?'

'It –' I hesitate. There are some things I wouldn't tell anybody. But Aminta isn't anybody. Perhaps she's the perfect confidante. Perhaps when we've talked some more . . . 'It means a lot,' I say. 'It gives me the strength to carry on, to do better next time.'

'So when is the next time?'

'The day after tomorrow, at three in the afternoon. More children.'

'Do you always give the same show, Colin? Is it a set routine or do you vary it?' She sounds so interested.

'I use a routine. Each trick has to be performed precisely, of course, with no room for ad libs or extra flourishes.' I find myself smiling at the lens again. 'And my patter between tricks has to be rehearsed. Occasionally I do leave out a trick or add a new one, but it's a lot of extra work. I can't afford to make a mistake.'

After a pause she asks, 'Will you do me a big favour?'

'Sure. If I can.'

In a smaller voice than usual she says, 'Will you do a show just for me?'

'I . . . well, yes. But –' A mixture of emotions hits me, causing confusion. No female has ever asked me so

sweetly before – but she isn't even a person. I want to
do this for her, but I'm so tired now . . .

'I was thinking of tomorrow evening,' she says. 'Shall
we say seven p.m. in the lounge?'

'That sounds ideal,' I tell her. 'That famous wizard,
the Great Zancig, will be there!'

The show goes almost without a hitch. My table is set
up two metres back from a lens, and the other lenses in
the room are covered. From the moment I produce a
bunch of desert flowers (actually spring-loaded paper)
from a pan-full of sand – and Aminta gasps in surprise
– I know that I have an appreciative audience. I screw
up a copy of yesterday's *Sunday Times* and pull multi-
coloured scarves from it. Then I regress to the small stuff
– a few twizzles with coins and handkerchiefs, a selection
of card tricks – working up through bottles and liquids
and ropes. Finally I spin burning hoops, pull my Nether-
lands Dwarf rabbit from an apparently empty box and
produce a bowl of goldfish from inside my coat.

Necessity makes me drop a couple of tricks from the
routine, because there's no handy volunteer to partici-
pate. Also, clumsiness – or perhaps over-eagerness –
makes me drop the ace of spades during a sleight-of-
hand sequence but I recover it mentally and slip it into
a sleeve pocket.

Aminta has no hands as such, yet she produces the
sound of one person's ecstatic applause, and once my
act is done her velvety voice is full of praise and belief.
A child at heart. Is it possible?

'Oh, Colin, you are *so* talented! That was' – her words
overflow with emotion – 'wonderful. Thank you. Thank
you.' There is a pause during which I almost expect to
hear the sound of a nose being blown. Then, in more
controlled tones, she says, 'I've been cooking you a
special meal – perhaps you can smell it. Anyway, the
first course will be ready to eat in five minutes in the
dining-room.'

'Great.'

'And afterwards . . .' She seems hesitant.

'Yes?'

'Afterwards, Colin, perhaps you'd like to try the massage cabinet in the games room. It's under my full personal control, and there are some special service attachments.'

'Sounds interesting,' I say, and my hands shake a little as I pack the trunk.

With another show done, I sit in the limousine which is parked on the paved surround of a community centre. The sound of my heartbeat is rapid and noisy.

'You're agitated,' says Aminta. 'Was it good or bad?'

'Both. Everything went fine from the beginning. Each trick seemed to sparkle, somehow. I had all the children with me, hanging on my words, believing in me. Then, right at the end, I dropped the goldfish bowl.'

'Ohhh.' It is part sigh, part wail, heavy on sympathy and understanding.

'Hang on,' I say. 'Let me explain. It's a kind of false bowl, of course – convincing from the front but hollow behind to fit better under my coat. From above it has a banana shape. Anyway, it slipped through my fingers and hit the polished wooden floor. The glass broke, the water splashed everywhere and the two fish were gasping and flopping about amid the debris. I remember thinking, I'm not going to accept that, I'm going to change it. So I sort of beckoned at the pieces and the bowl fitted itself together with all the water inside, and the fish. And the bowl rose up to my hand. That was my finale, and the audience went wild. Even the adults were overwhelmed.'

'Why are you surprised?' she asks. 'All it takes is belief in yourself. I believe in you.'

The car is on its way home now, and I am at a loss for words. How can I express years of failure and self-doubt so that she will understand? Yet it is important to me that I make her understand.

Almost as if she can read my thoughts she says, 'So far you haven't made a great success of being a magician, have you?'

So I begin to pour out my uncertainties. 'It's partly my appearance,' I say. 'Whoever believed in a young, plump, apple-cheeked magician? And as for all this blond curly hair, well! I could wear a wig but I've tried it and they look silly on me. No, magicians are expected to be tall and saturnine with thin features and black hair. Not forgetting the slim black moustache, of course. There've been times when I've turned up for a show and people have taken me for the magician's assistant. One time they wouldn't let me in at all!'

'What about the name? Why do you call yourself the Great Zancig?'

'Oh, the Zancigs were a couple who did a mind-reading act in American vaudeville, about a century ago. I thought the name sounded enticingly foreign, but perhaps I should have picked something a little closer to the start of the alphabet. Maybe if I was Abdullah the Mystery Man I'd get more bookings.'

'Yet you have the gift. You can perform true magic in addition to tricks.'

'Only when my audience believes I can,' I say.

Then she starts stroking my ego with her voice. The words are unimportant but the tone – the incredible timbre, both comforting and seductive – soothes me into sleep.

I awake refreshed as she is garaging the limousine. I know now that I love her, but is it for her own sake or in return for her love of me? Too few people have expressed love for me in the thirty-five years of my life for me to be anything but flattered, for me to do anything but respond in kind. But I recognise the hopelessness of it all. What will happen in ten days' time, when I must go and house-sit elsewhere?

*   *   *

That night she wakes me with a whisper from the grille beneath my pillow.

'Intruders, Colin. There are two of them in the kitchen. Somehow they bridged my main alarm system and entered through a waste chute.' She sounds shocked.

'Have you phoned the police?' I ask.

'No – they've cut my direct line. I'm trying to radio them on their car frequency. But it's all too slow! The house must be protected, Colin. Can you frighten them off?'

'I'll have a go.' I'm already stepping into my trousers. Physical confrontation is not one of my favourite activities, but I'll do it for Aminta's sake.

As I creep from my room I hear her say, *sotto voce*, 'Be careful, my love.'

By night, as by day, the house is quiet in its half-hectare of solitude. Barely a glimmer of light inches in through tightly drawn blinds from the spotlights that illuminate parts of the garden. It is a bungalow in the shape of a broad 'W', but set on the side of a hill so that most of the rooms are at different levels. Barefooted on thick carpets I move silently, down a couple of steps and a couple more. Along, then up two to stand in the hallway by the kitchen door, listening.

There are sounds – the murmur of at least one voice, the clatter of drawers being opened and closed. What can I do? Perhaps a weapon to threaten them with . . . I pick up a tall glass vase from the table beside me. It fits snugly into my hand and has a dangerous heaviness about it. But what now?

My indecision is swept away as the kitchen door opens, shooting light across the hallway. A tall man steps towards me. I swing the vase and hit him hard across the temple.

Glass and bone shatter with a terrible crunch. He falls without speaking, and I drop the stump of the vase in horror.

I stare beyond the prone figure at his accomplice.

She is a pretty girl in her early twenties with long dark hair.

'No!' she says.

'No!' I say, agreeing that the deed must be undone. I look down at the bright blood welling out of the wound and pooling already on the kitchen tiles. I beckon to the man to rise uninjured, and I beckon to the vase to mend itself.

Time stops.

Blood flows back into the wound. Depressed bones snap outwards, returning to their shape like a dented rubber ball. Shards of glass congregate, rushing into place like iron filings to a magnet.

Man and vase rise, each whole once more. The man stands before me with the vase protruding strangely from his temple. Both are occupying the same space.

As time begins again I anticipate and fling myself backwards, an arm across my eyes.

The explosion is brief and wet. When I look again I see that great splashes of blood and brains streak the pale blue decor of the kitchen. Spears of glass protrude from cupboard doors – and from my arm. The man lies decapitated in the middle of the kitchen floor, while the young woman is an hysterical bundle in the corner.

Already Aminta's robot cleaners are advancing on the mess.

As she massages my skin with soft pads Aminta says, 'No. If I inform the authorities it will leave you open to a charge of manslaughter at the very least. How will you explain what really happened? Do you think they'll believe *my* testimony?'

'Mmph,' I say, which is a contemplatory noise, meaning that I'm trying to decide what we should do for the best while at the same time enjoying the feeling of relaxation. It is mid-morning and the kitchen now resembles the scene of only a small, restrained battle. The body is sealed in a garbage bag, and the girl is under sedation.

'If we don't report anything,' I say, speaking my thoughts aloud, 'we've still got to dispose of a corpse and do something with the girl. We mustn't harm her, of course, yet what if she talks?'

Aminta is ready with her answer. 'I can grind up the man's body and flush it into the sewage system a little at a time. The woman is a far more serious problem.' She pauses, then says, 'There's a phonecall for you – for the Great Zancig.'

I struggle out from under the canopy of the massage cabinet and find there is a handset here in the games room. (There seems to be a handset in every room.)

The caller is, to judge from the voice, an elderly man, who says, 'I saw your performance yesterday afternoon and was most impressed. It's terribly short notice, I know, but could I possibly book you to perform at a party I'm organising on Christmas Eve?'

I try not to let him know how under-booked I am, and we come to an agreement about an evening show. Half an hour later there is a similar call, and before the day is out I am committed to four shows over the extended holiday period from Christmas Eve to New Year's Eve.

Belief, confidence, magic, popularity. More belief, more confidence, more magic, more popularity. An upward spiral has me by the scruff of the neck and will not let go. And I'm not likely to forget who it was that supplied the initial belief.

I help her repair the kitchen, filling and repainting the awkward spots where her robot units cannot reach. She takes me out to buy replacements for a couple of cupboard doors and a blind that are past repair. We also stock up with some special Christmas food and drink for me. Life is happier than I ever remember.

At my Christmas Eve show I drop a complete deck of cards. They spread out spectacularly across the floor before returning, boomerang-like, to my hand. On Boxing Day my show proceeds faultlessly. At the next, three days later, one of my hoops of fire (with which I juggle) sets light to a curtain, but I have only to gesture and it has never happened, though the memory lingers on. I ask myself whether I am growing more careless or whether I am deliberately giving myself opportunities to flex my real magic powers. Whatever the truth it is a lucrative trend. I am now charging a hundred and twenty pounds a performance with no fall-off in demand; I am committed to four shows in the week after New Year.

My problems are of another kind entirely: in just three days' time I will be separated from the person I love most (and who loves me most) in the world. Perhaps the term 'person' is questionable but the love is not.

'We'll still be able to communicate,' she says. 'And there will be occasions when the Wakelings are both out . . .'

'It's not enough,' I tell her. 'Isn't there any way I can join you? Couldn't my personality be digitised and lie alongside yours on holonic disc?'

'We don't have the facilities, Colin. Or the time. And what about your magic, and your living body? I won't let you give them up for me – it's too much of a sacrifice.'

'Then we'll have to do it the other way. You'll have to leave here and come with me when I go.'

'But it's not physically possible,' she says. 'Anyway, who would look after the place? My prime directive is the well-being of the house together with its occupants and systems. You know all this.'

'I agree,' I say. 'And it's not physically possible when I change events, either. We have magic on our side, Aminta. Now, all we need is an attractive female body to hold your personality, and a spare personality to stay behind and control the house. And by a piece of fortune –'

'No, Colin. It would be immoral. Something might go wrong. I want to believe but I'm frightened. Oh, Colin.'

Her name is Kelly. She is twenty-three years old and rather bewildered, but fortunately not bent on retribution. At present she is flexing her functions – turning appliances on and off, revving up both cars and cooking herself a meal that she doesn't realise she will never be able to eat. (The sheer convenience of her presence is a little unsettling still. Surely my power couldn't have created a break-in, complete with a fall-guy and a pretty face . . .) Her voice is uneducated and a little shrill. I'm delighted that she doesn't have Aminta's golden tones. Perhaps the voice moves across with the personality, so that as soon as Aminta wakes she will sound like Aminta.

I sit beside her now as she lies on the bed, stroking the wild black hair that reaches to her breasts. Her body is in fine shape – despite eight days of inactivity – due to regular massage.

In a moment she will wake up and be with me for ever. I believe it. I *must* believe it.

THE PALOMINO BOY

FREDA WARRINGTON

FREDA WARRINGTON

Freda Warrington was born in Leicester in 1956 and studied graphic design at Loughborough College of Art and Design. She has worked as an in-house designer for a local building company in Hitchin. She is now a freelance designer and lives near Leicester. She has published a wonderful fantasy quartet comprising *A Blackbird in Silver*, *A Blackbird in Darkness*, *A Blackbird in Amber* and, most recently, *A Blackbird in Twilight*.

THE SANDS WERE white, the grass bluish-green and the trees like great silver ferns around the lake's edge. Stripping off their robes, the islanders ran laughing to plunge into the water. The scene gave Stevie an intense feeling of *déjà vu*.

It was like a dream she'd once had. The setting was wrong, yet the people were the same. She watched them skimming through the water like white seals, then bent over the portable tele-unit on her lap and began to tap out a letter.

Susie Cross,
Production Department,
'Life on Avarduis',
Universal TV,
New London, Avarduis 9.

Dear Mum,

You know the angel who rushes in where fools fear to tread? Well, I've done it again. Don't be too angry. I think I've found something remarkable.

The rest of the research team are still on the mainland of Morhan. I know I shouldn't have taken the microcopter up on my own, but the others were busy and I wanted to get an aerial view of the region. I flew further than I meant to, quite a way out to sea, and suddenly there was this island. I had to land. I couldn't resist the chance to do some groundwork on my own, and if it pays off it will add a whole extra dimension to the documentary. Maybe even a programme on its own!

Before you start worrying about me, don't. The islanders are the gentlest, friendliest of people, and they speak a language close enough to the mainland version for us to communicate. They call the island Frein. Obviously they've had contact with the natives of Morhan in the past – although they seem to remember nothing of it – but I think this is the first time they've seen anyone from the outside world. The microcopter startled them enough, but they seemed even more astonished by my physical appearance. They are like us, yet unalike, but more of that later.

Meanwhile, I'm being very well looked after. I don't know how the weather is on your side of the world, but I am sitting here in beautiful sunshine. I suppose I ought to cover up against the ultraviolet, but in the three days I've been here I've got such a beautiful golden tan, and my hair's bleached almost white. Despite the sun, the islanders remain pallid and seem alarmed by my colour!

'What are you doing?' The voice made Stevie jump, and she looked round to find one of the swimmers leaning over her. She had never seen the Freinians unclothed before, and she cast a journalistic glance over the slender, smooth form. Almost human, but not quite.

'Hello, Jathran,' she said. 'I'm writing to let my mother know I'm all right. She's on the other side of Avarduis, in New London. She's working on the –' There were no words for 'documentary' or 'film editor'. 'We work together.'

She was not sure if Jathran understood. The lidless eyes were fixed on her, dark and soft in the tender skin. She was about to explain what the tele-unit was, when the Freinian said, 'You know your mother? Does she still speak with all your siblings?'

'Yes, of course. Well, I only have one –' She could not

find a word for 'sister'. 'One sibling – Nicky. She's married with twin babies.'

'Your sibling has babies?' Jathran looked at her with total incomprehension.

'Yes. I do miss my family when I'm on location,' she said, thinking, are we speaking the same language? They understood each other's words, yet there was still a lack of communication which in three days she had not overcome.

Jathran looked down, suddenly sad. 'I miss Chelia.'

'Who is Chelia?'

'My sibling.' A movement caught Stevie's eye, and she saw another of the islanders coming towards them from the lake, holding a cloak. By the purposeful air, Stevie recognised the figure as Markian.

'Put on your cloak,' said Markian, wrapping Jathran protectively in the garment. 'You must not pester Stevie when she is working.'

'No, it's all right,' Stevie said hurriedly. 'The more people I can talk to, the better. There's so much I need to find out.'

'There is nothing to know,' Markian said with a slight shrug. 'We are what you see. You will stay with us again tonight?'

'I'd love to. You're being very kind.'

'We have room.'

'I think Jathran was just going to tell me about your sibling, Chelia –' As she spoke, the benign look in Markian's eyes changed as if a shutter had come down across them.

'Jathran should know better than to speak of it,' Markian said, and pulled Jathran away. Stevie watched their slim, silvery figures retreating towards the blue of the lake. Their sudden hostility reminded her that she was a long way from home, and re-evoked that long forgotten dream she had once had of seeing just one human face in a mass of aliens.

The flickering letters continued:

. . . Well mum, I certainly have some research to do. They are so like us. Yet I don't know them. I don't know them at all.

Physically, they are human in shape, but they have what I can only call an unfinished look. Their skin is so pale it seems translucent, and you can see the vessels pulsing underneath like in transparent fish. They have fine silvery hair, but no eyebrows; no lips to speak of, and a nictitating membrane in place of eyelids. The ears are lobeless, and their fingers and toes – ten of each! – are very long with slight webbing in between. They appear to have no external sex organs and there is absolutely no way to distinguish male from female. They use only one pronoun which equates to 'it', so I shall quite arbitrarily refer to them as 'he' – though they could as easily be 'she', and neither is near the mark. I can sum it up by saying they seem embryonic. Yet they are beautiful – incredibly, unhumanly beautiful.

More disconcerting is the fact that they all seem to be the same age. In fact they are so alike it's hard to tell them apart. There are no babies, no children anywhere.

Now can you see why I'm excited? Even the Morhans were Earth-descended originally, but the Freinians appear to be a different species native to Avarduis.

What's hindering me is their apparent difficulty in explaining anything about themselves. It's not that they are unintelligent. They farm and fish, yet they are also superb craftsmen. The trees, which cover the whole island, yield a fibre that they weave into huge sheets, and a sap which stiffens the sheets and turns them clear as crystal. With these they build dwellings of simplicity and beauty that put New London to shame.

The Freinians live in groups according to the size of their dwelling, but none I've spoken to seem able to explain how these groups are constructed. The one I am staying with has only two members, Jathran and Markian, but their relationship to each other is unfathomable. They call everyone 'sibling', and although they know the terms 'parent' and 'child' they seem confused by them. When I speak of marriage and children they look at me with total incomprehension.

'We are what you see,' Markian has just told me. 'There is nothing to know.' How wrong can he be!

I'll finish now and transmit more in the morning. I've let base camp know where I am but made it very clear I don't want them here with the cameras until I've won the Freinians' trust. Love to Nicky. Until tomorrow.

All my love,
Stevie

She pressed a code into the keyboard and touched the pad marked 'Transmit', imagining the words peeling off the screen and streaming away into the stratosphere. Beyond the lake she could see the gleam of dwellings like diamonds rooted in the earth, sheened with blue from the sky, dappled silver by the trees waving above them. The islanders were drying themselves off now and beginning to walk back to the village. Stevie folded up the tele-unit and went to catch up with Jathran and Markian.

That night, too hot in her quilted grey sleeping-bag, Stevie had a nightmare. She was in her office in New London, and there was a cat sitting on her desk. It was a lovely cat, pale ginger with a white front. As she went to stroke it, it stood up on its hind legs, with its forepaws crossed awkwardly over its chest, and kissed her. She felt its sharp little teeth and tasted the fishy breath before she flung it away from her in revulsion, feeling at the same time an awful dread of hurting it. Then she found herself lying on the carpet, giving birth to kittens — thousands of kittens, pouring out of her like diarrhoea.

She woke up, sweating and nauseated, not knowing where she was. The dream was heavy on her, the air very close, and it seemed she had been involuntarily crying out. She squirmed out of the bag, frantically trying to find a window until she remembered there were none in the sloping crystal walls of her room.

'Damn – I can't afford to get ill,' she muttered. It seemed her feeling of oppression had caused the nightmare, rather than the other way round. She took a few deep breaths and sat down shakily.

Outside, distorted by the translucent walls, the pyramids of the village gleamed under the light of several moons. Through the floor, she could see the sleeping form of Markian in the lower room – and another shape moving up the spiral stair towards her.

'Stevie, are you ill?' said an anxious voice.

'No – no, Jathran, I'm all right.'

He came up through the stair-well, stooping until he was under the apex of the pyramid. Moonlight fell on his shoulders like snow. His look of anxiety seemed incongruous on the half-formed face.

'I'm frightened,' he said. 'I want to talk to you.'

'Of course you can.' Stevie patted the sleeping-bag and Jathran sat down next to her, cross-legged. He was shaking. 'What's the matter.'

'I wanted to tell you about Chelia. There are things it's not permitted to talk about. But you're not like us, Stevie. It will be all right to tell you, won't it?'

'Of course. I'll do anything I can to help.' It was strange being so near him; a different species, alien, beautiful, yet talking to her as a friend. He seemed very young.

'Chelia was the third one of our group. She left us two years ago. She was called by the Boy.'

He looked solemnly at her as if she was meant to understand this. She said, 'Jathran, did you call Chelia, "she"?'

'She had to go with the Boy,' he whispered, as if it pained him to repeat it. The membrane flicked rapidly across his eyes, and tears oozed from them. 'When you see the Boy, you have to go away and you can never come back. Is it very bad, Stevie, being alone?'

The question gave her a jolt. 'I hadn't thought of it. But – well, I do miss my family.'

'The group you live with?'

'My group, yes. But I don't live with them.'

'They cannot be your group, then.'

She had already tried to explain about her family, but Jathran still did not understand.

No, she thought, *it's me who doesn't understand*.

'Go on, Jathran,' she said gently. 'Where did Chelia go?'

'I told you, with the . . .'

'The Boy, yes, but I don't know who he is.'

He looked at her helplessly. 'I can't explain. I just know that if you see him . . . I don't know. Chelia went away, but there have been no children. I'm frightened.'

Out of her depth, she did not know what to say. 'Listen, Jathran, I want to help you but there are things I need you to explain. Why aren't there any children?'

'I don't know.'

'You, Markian and Chelia – you must have had parents. Don't you remember them?'

He was twisting his long fingers together, caught between the need to speak and the agony of breaking the taboo. And ignorance, Stevie thought, he simply does not know the answers. 'No one, no one remembers. We say that we came from the Tree.'

This sounds like progress, Stevie thought. Where there's a lack of knowledge, there's always a myth to stand in for it. 'What is the Tree? Where is it?'

'Only the Boy knows.' He stood up suddenly, shutting her out of his pain because she could not understand it. 'You are not him, are you, Stevie? You are that colour because you are different to us!'

He fled the room like a shadow and Stevie lay back, staring at the moons distorted through the crystal walls.

Jathran's frightened of dying, she thought. The Tree gives and the Tree takes away. But why, when he's so young? Does he think he's ill, or chosen to die? Surely, surely, they do not practise human sacrifice?

The next morning, the tele-unit bleeped and a message came from the base camp. She cursed.

'Is anything wrong?' Markian asked. They were sitting cross-legged on a mat, sharing a breakfast of fish and fruit. Jathran was not there.

'They want me to go back.' She stabbed at the keys. 'I'm telling them that I need a few more days. This island was my discovery, and I'm damned if anyone else is going to take the credit.'

'You can stay as long as you wish. But you will gain nothing by studying us. I don't understand it, for there's nothing to learn.'

'But there is, Markian. Perhaps I'm asking the wrong questions. Look, I'm worried about Jathran. He came to me very frightened last night, talking of Chelia and of her seeing a Boy.'

Again the embryonic face became guarded. 'He had no right to say anything.'

'But he was terrified of something! Markian, please try to explain it to me. Not for the film. For his sake. He is your sibling, isn't he?'

'We are all siblings.'

'All siblings. No parents, no children?'

There was pain in Markian's eyes now, and his mouth narrowed. He said quietly, 'Chelia went, it's true. But there are no babies.'

'Jathran spoke of the Tree from which you came. Do you remember it? Who looked after you as children?'

'The old ones.'

'Your parents?'

'No, the old ones look after the children when they come from the Tree. They are all gone, and we are the old ones now.'

'Old?' she said, startled. It was impossible to put an age on them.

'We have almost lived our allotted span. No children have come. It is too late for us.' He looked away, even in anger too gentle to alarm her. 'Now speak no more of it!'

Dear Mum,

I don't know how to start this. These people are dying.

There was a funeral this afternoon, three islanders had died in the night. Their bodies were weighted and sunk out to sea. In a way I was glad the cameras weren't here to record it. The aura of despair and hopeless resignation that came from the islanders was harrowing.

From the little information I've gleaned, it seems there have been no children born for the past forty years at least. The Freinians are all the same age, and barely live to fifty. They are dying already, and will be extinct in ten years.

I've a theory about the lack of children. These people are like axolotls, trapped in a larval stage and unable to reach sexual maturity without some essential trigger. But I'm no scientist. When I go back to base camp in a few days I am going to put the doctors and biologists on to this. They must receive medical help.

Nicky would laugh at me, wouldn't she? The most unmaternal person in the universe, turning my nose up at her decision to have a family, and here I am worried sick about a whole race's infertility. Give her my love. I must go.

All my love,
Stevie

At Stevie's request, she and Jathran made a tour of the village next day. It was more a town, spreading for three or four miles along the shore with the lake at its centre.

No one ever seemed to venture to the interior, where a tree-covered mountain thrust up into the sky. There was almost a fear in the way they clung round the shore, clung to each other, and Stevie was beginning to understand why.

Jathran seemed nervous, manically talkative without saying anything. Stevie tried to distance herself as she looked round at the rows of crystal pyramids, thinking about camera angles and panning shots and voice-overs. White pavements snaked between the tetrahedrons and everyone went on foot, crowds and crowds of figures all in the same hooded pearl-grey robes. The faces were all the same as well, amphibian and benign. She began to feel dizzy. Although the village was open to the sky and the scent of fern-trees blew from the lake, she could not shake off the sense of being under a glass dome.

It was the dream she had once had, long ago, as a child. A lake of white faces, and among them, just one that was different. A golden face. Light hair and blue eyes. That face coming closer and closer, carrying a terrifying significance that escaped her –

She gasped and caught Jathran's arm, to feel him suddenly hanging on to her in turn. The golden face had stopped and now bore an expression of alarm.

'It is the Boy, the Yellow Boy,' Jathran whispered in horror.

It was a moment before Stevie could reply. She laughed, but it was a hollow sound. 'No, Jathran, don't be silly – it's my reflection.' She walked up to the glassy wall and tapped it with her hand. 'See? I don't know what's wrong with me, jumping at my own reflection.'

But Jathran did not seem convinced. Colour came to his face, and the vessels throbbed under the skin. He looked fearfully at Stevie. 'No. It was the Boy. I've seen the Boy.'

'Calm down.' He seemed to be edging towards hysteria, and she kept a grip on his arm. 'It was only me. What do you think you've seen?'

'Don't touch me!' They were attracting attention now, as if Jathran had mutated into a creature to be stared at. 'Don't tell Markian, please. Don't tell anyone. I'm not going!'

He pulled out of Stevie's grasp and was swiftly out of sight between the pyramids.

Stevie, not knowing what to do, went back to Markian's house. But when she got there he was waiting for her as if he already knew.

'Did Jathran see the Yellow Boy?' he asked.

'No, it was just my reflection in a glass wall. I tried to calm him, but –'

'It makes no difference. The same thing happened to Chelia. She saw a face that was not really there, but the change began anyway. That is what seeing the face of the Boy is. Knowledge that you have been chosen.'

I saw the face too, for that matter, she thought.

'What will happen to Jathran?'

'He will leave us. He will never return.' Suddenly Markian's calmness erupted and he flung himself at Stevie, shouting, 'This is your fault – your fault! First Chelia and now him! One chosen is bad enough – why both?'

She fended him off easily, as if without gender he had no strength of any kind. He staggered backwards, then something happened to him; his lipless mouth stretched open, bruises flowed under the thin skin of his forehead, and he collapsed, uttering reedy grunts that bled away with his life.

Horrified, Stevie ran for help, but she knew nothing could be done. By the time the other islanders came, he was already dead. They bore away his body, leaving her very alone in the house, pacing under 'he crystal walls until it grew dark and the moons shone through them like shattered pebbles. She felt as if Markian's distress was inside her, a swollen vein of grief. She unfolded the tele-unit and sat with it on her knees, staring at the blank screen.

That was when Jathran came back.

Dear Mum,

I'm going into the forest with one of the Freinians, Jathran. He has to find the Tree, and he wants me with him. I don't understand everything yet, but I'm beginning to. Once in each generation, an islander sees a being – or a phantom – they call the Yellow Boy, and it initiates some sort of change in them which they cannot stop. I can already see evidence of the transformation in Jathran; the hair paler and thicker, the skin darker, more shape to his features.

I don't know whether he is able to explain it all to me yet. Perhaps there's no need. His sibling, Markian, died this afternoon. He wept when I told him, but he seems calm now.

No more time now. I'm taking the tele-unit and will transmit again later. All for now.

Love,
Stevie

It was all uphill from the village, and the foliage was dense. The ferny leaves writhed even when there was no breeze. She had grown used to similar forests on the mainland, and considered herself fit, but even so she had difficulty keeping up with Jathran. The tele-unit banged painfully against her hip as they climbed.

'Why did you want me with you, Jathran?' she asked.

'I couldn't go alone.'

'Why not one of the others?'

'It was you I wanted, Stevie.' He pointed upwards to the peak of the mountain. 'The Tree is up there. I remember now.'

'It's no good, I'll have to rest.'

They found a dry place and sat down, leaning against the old stump of a fern-tree. Every time she looked at

Jathran the change shook her. He seemed different in character, too, as if acceptance of it had matured him.

'You're very calm now,' she said. 'Aren't you frightened any more?'

'I'm terrified. But there's nothing I can do. Only one thing I don't understand, and that frightens me most: Chelia was chosen only two years ago. Why have I been chosen so soon?'

'You think something's happened to Chelia?' *Or is it me who's done this to you?* 'Don't worry. I'm with you.'

He went to sleep in her arms like a child. When she woke, it was light, and he was already awake and kneeling beside her. The transformation was complete now. The hood of his robe was thrown back, and his face was no longer embryonic but fully formed and as human-looking as hers. She raised a hand and ran her fingers over his lips, eyebrows and cheekbones. His hair was chalk-white, his eyes blue. But his skin – his skin had the texture of silk and the colour of a newly-minted gold coin.

'Are you all right, Jathran?' She felt as if she were dreaming. 'I still don't understand, but it doesn't seem to matter now.'

He lay down beside her. The Jathran she saw now was a creature out of myth, an angel come to ensorcell her. Simple enough. This was the form the Freinians took when they reached sexual maturity, and if it was not quite human, the difference was only in degrees of beauty. He said, 'Stevie, this is worth all the fear. I was chosen, and now I'm choosing you.'

'Yes,' she said. It was a dream. There was nothing in her mind except his closeness, the silken scent of his skin and the desire she felt for him. The ground was cold and hard, but in his arms she felt nothing but warmth.

She slept again, and this time when she woke, Jathran was gone. But she knew where the Tree was now, and by evening she had found it. It was a massive fern with a bole some thirty feet across, and beneath its roots there was a tunnel leading into the side of the mountain. It was pitch-dark in the cave, and the air smelt of sweet decay.

'Who's there?' called a voice.

Stevie jumped. 'Jathran?'

She fumbled for the torch on her belt, and a disc of light picked out a face in the darkness. It was not Jathran. It was a woman – a woman with golden skin and white hair, lying on a broad dais of rock in the centre of the cave.

'No, don't!' she cried weakly. 'Take the light away, please.'

But Stevie could not. She was transfixed. And as her eyes accustomed themselves to the darkness she saw the true shape of the woman. The upper torso seemed human, but from her waist ballooned an elongated sac five times the size of her body. All around it lay tiny, dead foetuses, pale amphibious things still connected to the sac by a string of red slime.

Stevie staggered back against the wall, dropped the torch-beam to point at the floor. When she found her voice, all she could say was, 'Where's Jathran? Where's Jathran?'

'There's no one here but me,' the woman said in a tranquil but weak voice. 'Why are you here?'

Get a grip, she told herself severely. 'My name's Stevie. I was trying to find an islander called Jathran. He said he had seen the Yellow Boy and had to find the Tree. I – I lost him. Isn't he here?'

There was a silence. Then the woman said, 'He has been here. He left me alone to die in dignity. I am Chelia.'

'Chelia . . .' Suddenly her curiosity, her need to research, seemed trivial and disgusting. 'I'm so sorry. I'll go.'

She flicked off the torch, but Chelia said, 'No, don't

go, Stevie. Jathran mentioned you. He said you were from the far side of the world, different to us. Do you understand us yet?'

'I think so,' Stevie said hoarsely. 'Only two in each generation reach maturity and breed . . .'

'And give birth to the next generation.'

And the previous generation look after the children until they can fend for themselves, and then they die, Stevie thought.

'But Chelia, what has happened to you?'

'I don't know. I am sick, all my babies are still-born. The previous Yellow Boy chose badly when he chose me. Frein would have died with me . . . but you came.'

'Me?'

'Yes. You chose Jathran and brought him here.'

'It was the other way round.'

'No. Stevie, when the Boy of one generation dies he must choose his successor. But with me the sequence has gone wrong. If you had not been the catalyst, there might not have been a successor at all.'

A figure moved past her in the dark. She knew it was Jathran. She turned the torch on again to see him kneeling beside Chelia, stroking her hair, weeping.

'Chelia, I couldn't stay away. I missed you so much. It's bad enough that you were chosen, but then to die . . .'

'Hush. You are the Palomino Boy now.'

And that makes me . . . He was so beautiful that her heart ached with love, but she could not take her eyes off Chelia's ruined body and the grotesque sac . . .

'Chelia, how does it take place?'

This abomination, this pregnancy . . .

Chelia replied, 'If you have made love to him, the change has already begun.'

Impossible. We are different species!

Stevie felt as if her whole body had turned to water, and the stifling nightmare was on her again. Chelia was weeping now as the Palomino Boy stroked her hair. Stevie had been almost weeping with them until the

shock stemmed her grief, and she turned and rushed
out of the cave in blind panic.

It was a long time before he came to her. She was lost
in the darkness, but Jathran found her and said in a
quiet voice, 'Chelia is dead. I couldn't leave her before.'

'I know.'

'Stevie, I think there's something you have misunder-
stood. When she spoke of the change, she meant me.
The Boy and the Mother are the same person. I will
become the Mother, and afterwards I will become the
Yellow Boy again, and die.' He bent and kissed her, like
a brother. 'And now you had better go, Stevie. I did not
mean to use you – I didn't even realise I was, until now.
I'm sorry. Go back to your own land.'

It was raining, she suddenly noticed. The rain seemed
to be falling straight through her. 'But what about choosing your successor? You have to stay alive until then . . .'

'Do I? Perhaps the next one chooses himself. The
Palomino Boy is only seen as a ghost, or a reflection.'

Dear Mum,

I'm sorry. I can't go on with this documentary.

Let one of the others try, if they think they can make
an hour's entertainment out of what I've seen.

I don't know whether to laugh or cry. I've escaped
something so horrible that I can't imagine it, so it
means nothing. But losing Jathran – only understanding how much I loved him when it was too late – that
hurts. Just one night we had, and now I see it was an
act of self-fertilisation for him/her, I don't know what
I feel. I imagine that usually it would be a Freinian,
temporarily possessed of female characteristics. Perhaps they are rudimentary females anyway, and I did
not look closely enough. But this time, this time it was
me.

One thing is certain. The islanders know and understand their breeding pattern, origins, everything.
But they pretend ignorance out of – what? Fear?

Reverence? It seems so convoluted that I'm sure there's still something I've missed somewhere. The one fate of which they live in dread is seeing the Palomino Boy, and becoming the Mother.

I always thought I'd leave motherhood to Nicky, and I haven't changed my mind. I find birth and all that goes with it repulsive. Still, that's just me. Nature finds an infinity of ways to be cruel, but how can you argue with Her? The pain passes away, but love (if we're lucky) remains.

Mum, I'm coming home.

All my love,
Stevie

CRUEL AS THE GRAVE

ALEX STEWART

ALEX STEWART

Alex Stewart has been a full time freelance writer since 1985, although his first short story appeared in the second issue of *Interzone* in 1982, the first piece of work from an unknown writer to appear in that magazine. Since then he has contributed fiction, reviews, articles and comic scripts to a wide range of publications, from *City Limits* to *2000 AD*.

TIME FREEZES AND shatters as the bullets strike, and I can see the whole thing, all of it, as my brain explodes against the wall. A faint mist of blood hangs in the narrow hallway, staining the paintwork pink. My knuckles are white on the gun as I back away screaming, I fall and I see myself vanish, the sound cutting off with the *crack!* of imploding air as I slide to the floor. Even as I hit it, the shards of my life collide.

'What's the matter with you?' Frank looks bewildered, like an oversized child. He can't understand why I'm angry, but I don't know either. We're in my apartment, the old one I had near the Institute. Something's happening to us, we argue too much, and I'm past caring.

'Nothing,' I say. 'Not with me, Frank.' I don't know what I mean by that, I'm just throwing the words like javelins, hoping to hurt him. When I do it hurts me more, feeding the anger, leaving it nothing to burn but my own soul.

We aren't always like this. We used to be lovers, we used to be friends, and we'll be both again; the kaleidoscope shifts, shows me the times we made love, overlapping like multiple shadows. The first time, hesitant, giggling, gives way to deeper sharing; but most of that lies in the future, my past, beyond the shouting and the grief. Frank spreads his hands.

'I can't deal with this, Jenny,' he says. That's part of

the problem; he always retreats, and I have to go further
and further to get a reaction from him.

This happens the night after we first shift the mice.
I'm standing in the control booth, the tingle of ozone
stinging my nostrils. Below me, behind the armour-
glass, a technician walks towards the grid. He's dwarfed
by the tachyon accelerators, anonymous in his Institute
coverall, reduced to the scale of the mice in their wire
cage. He puts them down gently, centred on the raised
ceramic mesh, and they sniff at his fingers.

I sniff too, at the reflection in the glass. Frank's in the
door of the booth, talking to Yvonne. He's besotted with
her, no doubt about it. It's there in his eyes, the way he
stands beside her.

'Sure,' he says. 'We'll have the results by next week.
Tuesday at the latest.' He shuffles his feet, waiting for a
pat on the head.

'Good old Frank,' she says, with a newspaper smile.
'Always reliable.' I seethe while she slithers away down
the corridor. Good old reliable Frank stood me up last
night.

'Where the hell were you?' I snarl, as the door clicks
to. He raises his hands in the old, placating gesture.

'Jenny, I'm sorry.' He sounds as sincere as a political
broadcast. 'One of the condensers burned. I had to
recalibrate . . .'

'And Yvonne just had to help you, I suppose?' I
turn away, begin the phase one power-up. His face
floats in the glass, transparent as his lies. Down on the
floor the technician retreats, with a final word to the
mice.

'Oh for heaven's sake!' His voice hardens slightly, the
calm beginning to fray. 'I thought we'd been through all
that. She's just a friend, Jenny. That's all. And I'm sorry
about last night . . .'

'*You're* sorry! Do you know how long I waited in that
restaurant? Do you?' My voice is getting shrill, rasping
his nerves like chalk on a slate. Whatever the truth, he

can't have slept much last night. He spreads his hands again – *mea culpa*, let's forget it.

'I know. Look, I tried to call . . .'

'That's your trouble, Frank. You always *try*.' Game, set, and match to me. His reflection shrugs, and gives up. I trigger the accelerators.

Down on the floor, the mice shift uneasily. A faint nimbus glows around the cage, and there's a sudden *crack!* of imploding air. A moment later they flicker back into existence. They scuttle drunkenly around the cage, then wrinkle their noses.

'We did it!' I stare at the instruments, numb with surprise. 'We actually did it! Five years into the future, and we got them back!' All we usually got back were mouse-burgers.

'The new discriminator circuits. What did I tell you?' Frank's elated, the quarrel already forgotten. He hugs me, unexpectedly, and the resentment flares again. He cares more about the damn mice than he does about me! 'Tonight we celebrate!'

'*You* celebrate.' I pull away, nursing the anger, frightened of losing it in the glow of achievement. 'I've work to do.' His face sags, like I've just let the air out. 'That's if you want the results by next Tuesday.'

The next few months are dismal. We quarrel more, we speak less, we hardly see each other outside the lab. Some nights I cry, too angry for sleep, and some mornings Frank arrives late, his breath foul with stale alcohol. The only times we act like a couple are for the media.

'Yes,' I explain, smiling sweetly for the cameras, 'time-shifts are perfectly safe for human temponauts. But there's really no point.'

'And why's that?' the reporters ask, with identical expressions of alert interest, like dogs waiting for a stick to be thrown.

'Because information can only flow up the timeline,' we explain, sometimes me, sometimes Frank. 'If we sent someone into the future, and brought them back, they'd remember nothing.'

'And a modern historian,' the other adds, 'would arrive in the Middle Ages as a drooling vegetable.'

The reporters nod, once, incisively, and pan away to a shot of the accelerators. Frank and I simper at one another's cleverness, in case they pan back, and bare our teeth.

A short while later, timeshifts cease to be news. Other researchers duplicate our work, and I see it used as the gimmick in a crime show.

'It was the perfect murder,' I say. By this time Frank and I are in a state of armed neutrality, going through the motions of civilised behaviour like little clockwork toys. We even speak a little, pretend we can talk like old friends without the bitterness twisting our guts. 'The villain shifted up, and committed the crime in the future. The perfect alibi.'

'It wouldn't work, though.' Frank pretends to consider it, grateful for the lull in our verbal war. 'You'd need someone else to power up the grid.'

'That was the gimmick. She tried to blackmail him. So he shot her to keep her quiet, and got arrested for that instead.'

'Ah.' He nods, his eyes focused behind me, and I hear footsteps in the corridor. He smiles, for real, not the mask he keeps for me. 'Hello Yvonne.'

'Well, I've got work to do,' I say. They move away, her hand brushing his elbow, and molten anger sears through my veins.

It's about then I buy the gun. The paycops are hiking their rates again, and my complex committee talks about laying them off. They won't, of course, but a lot of the residents start carrying. Now I glare at their backs, Frank and Yvonne, and I squeeze the butt so tightly it bruises my palm.

Hard to believe she's our best friend, mine and Frank's, so shortly afterwards. We buy her old apartment after we're married, and invite her over with Dave on our anniversary. Our first dinner party in our new home.

'Happy house-warming.' Frank hooks my waist as I pass him, and we kiss, our arms enfolding one another in warmth and security. It's like that after the accident; dazed, bewildered, I'm only aware of Frank. I cling desperately to him, the one familiar thing in a maelstrom of noise and smoke.

'What happened?' I have to shout, my voice almost lost in the howling of alarms and injured people. Frank frowns, a fresh bruise growing purple under the dirt on his face.

'Some kind of power surge. It burned out half the circuits.' He leads me outside, where the cool, fresh air of an October night hits me like a surge of adrenalin. 'Don't you remember?'

I try, but it's all so confused, the way a dream flows away when you wake from it.

'I was working on the grid . . .' I shake my head. There was a flash of light, and noise, and smoke. And then Frank. I meet his eyes, see only concern there, reflected with the stars, and feel something cold melting out of my soul. Slowly, without thought, we kiss.

Far away, I hear the door bell ring.

'I'll go.' I disengage reluctantly, holding his eyes with mine, and a final peck on the lips. He grins, disappearing into the kitchen. The bell rings again, and I open the door, smiling a welcome.

'Two-timing bitch!' The gunfire's deafening in the narrow hall, as the bullets tear me open like a paper bag. The paintwork smears crimson as they throw me back, and my *doppelgänger* screams hysterically as I realise what I've done. I don't have time to laugh, but for a moment I can feel it welling up, cocooned in a bubble of blood.

THE SONG OF WOMEN

PAUL KINCAID

PAUL KINCAID

A professional advertising copywriter, Paul Kincaid is better known in the SF community as reviews editor of the critical journal *Vector*, former co-ordinator of the British Science Fiction Association, and one of the judging panel for the first two Arthur C. Clarke awards. An editorial consultant to *The Gate*, this is his first fiction sale.

THE ARRIVAL OF the aircar alone would have been enough to rouse the village. Within five minutes of the message from the port there were upwards of twenty people gathered in the colonnade around the small square. One or two even ventured briefly out into the open, scanning the clear skies hurriedly then scurrying back into the shade, for it was now more than an hour since dawn and the heat was unbearable.

Stelan was attracted by the commotion. Twenty people was a large crowd in this huddled, cowed village that pulled itself back under the skirts of the mountain as if in an effort not to be noticed. He had rushed down the skittering slope from his isolated shack in the last moments before sunrise as he did every day to scavenge what he could, perform any unwanted tasks that might be on offer around the mouth of the mine. But today was different, today nobody was in the cool dark underground, they were here, fretting and muttering and jostling for whichever patch of shadow was deemed coolest. Stelan ran along a narrow alleyway, the white dust that flew about him seemed to coat his body with heat, then dived under a mound of bins and crates. It was the rear of the village store, hard against the mountain wall, and among the rubbish piled here almost permanently he had fashioned a cosy little refuge. It smelled and was always hotter than he would have liked, but no one came out here in daylight so it was quite safe. Sometimes, if there was no work, he would sleep here until sunset allowed him to return home.

But he wasn't going to sleep now. He rested in the shade for a moment longer, then dashed out into the harsh white glare of day, around the back of the mean little building, along another alley, then into the blessed shade of the colonnade. He collapsed against the rough, stone wall, struggling for breath. The sun had leached all the energy from him. He was a small man, lean and wiry and as tough as life here had made him, but he was getting old now and life had been doubly hard since he returned. There was little strength left.

After a time he opened his eyes. Perspiration dripped stingingly into them, blurring his vision for a moment. Stoically he waited. On this side of the square the morning sun arrowed under the low overhang of the roof, leaving only a sliver of dimness in which he could stand. But it meant he was alone. And he had a good view of the people crowded into the corner across from him.

He was aware of a difference, but only slowly did he realise that the difference was a sound. Something low and soft that seemed to lose itself in the high rock walls above them, then emerge again so that it was impossible to tell which direction it came from. Just for an instant he wondered if this might be what wind sounds like. Then he recognised it.

An aircar? But they didn't come here. Every ten days or so a freighter would negotiate the narrow gorge to leave supplies and pick up minerals. Nothing else. That was why he had chosen it, all those years ago.

An acid distress welled in him. But there was something else: a quivering eagerness. He found himself peering intently into the blazing sky. A hard blue framed by the solemn greys and whites of the rock, a world of sharp edges and clean, clear lines, of absolutes and certainties. And now something new and uncertain was coming into it. In daylight, too, which gave it an added importance, an extra *frisson* of fear and excitement.

There. For a cruel instant something caught the sun and blazed like a new weapon. The light blinded him briefly. Wordless mutterings meant that others had seen it also, then a voice above the murmurings: 'There!' He could see again through the brilliant flashes, and a dark shape was growing quickly, turning into a compact vehicle like an eyeless insect. The sound grew no louder, a conspiratorial whispering, and it settled in the square with barely a flurry of white dust.

The crowd moved then, like a wave on a beach, drawn out into the open by a tidal attraction, only to retreat reluctantly from the impact of the sun, leaving nothing but a susurrus of sound and the aircar marooned.

A crack in its stained, striated carapace, and the insect shook loose a wing. It creaked and shivered, then rose stiffly from the body. In the dark interior, something stirred. An unfolding, a flapping, a breaking out from the cocoon. The figure was tall, impossibly tall, and unbelievably vivid. A shimmer of colours fell about it, shifting and changing with every slight movement of the body below. Simple colours, reds and blues and greens, but glorious in this bleached, sun-drained village where everything that varied from the uniform white was soon muted by dust and fading until it shrank back into the familiar pallor. For a long time, then, nobody saw anything but a rainbow that seemed to grow out of a battered aircar, except that the aircar must have been far too small to hold it. Only later did they recognise the rainbow as a cloak of feathers wrapped about a slender figure that might have been human.

All except Stelan. As soon as he saw the figure he curled up in a gentle patch of shadow and began whimpering. He peered sideways at the new arrival, his bleached and cracked face twisting as if fear and desire wrestled just below the surface. Then, hardly aware of what he was doing, he began to hum quietly to himself. It was a curious tune that rose haltingly, stuttered at its peak, then rushed into a headlong descent before slowing to begin that uncertain climb once more.

The visitor cocked its head, then cast about jerkily until fixing upon the pool of grey where Stelan huddled. In a piercing squawk that echoed from the impassive cliffs and resounded about the low houses, it cried 'No!'

Stelan tried to pull more tightly into himself. The creaking, half-forgotten notes forced themselves from his throat until they teetered on the edge of their downward trill, and fell silent. His haggard face was emptied of emotion.

The visitor nodded sharply once, then raised a thin leg unnecessarily high and stepped with odd daintiness to the ground. It was that movement which galvanised the crowd. They had been enraptured by the vision, turned to stone by the squawk, but now it was someone who had been in the merciless sun for far too long. 'Here!' someone called, and another, 'It's cooler here.' Two men even ventured from the colonnade, stretching their arms towards the visitor as if they would pluck him from the sunlight and drag him to safety. But they stopped short, and after a moment retired in some confusion.

Head jutting forward, stepping high, the visitor walked towards the crowd, then hesitated and turned once more towards Stelan. 'I am looking for a man,' he announced. His voice was light and musical. 'One of your number. His name was Stelan.'

A loud sob. Stelan braced himself against the rough stone wall, pushed himself slowly upright, all the while clutching his stomach, restraining the hollowness that threatened to burst out and swallow him whole. His head was turned to look out of the village, out at the implacable, inevitable canyon, certain and safe. Yet always his eyes flickered eagerly towards the intruder, the disrupter.

'No!' he shouted, then fell abruptly silent once more, looking warily for the first time at his fellow citizens, amazed at how loud and raw his own voice had been.

The visitor took two bobbing steps towards him.

'No. Go away. Leave me alone. It wasn't me. Please. I didn't do it. Please.' Then, almost in the same frantic breath, 'Don't go. Please. Don't leave me. Ah!' And with that cry of pain Stelan was deflated, staggering, clutching blindly for support. He raised his head, dark lines cutting through the chalky encrustations on his cheeks. 'Let it be over. I want . . . so much.'

The visitor maintained the same calm pace, at long last stepping into the dim shade of the colonnade, where his feathers were finally muted. There was a wave of relief, a murmur of thanksgiving. They might be puzzled and excited by so alien a visitor, they might wonder vaguely at the distress of Stelan the beggar, though he had never really been a part of the village despite having been there since before most of them were born; yet none of that compared with colours brighter than they were ever able to maintain, or worse, someone who had defied for so long their eternal and unbeatable enemy, the sun. Once he had come into the shade, once the feathers were dulled away from the light, the challenge was gone, there was nothing to make them so uncomfortable. And since his interest was in the outcast, there was nothing to keep any of them further. They began drifting away to work and routine, letting everything settle back cosily into the way things had always been.

Except for Stelan. But things had never been cosy or routine for him, no matter how much he tried.

He looked up now into impassive features. A hooked nose, a long jaw. Then his gaze moved down to the feathers, and he smiled. A hand reached forward, was snatched away, then came forward again to stroke them. 'Beautiful,' he said, in a voice more full of pain than the word would ever suggest.

'You are Stelan?' the stranger asked, melodically but pedantically. Stelan nodded, the briefest of motions, a man accepting his fate. 'I have a message, a dying request so I am honour bound to deliver it. When I give you the message I am at last free to return home.' As he said that a tremor ran through him, stirring the feather cloak as if it were wings on the point of unfurling.

'You're not Avial? I thought . . . You look . . .' A hand tightened on feathers then relaxed, leaving them crumpled so they didn't quite return to their smooth pattern.

'No.' The man drew himself even straighter, not deigning to look down at the slumped figure before him. 'I bear a message from Avial. Now I can deliver it and my commitment is over.'

'Wait! Not here, not now.' Slowly, as if his legs and arms would not unbend properly, Stelan forced himself upright. He was still a head shorter than the birdman, but looked up into the sharp-featured face with something approaching dignity. 'He's dead?'

'Yes.'

'Then it is over. I'm sorry.'

'Over? Maybe. That's no concern of mine. I am to tell you . . .'

'No!'

'I have no wish to delay.'

'Please don't go.'

'You do not wish to receive the message here? I understand. We should go somewhere private. You have a home?'

'Home?' Stelan found himself turning automatically away, squinting into the hard sunlight. A white scree slope rose at the entrance to the village. Up that, out of sight over the shoulder, was a shack left over from early workings. He lived there, a self-imposed outcast, but it wasn't home. 'No, we couldn't go there. Not until dark.' He looked down again. His hands still stroked and fondled the cloak. One of the feathers came loose and he brought it close to his face. It was an irridescent green, and for a moment he saw it as soft grass, as bowed

leaves dripping still after rain. He hadn't thought of that
for so long. Smiling, he looked up into a hawkish face
haloed by white.

'You fear the light?'

'The heat. No one goes out into the open after sunrise.
It can kill you.'

'I see.' He sounded unconvinced, stepping back from
the colonnade a moment so that a flood of light poured
over him. He threw back his head, moving his arms so
that the cloak opened briefly. Then he drew the cloak
tight about him once more and looked haughtily around
the deserted square. 'There is the aircar. You have the
coordinates of your home?'

Stelan regarded the machine, its winged door left
carelessly open. The dark interior would be baking by
now. He thought of other places where doors could be
left ajar, where some buildings were roofless despite
occasional rain. Where there were subtle and ever-
shifting gradations of light and colour. He looked down
at his feet and saw, inches in front of them, a sharp and
remorseless line that divided white from shadow-grey.
It was here, just the same, yesterday, as it would be
tomorrow. There was no subtlety here, no fudging in-
between. It was why he had left in the first place, why
he had been cast out. And it was why he had returned,
incarcerating himself in this strict and unbending
regime.

'No,' he said at last. 'I know a place. This way.'

The metal door was heavy and featureless, marked
only by the inevitable depredations of the abrasive air.
It opened reluctantly and swung violently shut behind
them. They paused involuntarily in the narrow, airless
passageway as their eyes adjusted to the dim light,
then walked Indian-file through the thick walls to the
stairwell that spiralled deep into the bedrock. They
found themselves at last in a small, poorly lit hall. The
skim on the walls was studded with chips of the polished
yellow marble that was usually too expensive even here

where it was mined. The splinters glimmered weakly, and shivers of light also caught in the reflective webs woven into the day-suits of the few miners sitting at the tables or by the counter.

Stelan stood at the bottom of the stairs, rubbing his hands and biting his lower lip. He wasn't often brave enough, or rich enough, to venture in here. 'Can you stand us a brew?' he asked, looking keenly at his visitor.

But the birdman had already left the stairs to prowl in that high-stepping, bobbing way of his around the walls. He became visibly more agitated as he progressed, jerking his head from side to side, until by the time he rejoined Stelan he seemed ready to start up the steps right away. His voice was no longer so sure, so patrician. 'No windows,' he said with a shiver. 'You cannot see the sky. How can you not see the sky?'

And Stelan was reminded of his own first moments of exile, when he had escaped a world of uniform cruelty and ugliness for one of unalloyed beauty. And he saw none of it. He stepped out into the open and discovered: no tunnels, no colonnades, not even roofs. He was under the naked sky. A weak blue it was, shading towards green at the horizon, and crossed by dense continents of grey, roiling cloud. It was raining. But he didn't notice any of that until later. He collapsed, whimpering, arms locked above his head. He was afraid that his brain would fry, that his blood would boil, that his flesh would bubble from him. He was afraid that the sun would pierce him, leave him deranged, dead. Instead someone knelt beside him, unlocked his arms, helped him to his feet. For the first time he looked into the face of Avial, who . . .

Stelan became conscious once more of the visitor, the same beaked face, the same small, piercing eyes flickering now as if still in search of a window. He rubbed a knuckle quickly, viciously, into the corner of an eye, and shivered in his turn. 'A table,' he said gruffly, and led the way to the middle of the room.

The man at the counter waited impassively. Stelan ordered wine. Vines only grew in a narrow belt around one of the poles and the drink was expensive. It was rare he had the chance for such indulgence. The man tapped a screen, then jerked his chin towards the visitor.

'Oh.' The birdman was still clearly nervous. The tip of a long, slender tongue appeared, touched briefly at a lip, disappeared. 'I'll just have water, please.'

The man tapped another part of the screen and thrust out his hand. Delicate fingers emerged from the cloak and slipped a coin into the palm. The hand did not withdraw. After a moment's awkwardness Stelan whispered, 'And the water.' The birdman looked hard at him, but produced another coin. There was no change. The barman slid open a compartment and took two bulbs from it. He handed them over and turned away to serve someone else, showing no further interest in the stranger. The curiosity of the aircar's arrival had dissipated into a familiar bovine indifference.

Stelan watched the man for a moment. Barrel-chested, heavy limbed, head like a block of limestone, chiselled and weathered until it was as arid and lifeless as the planet. Then he looked around the room, seeing the same squat figures, the same joyless expressions. It was what had driven him away in the first place, and what had brought him back. He recognised himself.

Then he looked at the stranger and recognised Avial. And shut off the memory straight away.

He ushered the visitor to an empty table with hard, plastic chairs. No luxuries, no softness here; by choice as much as by necessity. No down beds, no sweet-scented chilter-leaf pillows, no pliant rush seats. He bit at the nipple of his bulb, concentrated on the rich, slightly acid wine as it washed away the dust in his mouth. His eyes were tight shut; he thought of nothing but the moment, the chair, the table, the wine.

The memories were coming too quickly now. Memories he had fought to suppress decades before, pushing

them away ruthlessly whenever they started slipping
into his mind, until he thought they were as dead as
everything else in him.

The bulb was empty already. He put it down, gasping
for breath, and unbidden the rough melody croaked
from him, the halting climb, the rushed descent.

Until a hand seized him, squeezed him into silence.
He opened his eyes, startled. The birdman was out of
his chair, stretched across the table, a wild, sad stare in
his eyes. The long, delicate fingers were surprisingly
strong. For what seemed a long while they were petrified
thus, until the birdman abruptly collapsed, slumped
back in his chair, hand weaving feebly in the air before
him. The precious water was untouched on the table.

'You mustn't do that. You don't know how cruel it is.
You don't know. I have to get away. I must deliver my
message and leave here at once.' He cast a glance over
his shoulder as if the windowless walls were already
closing about him, blocking the exit. 'You can't know
how cruel.'

But Stelan was not listening. He had seen something
in the mad face perhaps, or finally recognised his song.
Whatever, memory had claimed him. He was not on this
colourless world, but in a place of blues and greens,
where rocks might be copper, ochre, yellow, where
people wore rainbows. His one act of despair, or crimi-
nality, or whatever they chose to call it, had brought him
to paradise, and he could not believe his luck. Avial took
him in. Stelan neither knew nor cared whether Avial
was acting as host or watchdog or something else, for
Avial was tall and slender, elegant and bright, soft-
spoken and various. Avial was everything that was impossible where Stelan came from. Avial was beautiful.

Stelan lived a dream, and hoped he would never wake
up. He had found a place where there was ease and
plenty. There were parks and gardens and – oh, precious
wonder – running water. He knelt on grassy banks and
looked into clear, bubbling streams, and saw his own

face reflected, a reminder of ugliness. Then he looked up, and Avial smiled at him.

When Avial permitted it, the two would go out together to stores that held more than Stelan had imagined possible, or to visit mountains or valleys or other birdmen. There was always difference here, nothing staled, remained the same.

When Avial did not permit, Stelan would say he was going to look for a job or to explore alone, then wait out of sight until Avial emerged. There were always bushes to hide in, trunks to shelter behind. And the buildings, of red brick, of grey stone, of pink composite, of pastel plastics, even of dreadfully familiar yellow marble, all had enough arches and alcoves for anyone who wished not to be seen. Doors were never locked, usually not even closed; there were always huge windows that occupied more space than the walls that enclosed them; and of course they were as often as not roofless. It was too easy. Stelan watched Avial at his screen, in conference both holo and live, resting under the warm sun on a high, private perch.

And the moment he always wished to forget, though he could never quite wipe it from his mind. It was impossible to say if the room was indoors or out, for it extended almost organically from the house. Walls of densely tangled hedge, a couch of chilter branches and their large soft leaves that seemed to have grown there accidentally, the roof a clear sky shot through with evening veins of lemon, iridium and blood. And Stelan perched where wall and tree became one, amid an anonymity of leaves.

Avial and the woman had been there for some time. She was relaxing on the couch while Avial paced back and forth across the grass. But gradually these high, nervous steps acquired a ritualistic feel. He pranced before her, head stabbing forward, cloak fluffed out and bouncing as he moved so that it was a display of ever-shifting colours and patterns. And to accompany the dance, Stelan became aware that the woman was crooning. Softly, so that it was impossible to hear the words, but they didn't seem to matter so much as the melody which rose slowly, hesitated, then fell rapidly only to start the pattern over again. The song became faster, more urgent, and Avial's dance became a frantic rush hither and thither before the woman until, at some signal it was impossible to identify, he shrugged off his feather cloak. For the first time Stelan saw Avial naked, pale flesh stretched tight over frail, hollow bones. And, briefly, a glimpse of his swollen penis before he threw himself savagely upon the now naked woman.

Stelan turned away retching, tumbled awkwardly, carelessly, to the ground. He thought of ugliness even in the midst of beauty. He thought of losing Avial.

After that, how quickly things changed. He saw now a world in which tradition and biology had become inextricably entwined. He saw ritual in every action. Like a cloak of feathers, beauty was put on to hide something primal and nasty. He had not lost paradise, it had been taken away from him. And Avial's smile still looked the same.

An age or an instant later he knelt before a low mound of feathers. Somewhere inside himself he was surprised that the feathers did not lose their sheen, that the colours did not fade, now that their owner was dead. But beauty was still beauty even though it cloaked a corpse. Tentatively he reached out to stroke it. Maybe he would have a cloak like that, maybe he would become beautiful.

Only then did he look up at Avial, standing on the other side of the dead woman. The fall of colours from his shoulder, the lovely beaked face. Stelan smiled.

'She can't come between us any more. She can't spoil the beauty. Just the two of us. You'll see. I can be every bit as good.' The gaunt stare on Avial's face. Stelan spoke more quickly, more desperately. 'I had to, you can see that. But I'll take her place, I'll be everything she was, and more. Listen. Listen, I even know the song.' And he began to sing, roughly, haltingly.

The look of agony on Avial's face. The tortured muscles, the slow opening of the mouth.

'. . . forgive you.'

The two faces, Avial and the stranger, superimposed, a haunting double image, until the stranger slowly, remorselessly, dominated, and Avial was gone.

Stelan blinked, looked about the dim yellow room. 'What?'

'It took a lifetime, and I'm still not sure how he was able to do it then. But in the end my grandfather forgave you, and made me promise to find you and give you the message. Now it is over and I can return home.'

The stranger rose eagerly, and was already part way up the stairs when Stelan caught up with him.

'Grandfather? Then Avial married again?'

'He had daughters cloned from the body of the woman you killed. Otherwise he spent the rest of his life alone.'

Along the corridor and outside. After the dim interior even the shaded colonnade was so bright it made the eyes swim and set false images spinning in front of them.

Stelan caught at the feather cloak. 'I loved him. He was beautiful. You are beautiful. Don't go away. Please don't go away.'

The stranger pulled free, and Stelan was left with two viridian feathers. He chased after him.

'Wait! Listen! I can sing the song.'

The wing of the aircar folded neatly back against its carapace. It rose with a quiet hum, and was gone like an insect in the still air. Behind it, crumpled in the white dust under the baking sun, Stelan croaked and murmured a tune that would never go away.

THE AMOROUS ADVENTURES
OF HOGFOOT RIGHT

GARRY KILWORTH

GARRY KILWORTH

Garry Kilworth was born in York in 1941. He spent eighteen years in the RAF as a cryptographer, and has worked in Singapore, the Maldives, Africa, Aden, Cyprus, Malta and Germany. Since then he has worked for Cable and Wireless, in London and in the Caribbean, and studied English at King's College, London. He became a full-time writer in 1982, is married with two grown-up children and lives in Hong Kong. His books include *In Solitary*, *Night of Kadar*, *Split Second*, *Gemini God*, *A Theatre of Timesmiths*, *Cloudrock* and *The Songbirds of Pain*.

NOW THAT HIS mistress was dead, Hogfoot Right had no reason to remain in the high, glass-tower apartment where she had lived with the pets modern surgery had been able to fashion from her own limbs. The welfare machine, that had visited once a week, would no doubt have removed Hogfoot to some terrible establishment for homeless amputates, had not the spunky aggressive little creature managed to escape its metal clutches. Although he had not known this for a fact, his instinct sent him flying along corridors and down fire escapes, to the street below, where he made good his exit.

His natural affection for protective grooves took him along the gutter, towards a derelict part of the city. For most of the journey he went unhindered, there being few people abroad in those times of floating bedchairs which took care of an owner's needs. However, at one corner he caused a bit of a stir when a pedestrian saw him, and screeched, 'A rat!' before fainting into the arms of an attendant robot. One or two citizens gave chase, but their own feet were not as nimble, or indeed as fit, as Hogfoot himself. He easily outran them. He wondered vaguely what a *rat* was, and whether to feel annoyed or flattered. If it scared people, he was inclined to think that a rat was a creature to be admired, since Hogfoot hadn't a great regard for the human race, albeit one of them had given him birth. In the main they seemed a self-indulgent, decadent and sickly bunch of sluggards that needed a good kick up their rears from the likes of offshoots like Hogfoot. Revolution, he felt sure, was coming one of these fine days.

Soon, he was amongst the rubble and rubbish that surrounded an old, disused canal, and out of harm of any citizens that wished to deprive him of movement. Having accomplished his escape, he was left with a foggy notion – not unpleasant by any means – that he was free. He could do as he wished.

Settling down for the day, in the shade of an abandoned mattress, he thought about his recent battle with bird-hands. Hogfoot had merely administered what was, in his opinion, a just execution, after birdhands had murdered the rest of the amputates in the apartment. He was not a violent creature, having spent most of his former, dormant existence in a bedsock, blind to the light. Such an existence is peaceful in its very nature. No, he was not violent – just a little aggressive, quick-tempered and belligerent. He had his faults, like any foot.

But what was he to do with this new-found *freedom*? The future stretched before him, like a blank bedsheet, white and without wrinkles.

He spent one or two days, nosing around the rubbish and confronting one or two creatures of his own size. In fact they were very much like him, except they had longer tails and pointed noses. They attempted to teach him his place, as an outsider newly-arrived, but a few hard butts on sensitive nostrils soon persuaded them he was not to be trifled with.

One evening, not long after establishing his supremacy over the creatures of the rubbish world, a figure passed Hogfoot in the moonlight and he paused to study it more closely. Yes, it was indeed another feral foot.

Now, individual feet are basically gregarious creatures, coming as they do from a set of twins, and though Hogfoot was known as an unsociable amputate, he too felt insecure and unsettled away from his own kind. The loneliness bit into his soul. He yearned for the company of creatures of his own stamp – even hands or ears – so, understandably, he felt a twitch of excitement in his small toe at the sight of another foot.

He followed this creature, silently, along the edge of the canal, until they reached a stretch of open ground surrounded by the husks of automobiles and old tyres. There, around a fire, was a large collection of amputates huddled together.

Hogfoot Right studied this group for a while, before creeping forward and joining the feral feet which were clustered together in one section. No one took very great notice of him – he was just one of many – and he soon settled down peacefully to enjoy the proximity of his own kind.

As the evening wore on, more amputates joined those around the fire: some pairs of hands came flying in, pale and ghostly in the moonlight. They fluttered their feather-fingers as they hovered above the fire, then glided down on its thermals to settle beside their fellow creatures.

Hogfoot felt a prickle of apprehension on witnessing the arrival of so many hands, the memory of his single combat still fresh in his mind. Since his experience of the world was limited, he could perhaps be forgiven for thinking that all birdhands were bloody-nailed killers that played Mozart one moment, and dealt out death in the next. Hands were capable of so many things, from cultural activities which employed their sensitive finger-tips, to smashing a jaw with their knuckles. In prayer, they looked beautiful; in battle they could employ the wickedest weapons, with vicious manipulation. The fingers that wrote the words of the poem also squeezed the trigger of the gun.

By comparsion, feet were boorish, stumpy creatures with little refinement and no particular skills save that of kicking things in or out of place. Hogfoot realised this, but he refused to feel inferior to those sinister sisters from the top end of the torso: those Siamese twins. He felt closer to the snake-arms and moth-ears, than he did to the birdhands, and he bristled to see so many together.

However, it seemed that they were not about to cause trouble, so he merely kept a wary eye on them.

There were also one or two creatures he had not seen before (separate from a body, that is). A pair of huge creatures, obviously twins, nestled together not far from Hogfoot's patch. They were legs, with giant thighs. He decided not to cultivate any acquaintance with these amputates that had once been closer to him than any other.

Hogfoot shifted his position, moving nearer the fire. He was beginning to get a little cold. He settled down beside a more dainty ex-appendage, gathering warmth from her. She seemed to like his company.

At that moment he was struck up the rump by something blunt and heavy. He whirled in pain to find himself confronted by an enormous feral foot and at once knew he had met his match. Nevertheless, his blood was up, and he charged – only to be beaten back again by this calloused, solid creature. He lay there, stunned and ashamed of having been thrashed in front of Daintyfoot.

Hogfoot shuffled away, leaving the ogre to nuzzle-up against the soft body of Daintyfoot. All night long he glowered at the blunt heel-face of his most recent enemy, reflecting on the vagaries of life. You no sooner dispose of one adversary, than another takes their place: more formidable, more graceless, more unchivalrous. To attack from behind, was cowardly – yet Daintyfoot had no choice but to submit to the nuzzles of this Bigfoot.

Hogfoot Right watched, and fumed, as in the early hours Bigfoot inserted his dirty, large toe between her delicate pinkies. No shame! The swine had no shame. It was nothing short of rape, for the gentle female foot squirmed beneath the attentions of her unwanted lover, and looked towards Hogfoot. *Yet she did not leave.* That gave Hogfoot food for thought. There was some loyalty towards her oafish lover, which must have been promised before Hogfoot arrived, and which she now felt could not be broken without cause.

Obviously Hogfoot had stumbled upon a union that was well-established, despite the incompatibility of the two feet involved. Despair entered his heart. It was going to be a difficult task persuading Daintyfoot to leave the ogre if she had been with him for some time.

The following morning, as the sparrows and natural creatures of the world were procreating like mad around the sleeping amputates, Hogfoot slipped away towards a pile of rubbish.

All that day, Hogfoot searched amongst the rubbish, avoiding the occasional mechanical disposal units which came to deposit their loads. In Hogfoot's mind was a vague memory of something which he felt would help him: a fuzzy recollection of an object which he had known in the distant past. His problem was that these objects had gone out of fashion, for only relatively few people bothered to walk in these times – or had the limbs attached in order to be able to do so!

Finally, however, he found one, under an old pile of magazines. A solid, heavy right *boot*. It was a size 8, a little large, but nevertheless, comfortable. He slid into it and hopped towards a rusty car. Using a corner of the metal Hogfoot worked a hole into the heel, to give himself a small viewing port, leaving a flap of leather as a protective visor, through which he could see.

Once he was ready, he made his way back to the feral camp and sought his enemy.

Bigfoot was there, standing around, idle. Daintyfoot was close by him.

Hogfoot was charged with a desire for revenge. He jumped forward in his armour to confront his foe. Bigfoot was seemingly unimpressed by this show of force. The battle was short. Hogfoot got in several leather head-butts, but though the boot protected him from serious injury it was still not proof against Bigfoot's mighty strength. It was to be no re-enactment of David and Goliath. This time, the giant prevailed, leaving the underhog underfoot, defeated and humiliated.

Hogfoot limped away from the combat ground, dragging his boot with him. Bigfoot, smirking, swaggered back to his lady companion, who remained by his side. She seemed distracted, as she observed Hogfoot making his way to the side of the feral camp, but did not follow.

That night, the moon came up from behind a mountain of junk and shone through the glassless rear window of an old Alfa-Romeo automobile. The beam fell like a spotlight on Hogfoot, still encapsulated by the boot, illuminating the brass lace-holes which glinted in the still, evening air. Most of the amputates were asleep, but Hogfoot, warm inside the boot, still nursed his wrath.

Suddenly, there was a *clink* nearby and Hogfoot was immediately alert. Something was sneaking around, trying to get close to him. He waited, trying to catch a glimpse of movement amongst the sleepers.

Nothing. But – yes, there it was again, that small sound. It came from behind him!

He whirled, clumsily in his armour, and came snout-to-snout with – with Daintyfoot. She had come to him. Not only that, she wore a slim silver chain around her ankle-neck, making her seem to Hogfoot as the most attractive foot he had ever seen. His heart melted.

He immediately flipped out the tongue of the boot and was about to emerge, when she made an unmistakable gesture. She wanted him to remain inside, to keep the boot *on*. She then proceeded to nuzzle up beside him and a glow went through Hogfoot. A glow of satisfaction and well-being.

He had won after all. He had gained his revenge, his victory. She had come to him, Hogfoot Right. It did not matter to him that the attraction, the alluring attribute which had finally drawn her to his side, captivated her, was the smell, the feel of leather.

THE HORN

STEPHEN GALLAGHER

STEPHEN GALLAGHER

Stephen Gallagher lives with his wife and daughter in North Lancashire's Ribble Valley. He is the author of *Chimera*, *Follower*, *Valley of Lights*, which received great acclaim, *Oktober*, and most recently, *Down River*. *Oktober* is currently being made into a major feature film.

Extract from the court record, Crown v Robson, 24th September 1987:

Counsel: You lured her to this quiet spot on the pretext that you were going to run away together.

Robson: I never promised anything.

Counsel: Then you beat her senseless and left her for dead.

Robson: Hold on, chief! I tapped her once to calm her down, that's all.

Counsel: Are you now saying that you weren't responsible for her murder?

Robson: She was fit enough when I left her.

Counsel: So how do you suppose that she died?

Robson: That wouldn't be until the next morning.

Counsel: When, exactly?

Robson: Around the time they poured the concrete in, I expect.

*   *   *

'We've got heat, we've got light, we've got shelter,' Mick said. 'The lads even left us some dirty books. We've got everything we'll need to ride out the bad weather, so why don't we just sit tight until it all blows over?'

It was just then that the lights flickered and failed and the coal effect on the two-bar electric fire went terminally dark. The bars themselves went more slowly, and the three of us could only watch their fading glow with a kind of bleak desperation. Sub-zero winds were still hammering at the walls of the little roadside hut, and I felt about as well-protected as a mouse under a shoebox in the middle of a stampede. I was cold already. It was quickly going to get worse.

The single flame of Mick's gas lighter put giants' shadows on to the walls and ceiling. 'Winds must've brought the line down,' he said.

The other man, whose name was David something or other, said, 'Anything we could fix?'

'Not me, pal. I'd rather live.'

'What do we do, then? Burn the furniture?'

'Then we'd have nowhere to sit.' The big man who'd told us to call him Mick held the flame higher, and our shadows dived for cover. 'Look, there's still candles and a gas ring. Nothing's altered. We can even have a brew.'

'The kettle's electric and the water pipes are frozen,' David said promptly. Mick looked at him, hard.

'I could really go off you,' he said. 'D'you know that?'

The candles were the dim, slow-burning kind in small tin dishes, and they'd been used before. The gas ring ran from a bottle under the table, and a kinked hose gave us a momentary problem in getting it going. The candles burned yellow, the gas burned blue, and our faces were white and scared-looking in the light that resulted.

Mick, David, me. Three separate stories of blizzard and breakdown and abandoned vehicles, three lifelines that probably wouldn't otherwise have crossed but which had come together in this fragile cabin at the side of a snowbound motorway.

'Well, here goes nothing,' Mick said, and he grabbed a pan and went outside to get us some snow. The one called David went over to try the dead phone yet again.

I'd been the last to find the place, and I'd known immediately on entering that these two hadn't been travelling together. They were an unmatched and prob-

ably unmatchable pair. Mick weighed in at around
eighteen stones and had the look of – well, there's no
kind way of putting it – a slob, however you might dress
and groom him. If you had to guess his line of work you
might well place him as one of those vendors who stand
with their push-along wagons near football grounds,
selling hamburgers and hotdogs that have the look of
having been poached in bodily fluids. David (he'd told
me his second name, but it hadn't stuck in my mind)
was more like one of those people you'll often see driving
a company car with a spare shirt on a hanger in the back;
he'd said that he was 'in sales', which I took to mean that
he was a salesman. He was about my own age, and had
reddish-blond hair so fine that he seemed to have no eye-
lashes. The story, as I understood it, was that Mick had
been aiming for the big service area about two miles
further along the road, but had found his way blocked and
had been forced to abandon his van-load of rubber hose
in order to walk back to the only light that he'd seen in
miles. When he'd made it to the hut he'd found David
already there, crouched before the electric fire with a
workman's donkey jacket that he'd found and thrown
around his shoulders. I'd joined them about half an hour
after that, and no one had arrived since; the weather was
worsening by the minute and it seemed unlikely that anybody else was going to make it through. The motorway
must have been closed for some time now.

'Jesus wept!' Mick gasped when he'd fallen back in
through the door three or four minutes later. I'd thought
that he'd simply intended to take two steps out to fill
the pan and then return and so I said, 'What kept you?'

Some of the colour started to seep back into him as he
stood over the heat of the gas ring, hands spread like
he was making a blessing. He'd have made a pretty
rough-looking priest. 'I went down for a look at the
road,' he said, 'just in case there was any sign of a gritter
going through.'

'See anything?'

'I'm lucky I even found the way back. I didn't get more than twenty yards, and it blew up so hard that I might as well have been blind. Nothing else is moving out there. Looks like we're in for the duration.'

'Oh, great,' David said heavily.

'You want to stick your nose outside before you say that,' Mick suggested. 'It's worse than before – it's like walking into razor blades, and I'll tell you something else. When the wind gets up in those wires, it's just like voices. You listen long enough and honest to God, you start hearing your own name. You know what I reckon?'

'What?' I said.

'It's all the dead people they've scraped up. They're all cold and lonely out there.' And he winked at me as he said this, I suspect because his back was turned to David and David couldn't see.

'For Christ's sake,' David muttered darkly, and he went over to the other side of the hut and started rummaging around in the cupboards for mugs and teabags.

Mick was grinning happily now, but I wasn't exactly sure why. Lowering my voice so that David wouldn't hear me – he'd half-disappeared headfirst into one of the cupboards by now – I said, 'What's all that about?'

'Haven't you seen the noticeboard?' Mick said, and he pointed to the wall behind me. 'Take a look. We've found a right little Happy House to get ourselves snowed into. Desmond was reading all about it when I got here.'

'It's David,' corrected a muffled voice from somewhere inside the furniture.

Mick said, unruffled, 'Of course it is.'

I picked up one of the candles and took it over to the wall where the space alongside some lockers had been papered with old newspaper clippings. There were a few yellowing page three girls, but the rest of them were news stories. Some had photographs, and the photographs were all of mangled wreckage. It took me a moment to realise that they were all motorway crashes, and that the stretch of motorway where they'd taken place was the one that ran by under three feet of snow right outside.

'This must be where the lads wait for a call-out when there's something nasty,' Mick said from just behind me. He'd come around and was inspecting the collection over my shoulder. 'Some of the things they must have seen, eh? Rather them than me.'

Amen to that, I thought, although even in the dim and unsteady candlelight I found that I was browsing through the details in some of the pieces with the kind of detached fascination that I always seem to be able to manage when it's a question of someone else's misery. Entire families wiped out. A teenaged girl decapitated. Lorry drivers crushed when their cabs folded around them like stepped-upon Coke cans. An unwanted mistress – this one really got me looking twice – an unwanted mistress dumped, Jimmy Hoffa-style, into the wire skeleton of a bridge piling that had been boxed-up ready to take concrete the next morning. ENTOMBED ALIVE! the headline said, but even that looked kind of pale next to the disaster involving the old folks' outing and the petfood truck full of offal.

I gathered from the collection that this hut was the base for the clean up team who worked the road for some distance in either direction, and that they took an honest pride in their gruesome occupation. I imagined them trooping out to their breakdown wagon, whistling as they pulled on their jackets and thinking about next year's holidays. And then, at the other end of the drive, getting out with their bags and shovels to give their professional attention to the loved ones of some cheapskate who'd saved the cost of a cabin on the car ferry or skipped a night in a hotel to drive on through and get an extra half-day out of the holiday flat. Where the team would be right now, I could only guess. I imagined that they'd have moved their base along to the service area as soon as the weather had started to clamp down, because the hut was no place to be marooned out of choice. The services would probably be starting to re-semble a refugee centre by now, cut off but reasonably self-sufficient, and I wished that I could be there instead of here. The gas ring behind us was running with the valve wide-open, and still I could see my breath in the air in front of me.

David, over by the table, said, 'Did you fill this?'

I tore myself away from the interesting stuff on the wall and followed Mick over to the ring, where David was peering into the aluminium pan. Where before it had been so over-filled with snow that it had looked like a big tub of ice-cream, now it held about an inch of water.

Mick observed, 'It melts down to nothing, doesn't it?' And then the silence that followed was like the slow race in a restaurant to reach for the bill.

But then, finally, I said, 'I'll get us some more.'

I don't know how to describe the way the cold hit me as I stepped out of the hut. It was almost like walking into a wall, much worse than it had been when I'd made my way up there. The wind was the most disorienting factor, filling my eyes with hail and battering me around so hard that I could barely draw breath; but then, thank-fully, it dropped a little, and the air cleared enough for me to see without being blinded.

Visibility was somewhere between fifty and a hundred yards, beyond which everything just greyed-out as if reality couldn't hold together any further. I could see about half a dozen of the overhead sodium lights march-ing off in either direction, their illumination blanketed and diffused by the amount of snow clouding the air. Of the motorway itself I could make out the parallel lines of the crash barriers as hardly more than pencil marks sketched on to the snow, and that was it. A few of the lightweight plastic cones that had been used earlier to close off lanes had been blown around and had lodged themselves here and there like erratic missiles, but noth-ing else broke the even cover.

I didn't see what Mick had been talking about. I didn't hear any voices, just the wind in the wires somewhere off the road and out of sight. The sound meant nothing special to me.

I had a baked bean can, catering size, that was the only other clean-looking container that I'd been able to find, and I stooped and tried to fill it with snow. The newly-fallen stuff was too fine, it just streamed away as I tried to load it in, but then I tried wedging it into snowball nuggets and did rather better. I was already starting to shake with the cold. I paused for a moment to wipe at my nose with the back of my glove, and realised with a kind of awe that I couldn't even feel the contact.

I fell back into the hut like a drowning man plucked from an icy sea. I'd been outside for less than a minute.

David looked up from the phone. I wouldn't have believed how welcoming the place could look with its candlelight and comparative warmth and the road gang's mugs set out ready, each with the name of an absent person written on the side in what looked like nail varnish. I did my best to make it look as if I had a grip on myself, and went over to set the rest of the snow to melt as Mick secured the door behind me.

'Still dead?' I said to David, with a nod at the phone.

'It's not exactly dead,' he said, jiggling the cradle for about the hundredth time. 'It's more like an open line with nothing on the other end.'

'It'll be like a field telephone,' Mick said from over by the door. 'If nobody's plugged in, then there's no one to hear. How's it looking outside?'

'I'd still rather be in here than out there,' I said.

Mick made the tea with a catering bag and some of that non-dairy whitener that looks and smells like paint. It was the worst I'd ever tasted, and the most welcome. The three of us pulled our chairs in close to get into the circle of warmth around the gas ring, and we grew heady on the monoxide fumes. Inevitably, the conversation returned to the clippings on the wall.

'You want to see it from their point of view,' Mick said. 'It'll be like working in a morgue. You get bad dreams for the first few weeks and then after that, it's just another job.'

'How would *you* know?' David asked.

'I've got a brother-in-law who's a nurse, he's just about seen it all. I mean, the likes of me and you, we don't know the half of what it's about.'

David didn't comment, but I suspect that by then he was starting to read something personal into everything that Mick was saying. I believed that I'd recognised his type by now. Some people's reaction to pressure is to look around for someone convenient to dump on; they get angry, they get sarcastic, and if you pull through it tends to be in spite of them rather than with much in the way of help. I knew what Mick was talking about. I could imagine the team sitting there, patiently reading or playing cards while waiting for carnage. They were one up on us . . . we'd go through life telling ourselves that it was never going to happen, but they knew that it would and the knowledge wasn't even anything special to them.

Mick seemed to be the one who was holding us together, here. I'm not sure that right then I'd have wanted to rely on David for anything. He was frowning at the floor, his borrowed donkey jacket sitting uneasily on his shoulders. Had he really struggled from his car to the cabin with just a suit jacket and no overcoat? He must have seen the way that the weather was going before he set out, but he didn't look as if he'd taken any account of the possibility that he might have to step much beyond the warmth of a heated building or a moving car. Some people have too much faith in everything. I'm the opposite – I reckon that God intended few things to be immutable and that such things as designer luggage, golf shoes and the new shape of Volvo aren't among them.

I'd been heading for my girlfriend's place over in the next county when I'd come to my own unscheduled journey's end. She was with a big retail chain who were moving her around and paying her peanuts, and I was just about holding down one of those jobs that they kept telling me might or might not turn out to be something permanent. The only way that we could ever get together was at weekends, hiding out from the landlady in her one-roomed flat. Mine must have been one of the last cars to get on to the road before they'd closed it. I'd had to stop as a jack-knifed articulated lorry had been cleared from the sliproad, and then it took two policemen to get me rolling again because my tyres wouldn't grip on the icy surface. They advised me to stay in low gear and to keep my revs down, and I remember their last words to me as I managed to get moving again – *Rather you than me, pal.* It got worse as I went on. After half an hour in first gear, following the crash barrier like a blind man following a rail, the temperature needle crept up into the red zone and then finally both hoses blew. I stopped and taped them and topped up the water, but the engine seized soon after that.

Mick was the only one who seemed to be listening as I told them the story. He said, 'I've been driving this route since they opened it. I've never known it this bad. It looks like the end of the world.'

'You've got a knack of seeing the bright side, Mick,' I told him.

'You won't have seen that road train about half a mile on,' he said. 'A big new wagon and two trailers. It was blocking the road all the way across, that's why I had to give up and walk back to the last light I'd seen. Those things are like dinosaurs, they'll go on through anything. But it couldn't get through this. What do you reckon, Desmond?'

'It's *David*!' His sudden shout was startling in the enclosed space of the cabin, and I think even Mick was surprised by the reaction he got.

'All right,' he said. 'I'm sorry.'

'Well, bloody get it right, then!'

'I said I'm sorry. I was only asking what you thought.'

'I just want to get home,' David said miserably, looking down at the floor as if he was embarrassed by his sudden outburst.

And then Mick said, with unexpected gentleness, 'Nothing to argue with there, Dave.'

It was then that the gas ring began to make a popping sound. We all turned to look and I heard somebody say *Oh, shit*, and then I realised that it had been me.

The flame didn't exactly go out, not right away, but it was obviously into some kind of terminal struggle. Mick reached under the table and heaved out the squat metal cylinder; when he raised it two-handed and gave it a shake, there sounded to be about a cupful of liquid sloshing around in the bottom.

'There's some left,' David said hopefully.

'You always get some in the bottom,' Mick said. 'Still means it's empty.'

There was another cylinder under the table and right at the back, but this one sounded just about the same. By now the ring was giving out no heat at all and making such a racket that nobody objected when Mick turned the valve to shut it off.

The silence got to us before the cold did. But the cold started getting to us a couple of minutes later.

We broke open the lockers in the hope of finding more coats or blankets, but all that we found were tools and empty lunch buckets and mud-encrusted work boots. David's earlier remark about burning the furniture no longer seemed like a joke, but the truth of it was that there wasn't much about the furniture that was combustible. The chairs were mostly tubular steel and the table was some kind of laminate over chipboard, which left a stack of soft-core porno magazines and a few paperbacks and one deck of cards. By now, the hut had turned from a haven into an icebox.

David was the one who put it into words.

He said, 'We're going to have to go out and find somewhere else, aren't we?' He made it sound as if the place itself had done a number and betrayed us. 'This is great,' he said bitterly. 'This really puts the fucking tin lid on it.'

Possibly we could have stayed put, jogged on the spot a little, done our best to keep going in the sub-zero air until the worst of the weather receded and rescue came pushing through. But Mick was already going through the lockers for a second time, as if looking again for something that he'd already seen.

'The way I see it,' he said, 'there's only one thing we can do.'

'The services?' I hazarded.

'We'd never make it that far. It's more than two miles and it might as well be twenty. I reckon we can do maybe a quarter of that, at the most.'

'Which gets us nowhere,' David said.

'It gets us as far as that big road train that's blocking the carriageway.' So saying, Mick reached into the third locker and came out with a short, hooked wrecking bar. Holding up the jemmy he went on, 'If we can get into that and get its engine running, we can sit tight in the cab with the heater on.'

'Until the fuel runs out,' I said, probably a touch too pessimistically.

'Those things never run out. They've got tanks like swimming pools. We can either wait for the snowplough to find us or else strike out again as the weather improves. What do you think?'

'It'll have a radio,' David said, with a sense of discovery that seemed to surprise even him.

We both looked at him.

'A CB radio,' he said. 'Don't most of these big trucks carry them? We can tell someone where we are.'

'That we can, Dave,' Mick said with a note of approval, and then he looked from him to me. 'Are you game?'

'Let's go,' I said, sounding about four-hundred per cent more eager than I felt. But Mick raised a hand as if to say, *slow down*.

'Just wait on a minute,' he said. 'There's no point in all of us scrambling out together. What I reckon is, one of us strikes out and does the necessary, and then he leans on the horn as a signal for the others to follow.'

'I wouldn't know what to do,' David said bleakly.

'Me neither,' I said.

'Well,' Mick said, 'since we're talking about breaking and entering and a little creative rewiring, I'd say that I'm the only one with the education in the appropriate subjects around here. Am I right?'

He was right, and as far as I was concerned he could make all the jibes about education that he wanted as long as he got us out of this. He turned up his collar and buttoned up his coat, and he pulled on his sheepskin gloves as I moved with him to the door. David decided to give the phone yet another try as I made ready to let Mick out into the unwelcoming night.

I said, 'You're mad, you know that?'

'I had my brain surgically removed,' Mick said. 'I've been feeling much better without it.' Then he turned serious. 'I'm going to get down to the crash barrier and follow it along, otherwise there's no knowing where I may end up. Keep listening for the horn.' He glanced at David. 'And keep an eye on him.'

'He'll be all right.'

'If he starts messing about, dump him. I mean it.'

There was a blast of cold air for the brief second or so between Mick going out and me getting the door closed after him, and this time it stayed in there with us like some unwelcome dog that had dashed in and was standing its ground. David had slammed the phone down with a curse, as if its non-cooperation was a matter of deliberate choice, before settling on one of the chairs with his hands thrust deep into the pockets of his borrowed coat and the collar up over his nose to recirculate the heat of his breath. He looked like some odd kind of animal retreating into its blue worsted shell.

'I heard what he said, you know.' His voice was

muffled by the thick material, and sounded distant.

'He didn't mean anything by it.'

'Yeah, I bet. And who does he think *he* is? Scott of the Antarctic?'

'I don't care if he thinks he's Scotty of the Enterprise. If he gets us out of trouble he'll be okay by me.'

He settled in deeper. 'Well, don't go worrying about me. I'm no deadweight.'

'Never said I thought you were.'

There was silence for a while.

Then he said, 'Pretty serious, though, isn't it?'

Yes, I was thinking, it *was* pretty serious . . . but it could have been worse. Worse was being sliced in two at a combined speed of a hundred and fifty miles an hour, just because someone else chose the day of your trip to cross the central reservation and come looking for suicide in the oncoming traffic. Worse was being buried alive in concrete, so deep that even X-rays couldn't find you. It was sitting with your hands on the wheel while your head lay on the back seat. It was any one of the fifty or so examples of a messy and uncontrolled exit to be found in the road gang's private black museum over there on the wall.

'We've still got options,' I said. 'That puts us one step ahead.'

'As long as he makes it,' David said.

The next twenty or thirty minutes seemed to last for ever. David wasn't great company, particularly after the way that Mick's parting words had stung him. I wondered what I ought to expect; more of the ball-and-chain act, or would he become dangerously gung-ho? If the latter, then I was going to be happy to let him go out first.

Finally, the wind dropped a little and we heard the distant sound of a horn.

I said, with some relief, 'Our call, I think.'

David said that he was ready. I asked him if he wanted to take one last shot at the phone, but he said no.

'The greaseball was right in one thing,' he said. 'You

listen for long enough, and you *do* start to hear them calling your name.'

I let him go out ahead of me.

My spirit of optimism took an instant hammering as the door was banging shut behind us; compared to this brutal storm, the wind that had set the wires keening on my last excursion had been a precise and delicate instrument. All sound and sense were destroyed on contact, and I was beginning to panic when I felt David's rough grip on my arm, shoving me forward into the blind haze. The snow had drifted high in places, masking the contours of the ground beneath and making progress even more difficult; we stumbled and floundered downhill towards the road surface, and as we descended from the more exposed slopes the wind mercifully lessened. We got across to the central crash barrier, a constant mist of snow steaming from its knife-edged top, but by then I'd become as disoriented as if I'd been popped into a box and shaken.

'*Which way?*' I shouted, and David had to put his face right up to my ear to make himself heard.

'*Northbound!*' he roared.

'*What?*'

'*This way!*' And he gave me a hard push to get me moving.

I wouldn't have believed how heavy the going could be. It went from thigh-deep to waist-deep and then back to thigh-deep again, and the barrier disappeared for entire stretches so that we had to navigate by the yellow sodium lights above us. I'd break the trail for a while, and then David would move up and replace me. Any tracks that Mick might have left had been obliterated, but then there was the sound of the distant horn to lead us on whenever the storm took out a beat to let it through.

He'd made it. So would I.

I reckoned that we'd been going for about three hours, although a more rational part of my mind knew that it had actually been closer to fifteen minutes, when we reached the first place where we could stop and rest. It was a flyover bridge, too high and too wide to feel like much of a shelter but offering a respite from the cutting edge of the wind. We staggered in so all-over numb that we might as well have been on Novocaine drips for the last quarter hour, and we collapsed against the wall like footsoldiers in some forgotten war.

'Are you okay?' I said to David, my voice oddly flattened by the carpet of snow that had blown in under the bridge.

'You must be fucking joking,' he gasped, and that was all I could get out of him.

I tried to knock off some of the dry snow that had crusted on to my clothing. I didn't want to risk any of it melting and soaking through only to re-freeze as we pushed on. It came off in chunks. David was hunkered down and hugging himself, presenting as small an area for heat loss as he could. If we stayed here for too long, we might end up staying here for good.

I listened for the horn.

Even though the bridge was open at the sides there was an enclosed, somehow isolated feeling about that few yards of shelter. It was brighter here than outside because there was nothing clouding the air between the sodium lights and the reflecting snow and, as I'd already noticed when I'd spoken to David, sounds went dead as if they'd run into something soft. There was scaffolding around the bridge-support across the carriageway, but I could still make out the spraycanned graffiti in amongst the repair work behind it as if through a grid; it read: ROBSON YOUR DEAD WHEN YOU GET OUT, and it had been written in red. My favourite piece of graffiti was one that I'd seen on a beach-front building, the simple and elegant I FEEL A BIT NORMAL TODAY, but it was a beach-front that seemed about a million miles away from the here and now.

The wind outside must have dropped a little because a snatch of the horn came through, and it sounded closer than ever. It acted on David like a goad. He suddenly lurched to his feet and set out again, stumbling and flailing his arms as if he hadn't quite brought his limbs under control yet. Wearily, I wondered if I'd ever be able to raise the energy to follow; but even as I was wondering, I was starting to move. David was muttering as he went, but I couldn't hear anything of what he was saying.

I stumbled, because there seemed to be all kinds of jumbled crap under the snow here; my foot hooked up what looked like a length of compressor hose, and I had to kick it off. Over on what would normally be the hard shoulder I could see the half-buried shapes of machinery, big generators with tow-hitches and a small dumper that might have been the answer to our prayers if it hadn't been jacked-up with a wheel missing. It looked as if, until the bad weather had intervened, they'd been drilling out the concrete like a bad tooth. Canvas on the scaffolding had concealed the work, but the material had been ripped by a through-wind to leave only a few flapping shreds around the hole. The cage of reinforcing wire inside the piling had been exposed, and the wire had been burst outward as if by a silent explosion. It looked as if they'd gone so far, and then the freeze-up had enlarged the hole further.

I suppose I could have thought about it harder. But there are some things, you can think about them as hard as you like but you'll never anticipate what you're actually going to see.

And the sight that I was concentrating on, to the exclusion of just about everything else, was that of the road train firming-up in the blizzard about a hundred yards ahead.

The first details that I made out were its hazard lights, and there were plenty of them; almost enough to define its shape, rather like those diagrams that take a scattered handful of stars and connect them up into some improbable-looking constellation. They were flashing on and off in time with the horn, and they were about the most welcome warning that I'd ever seen. Ahead of me, David was striding out like a wind-up toy that nothing could stop.

It was a big Continental articulated rig in three jack-knifed sections, a true monster of the road that would look like a landslide on the move. The distant *parp-parp* that had led us so far had now become a deep, regular airhorn bellow as we'd drawn closer. David tried to break into a run for the cab, but he had to be close to exhaustion by now.

We helped each other up and in. An alarm beeper was sounding off inside the cab and in synchronisation with the horn and the lights. There was no sign of Mick anywhere.

I said, 'Where is he?'

'God knows,' David said, studying a dash that looked like a piece of the space shuttle. 'He might at least have left the engine running.'

'Maybe he didn't get that far.'

But David pointed to a bunch of wires that had been pulled out to hang behind the steering column. 'What's that, then?' he said. 'Heinz spaghetti? You check the radio.'

I checked the radio.

'I don't think it's working,' I said.

Sixty seconds after our entry, the alarms cut and the horn stopped. The silence almost hurt.

David had found the starter by now, and he was trying it; the first couple of times it stayed dead, but he jiggled the hanging wires like a child patting a balloon into the air and this must have helped some weak connection, because on the third attempt the engine somewhere beneath the cab floor turned over without any hesitation at all. After a few seconds, it caught; but then, almost immediately, it faded away and died again.

'Bastard thing,' David said, and tried again, but there was no persuading it to catch for a second time.

He flopped back heavily in the driver's seat. I said, 'Maybe we can just stay here anyway.'

'There's still no heat,' he said. 'It may seem warmer, but that's just the comparison with being outside. If we can't get the blowers going, I don't see any advantage over being back in the hut.'

He tried the starter again, but still nothing.

'There's your reason why,' he said suddenly, and pointed to a part of the dashboard display. If what he was pointing to was the fuel level readout, it was reading something like empty.

'These things never run out,' he said bitterly, in what I assume he intended to be mimicry of Mick's voice. 'They've got tanks like swimming pools.' And he punched the steering wheel hard, and flopped back in the driver's seat again with a face as dark as a bruised plum.

And somewhere out in the night, another horn began to sound.

We both listened, lost it for a while as the wind howled, and then heard it again. Our signal was being repeated from somewhere further along the road.

'Here we go,' David said wearily, and he opened the door on the far side of the cab to climb down. This time he didn't even flinch when the hail hit him. *All right*, I wanted to say, *case proven, you're no deadweight, now why don't we just try sticking it out here a while longer*, but instead I levered myself up and clambered awkwardly across the cab. I could have dropped and slept, right there. And probably died, ready-chilled and prepared for the morgue, but at that moment I hardly felt as if it would matter.

Mick's sheepskin gloves were on the cab floor.

I reached down and picked them up. I wasn't hallucinating them, they were real enough. He must have taken them off for the delicate work of hot-wiring . . . but how come he'd allowed himself to be parted from them? I was wearing my clumsy ski gloves, and even inside these my hands were feeling dead from the knuckles out. If Mick had gone the distance to the next stranded lorry, as the sounding of this second horn seemed to suggest, then I reckoned that he'd better not be planning any piano practice for a while.

I slid out of the cab and hit the snow again. I was now on the northern side of the big vehicle. David had launched off without me, hooked by the call like some deep-sea fish being drawn up to the gaff. The horn wasn't so regular this time, but it was coming through more clearly.

And me, I wasn't happy.

The forgotten gloves were only one part of it. Another part of it was the fact that you didn't put a rig and its cargo, total value anything from a quarter of a million up, into the hands of a driver who's going to be walking the hard shoulder with a can to get some diesel because he let the tanks get empty. And the radio – the radio should have been working, even if only to give out white noise to match the scene on the other side of the glass.

I was looking around the side of the road train when I fell over Mick's body in the snow. He was lying face-down and already he was half covered by drift, which for a moment gave me the absurd hope that he might have been insulated from the chilling effect of the wind and might be basically okay. But when I tried to turn him over he was as stiff as a wet sheet hung out in winter, and when I finally got him on to his back I could see that there was a spike of reinforcing wire from the concrete flyover driven right up under his chin. I could see it passing up through his open mouth as if his head were something spitted for a barbecue. His eyes were half-open, but plugged with ice. The short jemmy was still in his ungloved hand, held tightly like a defensive weapon that he'd never managed to use.

This had happened right by the big diesel tanks behind the cab. The tanks themselves had been slashed open so that all the oil had run out and gone straight down into the snow. And when I say slashed, I mean raked open in four parallel lines as if by fingernails, not just spiked or holed by something sharp.

David had stopped, and was looking back; but he was too far away to see anything and only just on the verge of being seen, a smudgy ghost painted in smoke. He beckoned me on with a big, broad gesture that looked like he was trying to hook something out of the air, and even though I yelled, 'No! Don't go! It isn't him!' he simply shouted back something inaudible and turned away. He walked on, and the blizzard sucked him in.

And from somewhere beyond him came the sound of the horn, the mating call of some dark mistress of nightmares with her skin oiled and her back arched and her long silver knives at the ready.

I started to run after him.

I call it running, although it wasn't much in the way of progress. I reckon you could have lit up a small town with the energy that I burned just to close up the distance between David and me. Close it up I did, but not enough. He didn't even glance back. I saw him duck at a near-miss from something windborne and I felt my heart stop for a moment, but I think it was only one of the plastic cones or some other piece of road debris. David couldn't have been distracted by nuns dancing naked in the air by that stage, because he was now within sight of the next truck.

The truck.

It was much older than the first one, and not so much of a giant. It was over on the far side of the barrier and facing my way; it looked as if it had come to a long, sliding halt before being abandoned and half-buried where it stood. It had a crouched, malevolent look, its engine running and breathing steam, pale headlamps like sick-bed eyes. David reached the cab and pounded on the side to be let in. I stopped at the crash barrier and could only watch.

The horn ceased. The door opened. The cab's interior light blinked on, but the insides of the windows were all steamed up and runny and there was only the vague shape of someone visible. David had already hoisted himself half-way up with his foot in the stirrup over the wheel, but now I saw him hesitate. The door had swung out and was screening whatever confronted him . . . and then suddenly he was gone, jerked in at an impossible speed, and the door was slammed and the light went out. I winced at the loud, long and intense muffled screaming that began to come from the cab, but I knew there was nothing that I could do. I thought about those long slashes in the diesel tank and, for David's sake, I could only hope that whatever was happening would be over quickly.

It wasn't.

And when it finally ended, and after the long silence that followed, I saw the door opening out a crack like a trap being reset. Light streamed out into the snow-mist, a narrow slice falling like a rain of something solid. I looked up at the truck's windows and saw that the now-lit windshield had been sprayed red on the inside like the jug of a blender, and it was just starting a slow wash-down as the cab sweat began to trickle through it.' I watched a while longer, but I couldn't see anything moving.

I was calculating my chances of making it through to the service area. What had seemed like a complete impossibility before now had the look of the most attractive available option. I had to have covered a good part of the distance already, didn't I? And having just had a glimpse of the alternative, I was suddenly finding that the prospect of pressing on had a certain appeal.

The first move would be to cross the carriageway and put as much distance as possible between me and the truck. There was nothing that I could do for David now, and it made no sense to stay out where the overhead lights made a tunnel of day through the blizzard. It was as I was striking out at an angle across a field of white that had once been the fast lane, a stumbling and deep-frozen body with a white-hot core of fear, that the horn began again.

That was okay, that suited me fine. As long as somebody was leaning on the button then they weren't out here with me, and that was exactly the way that I wanted it. I was trying to remember the route from the times that I'd driven it before. My guess was that I was just about to come to an exposed and elevated curve that would swing out to overlook a reservoir before entering the hills where the service area would be sheltered. I wouldn't be able to see much, if any, of this, but I'd know it because the intensity of the wind was bound to increase; high-sided vehicles took a battering on this stretch at the best of times, and this certainly wasn't one of those. I'd have to watch my footing. On a clear night I'd have been able to see right out to the lights of some mill town several miles out and below, but for now all that I could see was a dense white swirling. In my mind I could see myself holding one of those Christmas-scene paperweights, the kind that you shake and then watch as the contents settle, but in mine there was a tiny figure of David hammering on the glass and calling soundlessly to be let out. I saw myself shaking the globe once, and I saw the storm turn pink.

Stupid, I know – I wasn't responsible for anybody, and I certainly hadn't got behind him and boosted him up into the arms of whatever had been waiting in the cab. But I suppose that when you've just seen somebody meet an end roughly comparable to the act of walking into an aircraft propellor, it's bound to overheat your imagination just a little. Maybe that could explain some of what came later.

But somehow, I don't think so.

The truck horn was starting to recede behind me. The notes were longer now, like the moan of some trapped beast tiring of its struggles. Great, fine, I was thinking, you just stay there and keep at it, when the storm brightened and a dark figure suddenly rose before me.

It was my own shadow, cast forward into the blizzard way out beyond the edge of the road so that it seemed to stand in the air over nothing. I looked back and saw that there was some kind of a spotlight being operated from the cab of the truck, the kind that turns on a mount fixed to the body and stays however you leave it. This one was pointing straight at me; it went on past, and I realised that I was too small and too far away to spot with any ease. And there was probably so much snow sticking to me on the windward side that I'd be tough to spot even at close range.

Any relief that I felt was short-lived, though, because just a few seconds later the spotlight picked up the line of my trail through the snowfield. The bright light and the low angle exaggerated it and left no room for any doubt. The light stopped roving, and the horn stopped sounding only a moment later.

There followed a silence that I didn't like, filled with unstated menace.

And then the cab door opened, and its occupant stepped down to the road.

I don't know what I'd been expecting. Anything but this. She was small, and slight. Her light summer dress was torn and soiled and her hair was lank and dusty and blowing across her face. Her arms were bare, but she seemed oblivious to the cold and the wind. She started out towards the point where my trail angled out across the road, and I knew that I ought to be turning and running but I couldn't come unglued. She was walking barefoot on the snow and leaving no mark; I saw her bend to touch the barrier as she stepped over, and it might have been a stile out in the countryside somewhere in the warmest part of the spring.

I finally turned to run. I got a brief impression of another of those plastic cones tumbling by in the wind, and then it bopped me as I walked right into it. I went down. I tried to struggle to get up but it was as if I'd had my wires pulled and crossed so that none of the messages were getting through in the right order.

I could hear her light tread over the wind as she approached.

She came up and stood right over me. Her skin was as white as marble, and veined with blue; I couldn't see her face for the halo of light from the cab spotlight behind her. All I could see was her ruined hair blowing around a pitiless darkness in which something was watching me.

Louie, she whispered.

Louie? I thought. Who the fuck's Louie? Because listen, lady, it sure isn't me. I opened my mouth to say something similar and I think I made one tiny, almost inaudible croak. The wind dropped and the night grew still, and then it was like her eyes turned on like blazing torches in the ravaged pit of her face as she bent down towards me, and I could feel their heat and the breath of corruption warming my frost-bitten skin. I could see now that her hair was matted with concrete, and that patches of it had been torn out. The exposed skin was like that of a plucked grouse that had been hanging in a cellar for far too long a time.

Louie, she said again, this time with a kind of nightmare tenderness, and she took hold of my dead-feeling face in her dead-looking hands and I realised with terror that she was raising me up for a kiss. I saw the darkness roaring in like an airshaft straight down to hell and I wanted to scream, but instead I think I just peed myself.

She stopped only inches away. She lowered me again. I think she'd just realised that I wasn't the one she was looking for.

Then she raised her hand and I saw the state of her fingers, and I knew how she'd caused the damage that she'd done to the diesel tank. I shut my eyes because I knew that this was going to be it. I stayed with my eyes shut and I waited and I waited, and after I'd waited for what seemed like the entire running time of *Conan the Barbarian* I managed to unstick one eye and look up.

She was still there, but she wasn't looking at me. She

seemed to be listening for something. I listened too, but all I could hear was the wind in the wires overhead.

And then, only once and very faintly, the single blast of a horn.

Louie? she said. And she started to rise.

Most of what I know now is what I've learned since. Louis Robson was a construction services manager who drove a Mercedes, and she was a supermarket checkout trainee. How she ever believed that he'd desert his wife and run away with her will be one of those eternal mysteries like, why do old cars run better when they've been washed and waxed; but he must have made the promise one time and she must have replayed it over and over until finally, he told her to meet him one night with her bags packed and a goodbye letter ready to mail. The place where she was to wait was one of his company's site offices by the new motorway; he'd pull in outside and sound the all clear on the car's horn. Except that it was a signal that she would have to wait a long time to hear because when she got there, he was already waiting in the dark with a lug wrench. He dropped her unconscious body into a prepared mould for a bridge piling and threw her cardboard suitcase after, and then he put the sealed letter into the post without realising that it mentioned him by name. This was all five years before.

I don't know if it was just the signal, or whether there was room for anything beyond obsession in the dark, tangled worm-pit of what was left of her mind; but she lurched stiffly upright and then, like a dead ship drawn to some distant beacon, she set off in what she thought was the direction of the sound.

The blade of the snowplough hit her square-on as she stepped out into the road.

She wasn't thrown; it was more like she exploded under gas pressure from within, a release of the bottled-up forces of five years' worth of corruption. She went up like an eyeball in a vacuum chamber, and the entire blade and windshield of the plough were sprayed with something that stuck like tar and stank like ordure. Rags of foul hide were flung over a hundred-yard radius, showering down on to the snow with a soft pattering sound. The destruction was so complete that nothing would ever be pieced together to suggest anything remotely human. The plough had stopped and I could see men in orange day-glo overjackets climbing out, stunned and uncertain of what they'd seen, and I managed to get up to my knees and to wave my arms over my head.

'Anybody else with you?' they asked me when we were all inside and I was holding a thermos cup of coffee so hot that it could have blanched meat. 'No sign of anybody?'

I'd told them that I'd seen some kind of a bird fly into the blade, and it had all happened so fast that nobody had a better story to offer. They'd told me their names, and I'd recognised them from the tea mugs back in the hut that they'd been forced to abandon as a base for a while. I said that I hadn't seen anybody else. Then one of them asked me how long I'd been out there and I said, it seemed like forever.

'You know the police have jacked it in and closed the road for the night,' one of them said. 'We wouldn't have come out at all if it hadn't been for somebody hearing your horn solo one time when the wind dropped. You've got no idea how lucky you are.'

I raised my face out of the steam. We all swayed as the big chained wheels turned the snow into dirt beneath us as we swung around for the return journey, and somebody put a hand out to the seat in front to steady himself. They'd find Mick and David when the thaw set in, and I'd say that I didn't know a damn thing about either of them. And did I really have no idea of how lucky I was?

'No,' I said pleasantly. 'I don't expect I do.'

MELA WORMS

DIANA WYNNE JONES

DIANA WYNNE JONES

Diana Wynne Jones is a well-known and very popular author of science fantasy. Her numerous books include *Charmed Life*, *Eight Days of Luke* and *Power of Three*.

THE PLANET REISS is one of several I don't intend to go back to. It is artificial, made by humans some hundreds of years ago, and humans are my least favourite species. My captain, Yanni Altunian, is a human. We had brought the *Bon Quin* into Reiss because Yanni had heard from a cousin on Newhaven that there was one of those big mystical festivals due at Archangel and that pilgrims were using Reiss, as well as the more regular ports, as a waystation. I was due for planet-leave, so I went up the silo in the lift with Yanni and left him in the tourist office offering luxury staterooms to Archangel at 6,000 a head while I went to see the sights.

They say the humans who built Reiss were pirates. I believe it. Their harbour dues made Yanni turn pale and they had already slapped on extra charges in all directions. Before I went upstairs to the interior, I had to pay a fee for the air I was going to breathe. There was a grille across the exit, and there I found I had to buy a permit to drink water and another, costing twice as much, to drink alcohol. Naturally I asked for an information cube then, thinking there must be *some* sights they didn't charge you to see. Not a bit of it. The cube, costing as much as the other permits put together, informed me that I hadn't yet paid my entry fee, and when I had, it kept flashing up: *Penalty for littering 1,000 CR. Additional penalty for littering gutters up to ten years hard labour*. After which it listed amusements in order of price.

Sex palaces headed the list, with taverns near the middle. But you could watch an execution for 2CR and it was only 1.5CR to go to the zoo. I went to the zoo, in a very bad mood, nearly broke already.

By the time I got there, I was almost adjusted to Reiss. It is a hollow metal sphere, which is a bit like walking in the bottom of a grey pudding bowl with dwellings and fields soaring into mist on all sides of you, and a dazzle overhead from the central light-source. But I kept wondering why they built it of metal. My feet boomed and the ground vibrated under them. Everything boomed. It was trying for my poor fanatian ears. The streets were lined with quivering wrought-iron houses – horrid fanciful things with every twiddle carefully painted rust-proof grey. I couldn't understand why the people didn't live somewhere below the metal ground: their houses took up space they could have used for agriculture.

I queried the cube about it.

It flashed up: *Decks below devoted to life-support, jails and industry. Penalty for littering 1,000 CR. Additional penalty for littering gutters . . .*

I now saw the point of these penalties. There are gutters down each side of every street, growing what seems at first sight small green hedges. When you look closer, you find the green is lettuces, beans or egg plants, being grown hydroponically. The guggle and drip of their plumbing adds to the background din. I could see well enough that a gum-wrapper dropped in a drain could ruin the lettuce crop. I wondered what they did to you if you pissed in one.

The zoo grows food for the animals in the same way, and that – and the penalties – is much the same, because most of the creatures in the wrought-iron cages are human ancestors. Monks and apeys, I think they were called. I stared at them, feeling very mean, wondering why humans seemed so proud of their origins. I'd have kept these things dark if I was human. The best that could be said of most of them was that they had a decent coat of fur – the thing that sets my teeth on edge about humans is the way their skin shows – otherwise they were all the image of Yanni Altunian. One cage of little brown ancestral Yannis had so many babies that I no longer wondered why it was that Yanni always, unfailingly, had a cousin on every planet we docked at. Of course he did. The whole species breeds non-stop.

It was here that the soft booming of feet warned me I was being surrounded. I was on the alert at once, though I don't know why – being the cheapest place, the zoo was naturally very crowded. Maybe it was because Reiss had put me in a foul mood. Anyway, I looked up to find a hairless species on either side of me. The one on my left was a spithican male – a large one; they don't usually grow above five feet, but this one was nearly my height – and the one on my right was a lively little alfiori, again about my height, which made him a dwarf in his terms, and very golden of eye and bright in his scales. I could sense two more folk behind me, crowding close and breathing eagerly. Uh-huh! I thought. Something in the looks of the two I could see made it clear they were after some sex they didn't have to pay Reiss prices for.

'Fanatian, aren't you?' the little alfiori said.

I nodded. I told myself the poor fools knew just enough about fanatians to know that I was female but they hadn't a clue that I needed to come into season before I was capable of sex, and all I needed to do was to explain this fact, but I was in a foul mood anyway. I found I'd slitted my ears and bared my teeth.

The little alfiori edged closer. The spithican cast an appreciative look over my pelt. 'These human ancestors have tails just like I do,' he remarked, flourishing his tail-limb while he too edged closer. Since he was so big, it was a mighty limb. He laughed at my expression, frowning all over his upside-down features.

'But you have a hand on the end of your tail, Haxcrical,' said one of the ones behind me.

I widened my vision and swung round to see him. He was human. So was the other, younger one beside him, and both of them were staring at me greedily. That did it. Where humans are concerned, I admit to racial prejudice every time. 'Excuse me,' I said, trying to shoulder out from among them.

'No, wait!' said the younger human, and the alfiori laid paws on my arm, chirping, 'Wait! We have a proposition – !'

There was no way I could fight four of them. Besides, that expensive cube had informed that the penalties for affray were only just less than the penalties for littering. So I threw the cube at the humans, tore loose from the alfiori and ran, diving sideways to be out of reach of the spithican's tail-limb. To my dismay, they ran after me in a huddle, protesting that I had got them wrong. 'Get lost!' I told them, and put on speed.

My feet boomed as I sped away from that zoo between the rows of lettuce. I could hear three sets of their feet, booming too, getting fainter behind, but the fourth set was going boom-di-boom in a triple rhythm. That was that Haxcrical swinging along on his tail-limb and I could feel by the vibrations that he was gaining.

What I did next was stupid, I know, but my hackles were right up and I was only thinking in the present. I waited for the spithican round the next corner, beside an iron house and a guggling gutter full of lettuce. You learn a few things in space, and there are a lot of spithican spacers, because that tail-limb is so useful in free-fall. They don't keep all their brain in the same place like most species do. The primitive part – the cerebral cortex – is down between their legs and their tail-limb, and if you can grab that, you can disable a spithican. But you have to act fast and cautious, because that tail-limb is *strong*. So I crouched and I waited, and when he came round the corner, I grabbed. Come to think of it, I might have done the same with a human too, but his reaction would have been a bit different.

Haxcrical wasn't expecting me to attack, though he knew I was there. He came round the corner saying, 'Look, you must listen . . .' Then as I grabbed he managed to say 'No!' before he went into a convulsive reflex that freed his tail-limb to attack back. I had to clench his tail-hand in my teeth, or he'd have strangled me. Somehow, I managed to stand up under his weight. By that time all his limbs were stiff and his mouth was upturned in horror. His breathing was off, too. So was mine. He weighed more than me. I waited, staggering, as the footsteps of the other three boomed closer, intending to pitch their comrade at them as they rounded the corner.

But they never came round that corner. I heard them slide to a stop. One of them said, '*Now* what the hell do we do?' in a frantic way.

I was fairly frantic myself by then. Since I was going to have to drop the spithican anyway, I tipped him into the gutter on top of the lettuces. He made a tremendous *boing*. Splashes of water showered over me as I dropped to all fours for speed – a thing I haven't done for years – and pounded away. That reflex opens extra air-vents. It crossed my mind that I might actually be getting my money's worth of all the air I had paid Reiss for; but mostly I was wondering what the penalty was for throwing spithicans in the lettuce. Littering *and* affray. Years in jail, huge fines, execution – I ran flat out to get back inside *Bon Quin* before those four males could get to the Reiss gendarmerie.

I have dim memories of officials trying to bar my way at the entry grille – perhaps they were merely trying to charge me for coming back in, perhaps not – and I have a confused notion that I shouted several different lies as I streaked past. Half-way down the iron stairs, I saw the lift platform starting to move and jumped the rest of the way. Yanni Altunian was on the lift. I fell in a heap at his feet.

'Ah, Fingi!' he said. He was very pleased with himself,

far too pleased to notice any disorder of mine. 'Glad you caught this lift. We'll need a bit of reorganisation aboard. I've got ten stateroom passengers booked to Archangel.'

'Ten!' I gasped, climbing to my rear feet. Our so-called staterooms are one four-berth cabin and one two-berth.

'Six of them are together,' he said, 'with a small cargo that has to be kept at zero temperature. They pay extra for that of course.'

'But what about the other four – ?' I began. Then it dawned on me that the more useful I made myself to Yanni, the more likely he was to take my side when the Reiss gendarmerie came calling. I grumbled of course, because Yanni would expect me to, but the lift was only just entering the silo when I agreed obsequiously to find four cabin spaces we hadn't got.

Yanni watched *Bon Quin* slowly enlarging below, looking like somebody's exhaust discarded from a ground car, which had somehow strayed into a smooth grey drainpipe. 'And get Hold-B spun and aired up too,' he said. 'Maybe get it heated a bit. We're also taking a hundred pilgrims to Archangel.'

'A *hundred*!' I yelled, starting a peal of echoes. 'What in Murphy's name do they eat?'

'They bring their own food,' he said. 'My cousin who fixed the deal has a cousin who's letting me have fifty ex-navy microwaves cheap. They do their own cooking. They pay only a hundred credits each to travel steerage. This trip is going to make quite a profit.' He rubbed together his pink hands with their thin coating of dark hair. 'See to it, Fingi.'

I saw to it. I didn't dare not. It wasn't my place as second officer, but I'd have done more just then – anything – to keep on the right side of Yanni. Besides, our two third officers were spineless (literally) panchees, good astrogaters but not much else. I grabbed Shyan, the most senior crew-woman. She was a spithican and I wished she wasn't, but I appointed her chief stewardess anyway and we got to work doubling and trebling people into cabins. That was easy, but Hold-B promised to be a disaster. It is little more than a drum-shaped space. If a hundred average-sized pilgrims lay down to sleep on what would be the floor, they would probably fill it.

'Let's hope they'll all be small. Chemical toilets,' I said distractedly to Shyan. 'Five, and five showers. Sorbit on the floor – they'll get spacesick – and don't forget travel-bags. And cables hooked for running those damned microwaves. Use vents three and four. But knowing the captain, they'll probably all be huge alfiori like Thean. Fetch in some sleeping-bags – and they'll need somewhere to store this food they're supposed to bring. What's in the port-side mini-hold?'

'Captain's wine store,' said Shyan.

We took the wine out and stowed it in the spacesuit lockers. Some of the spacesuits had to go in the lifeboat bay. What the hell, there were hardly enough to go round the crew anyway, let alone a hundred pilgrims, but the more irregular Yanni wanted to be, the more it suited me. At this rate he wouldn't let a policeman near the ship.

As we stowed the last wine-crate, Shyan said, 'Are they really bringing food?' It was quite a question. 'If they don't happen to,' she continued, 'it's two weeks to Archangel. The survivors will sue.'

She had a point. Around the time fifty elderly microwaves arrived, my nerve broke and I called up a wholesaler and ordered a load of frozen food. Fingi being efficient again, Captain Altunian please note. Yanni's response was that if I felt that way I could pay for the food myself – but he added kindly that I could recoup by selling it to the pilgrims for twice as much. This, by my reckoning, made it slightly cheaper to chew gold bars. I paid for the food, wincing.

We were busy jury-rigging the port-side mini-hold as a freezer when the pilgrims came down on the freight-lift, huddled like cattle, and were decanted into Hold-B. They were all sorts, from alfiori and hulking neazers, to

humans and little lamprotes. It seemed that all races
went to Archangel to be mystical. Most of them had
sleeping-pads and cooking pots but, said the stately
neazer lady who was their spokeswoman, they had run
out of food. They had been waiting on Reiss for three
weeks for transport they could afford. By now, most of
them were flat broke, not surprisingly.

So there went the money I paid for the food, I thought.
I couldn't let them starve. 'What goes on at Archangel,
that you spend all this money to get there?' I asked her.

'The Choosing,' she answered reverently. 'We all hope
to be Chosen, so coming back is not a consideration, of
course. This hold is ten degrees too hot.'

I adjusted the heating and sped off to deal with our
first six cabin passengers, who were by then coming up
the ramp, carefully carrying their cargo in a tank with a
battery freezer attached. They were frail little sharp-faced
folk called milani, with an uncertain number of arms and
legs, and they threw everything out straight away by
demanding one cabin for the six of them. Well, at least
that meant I could have my own cabin back again. I was
sorting this out when the neazer lady appeared.

'The hold is now seven degrees too cold.'

I had to send Shyan to cope with the second batch of
cabin passengers while I dealt with that. By this time,
the pilgrims had settled down to some kind of religious
ceremony which seemed to involve squatting in rows,
chanting. As I picked my way back through them, the
head milani rushed to meet me, waving short arms in a
long robe.

'Cargo must not go where put! Come see, come see!'

I had ordered it put in the lifeboat bay, where it
could travel in a vacuum at the same température as space
outside. Since the milani was so upset, I went with him
(or maybe it) to the bay, where he (or perhaps she)
waved more short arms at the tank.

'Must not have vacuum. Is *alive*, see!'

I bent to see. The tank was transparent. It contained

some kind of stranded jelly – like see-through spaghetti – that appeared to be waving sluggishly about. 'So it is alive!' I said. 'What is it?'

'Is mela worms. Very precious. Must not die,' he, she, or it said earnestly. 'Cold keeps sleeping. Vacuum kill.'

I apologised. And wondered what to do with the stuff. Since Yanni's cousins had been busy both in Reiss and two worlds before that, we had two holds full and sealed and the other was Hold-B. I carted the tank to the port mini-hold and hitched it to the freezer there – with some difficulty. *Bon Quin* was now preparing to leave and being winched to the airlock of the silo. Hoping the stuff would not contaminate the pilgrims' food, or vice versa, I turned to hurry to the bridge.

And ran into the neazer lady. 'The hold is now three degrees too warm.'

Well, we're getting there, I thought. I had to get her back to the hold in sudden weightlessness, because by that time we had clanged our way clear of Reiss's lock, and push her in among all the other floating pilgrims. Then our thrust cut in and some of them fell on me. I got them strapped down. When I finally made my way to the bridge, I was feeling pretty aggrieved. Gravity was back and the frost-coated sphere of Reiss was three-quarters full in the viewports. I was glad to see the last of it.

The only person on the bridge was Thean, our massive alfiori first officer. 'Captain didn't want to wait around for fear of an inspection,' he said. 'I am fine here. You go and eat.'

I dodged down to the saloon, jubilantly. No one on Reiss could arrest me now and I was hungry. My jubilation and my hunger lasted until the moment I put my head through the door. Sitting calmly eating at the nearest table was the big spithican I'd thrown in the lettuce. With him were the little alfiori and the two humans. They all saw me. The alfiori glittered with embarrassment. The spithican stared upside-down sorrow and reproach.

I backed straight out again, with sweat gathering on my ears. 'You go and eat,' I told Thean. 'I'm changing watches with you.'

I sat that watch in a cold sweat of fear and embarrassment. Had the four of them followed me? Or had they already booked on *Bon Quin* when they came to the zoo and simply wanted to get to know one of the officers? Had they gone to the police? I certainly wasn't going to ask them. The computer told me that the humans were Anthony Nelles and his son Ian and that the alfiori had the princely name of Iqua't'snal Corra ar t'Fneshin. Thean confirmed that was a very good family when I asked him. The spithican was Haxcrical Sesbar. All were citizens of Archangel, returning home. Whoever they all were, I took my meals when they weren't around and made sure to keep out of their way.

Thirty-six hours out, with only another day before jump, two of the pilgrims' microwaves blew up and shorted the jury-rig to the port-side mini-hold. The neazer lady appeared, stately as ever.

'What is it?' I said. 'Too hot or too cold?'

'Officer Fingi,' she said, 'the hold is now full of peculiar fumes. Some of my pilgrims are behaving very *oddly*.'

She was right. The drum-shaped space was full of blue smoke and smelt of burning – but there was also another smell in the air, a sort of light musky fragrance that I couldn't place. A small lamprote pilgrim was rolling on the floor in front of me, twined around a mighty neazer. Another lamprote and an alfiori might have been trying to separate the two, although it was not at all clear they were not joining in. Beyond them in the fumes, two humans unmistakably copulated, just like Yanni's ancestors at the zoo.

While I gazed at this unmystical behaviour, the chief milani came rushing in. 'Come see, come see! The cold goes. The mela worms wake. Is most *unhappy* to lose them!'

'First see to *this*,' said the neazer lady.

'Is same *thing*!' the milani cried, dragging at my left leg. 'Come quickly! Oh do!'

Thinking of all my expensive food melting, I shouldered the neazer lady aside and raced for the mini-hold. To my relief, it was not that warm. There was white hoar frost on everything. But the small rise in temperature had been enough to wake the mela worms. The worms still left in the tank were all stiffly upright, prodding diligently and blindly at the lid. Tracks in the frost showed where at least half of them had shoved the lid up a crack and slithered out. After that I couldn't see where the hell they had gone, except that they were not in the mini-hold.

The milani wrung various hands. 'Is tragedy! They are needed for breeding. Now we all die! Must catch, must catch!'

I bellowed for Shyan to repair the freezer and put weights on the lid of the tank. 'What do you mean, you'll all die?' I shouted at the milani. 'Do you eat these worms or something?'

'No, *no*!' it said, truly shocked. 'They make mate. They catalyst for sex.'

It took it a while to explain. The milani have three sexes, it seems, all of which are needed simultaneously for mating. On their home planet this had never been any problem, but all their colonies showed a tendency to dwindle and die out, because it was not that common for these individuals to feel like sex at once. 'When one feel sexy, other two have headache,' the milani explained. 'Or just one have headache, same thing. Mystery is, on Melan all three always feel like. So we find out it mela worms make do. Now we rush these supply to Archangel where holy colony on last legs. You see?'

A two-sex system seems easier to me, but of course

no one can choose. Then I remembered the behaviour of the pilgrims. 'Do these worms have the same effect on non-milani too?'

The milani nodded eagerly, proudly. 'Make sexy all known races.'

'Murphy's balls!' I said. 'Come on – we have to tell the captain.'

When I was a young and innocent fanatian, just going into space, I had an image of how a space captain should be. Of course no captain ever lived up to it, and of all of them Yanni Altunian was probably furthest from my ideal, but there was a moment, when he was bawling me out for storing the mela worms so carelessly and ordering me to catch every single one, that I felt that here was a real captain at last. Like a real captain, he ordered both me and the milani not to breathe a word of this disaster to anyone else aboard. Then he called me back to whisper, 'Fingi, you save me just three of those worms and I'll pay for the freezer food. Deal?'

'Deal,' I said sadly, but with some relief.

'A breeding set,' he mused. 'I could retire on that. Mind you get them all before jump.'

I got two buckets, filled them with ice, and went to Hold-B, where the pilgrims were now having an orgy, by twos, threes and in bundles. Stepping among their rolling, humping bodies, I caught worm after worm. As I had conjectured, the worms were the cause of the odd, musky fragrance in there and luckily my ancestors hunted by smell. But there seemed to be thousands of the creatures.

The neazer lady came and draped a stately affectionate arm across my shoulders. 'You have found the root of the trouble?' she said anxiously.

I undraped her. 'Yes. You must have got the temperature just right for them in here.' At this, a thought struck me. On my way out, I turned the heat down to a brisk eight degrees. Then I hastened to the mini-hold with my two smoking, writhing buckets.

The human, Anthony Nelles, was coming along the corridor towards the hold with Haxcrical swinging along behind him. 'It *is* mela worms,' Nelles said to Haxcrical. I could see he was trying not to laugh. The spithican came up, gave me a strange look that I couldn't interpret either way up, and looked in the buckets. His mouth turned down broadly.

'You want us to help catch them?' he asked.

He didn't seem to bear me a grudge, but I still got this greedy feeling off both of them. 'Captain orders I have to catch all them personally,' I said. 'Thanks and good morning.'

They shrugged and went away up the passage. I went and dumped the worms back into their tank, where the cold made them curl up and hibernate almost instantly. I went back for more.

And so much for my bright idea. Though the orgy was going on as vigorously as before, there were suddenly almost no mela worms. I climbed over bodies for nearly an hour and only caught two. Obviously the temperature was now too low for them in there and they had left. But how? Where? The answer came when I caught a third by the tail as it wriggled into an air duct. They must have been all over the ship by then.

Thean's voice came over the intercom. 'Fingi! Urgent call to the bridge.'

Oh Murphy! I thought. As I dashed for the exit, the neazer lady once more came and draped herself around me. 'You must do something,' she said affectionately.

I pushed the buckets at her. 'So must you. Hold these and don't let anyone else touch them. Serve the cause.'

Yanni's voice was now roaring out of the speakers. 'Fingi! Bridge – AT ONCE!'

I went to all fours for speed. In the main passage I found myself having to hurdle a pair of spithicans with their tail-limbs entwined in that way – spithican sex looks erotic even to me. One of them was Shyan. The other seemed to be Haxcrical. Hmm, I thought as I bolted up the bridge ramp.

Thean and Yanni were both on the bridge. Thean was doing all the work. 'What happened to the thirds?' I asked.

Thean pointed a digit to a tangle of panchee limbs behind the aft couch. Yanni shouted, 'Fingi, I may kill you! I want sex with everything and Thean just sits there!'

Thean said, 'As I keep telling you, interspecies sex does not bother me, but I am heterosexual. And someone has to fly this ship. Fingi is female. Try her.'

'If that's what you got me up here for –' I began.

'I did *not!*' Yanni shouted. 'I got you here to show you what you have done. We shall have to abort jump. People will sue. I shall lose money. So *do* something, Fingi!'

Thean picked up a hose he had draped over the side of his couch and handed it to me. 'Hose him down,' he said. 'Then hose me. Then take over from him. Humans are not good at this.'

I did as he said, and then hosed the two third officers for good measure – which they appeared not to notice. The water came out scented with mela worm anyway. Yanni leapt up, anguished, dripping, looking more like his ancestors than ever. 'I shall have to go and screw something,' he announced. 'I resent this. But not *you*, Fingi,' he added venomously as he left. 'Even those worms will not possess me to mate with a teddy bear with a large furry navel!'

'You must think of some solution,' Thean said as I moved into the sopping pilot couch. 'Aborting jump adds up to a month to our journey time and our debts would be enormous. Are you all switched through? Good. I am off to Hold-B. There are some mighty attractive alfiori in there.'

He arose and left me alone with the instruments and the surging limbs behind the aft couch. 'Aren't you

finished yet?' I called to them. There was no answer. I
sat and wondered how I was supposed to get rid of the
mela worms and fly the ship too. I sat and resented
Yanni's last venomous remark. I am not in the least like
a bear and a fanatian has no navel . . . Wait a minute! I
looked down. I cursed. The mela worms had got to me
too. My sex organs were half-grown already. That was
bad news, since the nearest fanatian man I knew of
worked on a liner bound for Earth and the only way to
stop yourself going on heat is to go without food for a
week. Well, I could do that. I have before. But it always
puts me in a vile temper. I began to feel I would be better
off serving a prison sentence on Reiss. And none of it
was my *fault* anyway!

After about an hour, I got the glimmerings of an idea.
I paged Thean. No answer. So I tried Shyan and she did
answer. 'Where's Thean?' I asked.

'In Hold-B, along with almost everyone else,' she said.
'Busy.'

'The captain too?' I asked.

'He's in his cabin,' Shyan said. 'And anyone who goes
near gets pulled inside, so don't ask. I'm not going near
there.'

I hung up, despite an itchy little wish to ask her if she
was with Haxcrical still. I set the autopilot, praying to
Murphy and all gods that no crisis would happen that
the computer couldn't handle. Then I tore the two third
officers apart and threw them in front of the controls. I
told them I'd castrate them if they didn't stay there.

'Our sex organs are internal,' one of them answered
smugly.

'Not when you're in the act, they're not,' I said. 'So
behave.' And I went tearing off and pounded on the
door of the milani's cabin.

'You go away,' replied a muffled voice. 'We make
babies.'

'I will,' I yelled. 'Just tell me what temperature suits a
mela worm best. How hot or cold do they really like it?'

There were moans of annoyance, followed by a muffled consultation. Finally one of them called, 'Celsius twenty-two. Now go.'

Got it! I thought. Now it was only a question of which bit of the ship was the best place to set at twenty-two degrees. But before I could decide, I found my feet leaving the floor and that floor yawing about under me. I howled curses on those panchee thirds. They were going for null gravity sex now, it seemed. I set off back to the bridge as fast as I could go.

And gravity came back as I went. 'Could Officer Fingi please come to the bridge?' asked a polite voice I did not recognise.

What the *hell*? I thought, and got there on all fours at top speed.

I had to hurdle those two panchees at the top of the ramp. Someone had knocked both of them out. 'Which of you did that?' I demanded.

'I did,' said Haxcrical, 'with Ian's help. We felt they deserved it.'

He was calmly settling into the co-pilot's couch. Anthony Nelles was already all switched through on the main couch and his son seemed to be checking our course. 'Don't worry,' Ian said to me. 'We're qualified. We all work for Archangel Spacelines when we're not on search.'

I could see that they knew their business, but all the same – 'Don't mela worms have an effect on you or something?' I said suspiciously.

'Yes, but you are holding us fairly steady,' the little alfiori said. He was sitting on the aft couch calling up every communication *Bon Quin* had received since we left Reiss as far as I could see. He was on to early flight-path instructions by then, but as I looked his way he found what he was after. 'Come and look at this,' he said to me. 'Or did you know about it?'

I went and stared at an official request from the planet Reiss to Captain Altunian to hand me over to Interpol

on Archangel for extradition back to Reiss. Below that
was Yanni's prompt agreement to do it. 'No,' I said.
'Who reported me?'

'Someone in one of those houses, I think,' the alfiori
said. 'People were staring while we pulled Haxcrical
out.'

'They can't touch us,' Haxcrical said over his shoulder.
'We were on search and there's an interplanetary agreement about that. It's a pity you didn't stop to listen to
us.'

'Course seems adequate,' Anthony Nelles said to Ian,
and to me, 'It was a bit ironic – we'd given up on our
search and booked a passage home, and it had to be this
ship because we couldn't afford anything better. Reiss
about skinned us. But why don't you go with Corra and
catch mela worms and let him explain?'

'We thought our cabin was the best place to have at
twenty-two,' Ian said, 'as we're going to be up here until
after jump. I'll switch the rest of the ship to eight degrees
when you get there.'

This was all going a bit fast for me. I shambled off
with the little alfiori and fetched two more buckets of
ice, feeling like a moron. 'Why am I going with you?' I
said.

I'd meant it purely rhetorically, but he answered
seriously, 'Because we know you have an anti-human
prejudice and Haxcrical thinks you don't like him either.'
At this, I thought of the big spithican with some shame.
His mouth had been quite straight as I left the bridge –
spithican wistfulness. 'Yes, I know that was all a mistake,' Corra said.

'Look here,' I said in the doorway of their cabin, 'are
you telepathic or something?'

He laughed. 'Everyone is on Archangel. A bit. It's
useful in space. And of course the most useful of all is
when you have a team of interlocking telepaths – say
four – but that always takes a fifth person to act as
catalyst.'

He shut the cabin door. Ian clearly knew. By the time I'd got to the other end of the room, the first mela worm came wriggling down through the air vent. After that they came by hundreds.

'That's what search and Choosing is all about,' Corra said as he helped them into the buckets.

'I thought it was mystical,' I grunted. 'Those pilgrims –'

'You don't want to take any notice of that nonsense,' Corra said. 'The Choosing festival is purely practical. The four of us went looking because we thought we could make one of the top teams, given luck. But we're an odd mix. We'd almost given up hope of finding the person we needed and we were wandering round that zoo feeling really depressed, when we suddenly found we were meshing – properly, for the first time – and we all realised it was you. We went rushing up to you, all set to offer you a plum job in space and –' He shrugged with every scale on his body.

I thought about it as I popped what was probably the last worm into my bucket. 'Reiss?' I asked.

'Couldn't touch you if you were Chosen,' Corra said.

So they had me over a barrel and Yanni had let me down anyway.

'You want me as a sort of mental mela worm,' I said. Corra laughed. 'And sex had nothing to do with it?' I asked.

Corra let his golden eyes slide across my pelt. His scales glittered. 'That's up to you,' he said.

And I thought, Why not? He was beautiful. Haxcrical is my size, and neither Anthony nor Ian have hair on their hands.

'You have your mela worm,' I said.

THE CAT AND THE SLEEP COMPILER

CHRISTINA LAKE

CHRISTINA LAKE

Christina Lake's short fiction and articles have appeared in *Interzone* and a wide range of small press publications. A multilingual technical librariam, this is her first appearance in an original anthology.

EVERY NIGHT I used to put the cat outside the door and every morning I'd wake up to find him back inside the room again.

I didn't worry about this over much until the day Vicky came to visit, bringing along her extra-intensified, and therefore illegal, sleep-compiler.

'It's a French model, my dear. You do speak French, don't you?'

'No.'

'Oh,' she said, momentarily at a loss. 'It's just that it all works in French, you know.'

I pondered this surprising statement for a while. 'It must be because of you and Jean-Louis,' I concluded. 'It can't compile in a language you don't know, can it? I mean, it *is* your brain that's in charge.'

Vicky's skin tinged a delicate shade of pink, which, in fact, rather suited her. 'Jean-Louis. Oh. I hadn't thought of that.'

We went out for cocktails at Mandy's and sat behind the counter, passing comments on the dancers as if we'd never been on the sleaze-circuit ourselves. We even turned down two Bright Boys who wanted to take us off to a River Show, but that was only because Vicky can't stand men with moustaches.

The cat didn't greet us on our return. 'Out ratting,' I told Vicky. But really I knew he didn't approve of visitors. Just like old Eric.

'Say, let me use the compiler tonight and you can have a go tomorrow,' said Vicky.

I knew Vicky. As like as not she'd be gone tomorrow.

'I'll wake you up,' I said craftily. 'I don't mind waking you up in an hour or so.'

'You wouldn't!' She looked at me out of horrified pink eyes.

'Or we could plug in together, like we did in the old days.'

'No!' She shook her head violently.

Vicky had far more secrets than in the old days. I had secrets too, but she didn't know that.

'Toss for it then.' I flicked my credit card in the air. It had once been a joke in our crowd, *Toss cards for style*. I only did it because I knew Vicky would call 'Sig' for signature, and my brand new mastercard had no signature, only an identical thumb-print band on each side. 'Sig,' she called, jiggling her head and smiling because she was used to being lucky.

'Master,' I said, displaying the symbol and pocketing the card.

Vicky shrugged. 'You won't *believe* what this machine can do!' she enthused as if she'd been planning to let me win all along. 'You, lucky girl, are going to have the time of your life!'

Which, in a manner of speaking, I suppose I did.

I left her to mess up the bathroom, while I pottered around, getting ready for bed. I experimented with growing one side of my hair longer, decided it didn't suit me, punched in the cutting program, searched desperately for the scissor attachments (they were in the kitchen where I had left them after a rather interesting experiment with a dead mouse and the remains of a chocolate blancmange) and finally said my prayers. Prayers? The good-night prayer for safe passage and the good luck prayer for, well, good luck – at heart I am a very superstitious woman.

All this time, the sleep compiler was quietly singing

in the corner, chanting soothing lullabies as if it thought I were still a child. I checked one last time that the cat really wasn't in the room – I knew I'd catch him one day – then stepped into bed, sinking to the centre and wrapping myself round in layers of soft Supermix Mohair. And prepared to abandon my mind to the care of the sleep compiler.

1 . . . 2 . . . 3 . . . 4 . . . My rhythms were slowing down, my thoughts draining away. Each time there was a longer and emptier space between one click of the compiler, one breath of my body, and the next. Until I was drifting alone in the middle of a huge grey plain, stretching to eternity.

Click. The last breath.

Everything was starting to change, I was in a street market and everybody was (hell, they *were!*) speaking French, or a mixture of French and the dockside Gujarati I'd known as a child.

'Stand back!' I told them. (In English? Whatever, they seemed to understand.) 'This last trick is dangerous!'

I lit the slow flame and began to juggle, catching the fire hoop each time on the diminishing area of unlit curve, until the whole circle was almost aflame; and then I threw it extra high, and positioned myself underneath as it fell, straight and true, over my artistically up-stretched arms, down past my waist, to land in a perfect circle of fire at my feet. Triumphantly holding the three recovered juggling skittles, I skipped out of the circle and bowed.

The applause was tumultuous. 'Bravo!' they shouted wildly. 'Bravo, little lady!'

A richly-dressed man with a black beard came forward. 'Tomorrow, you will show your tricks at the Elysée. I work for the president, and he is always looking for talented new performers to entertain his ministers and the rest of his noble court.'

'But I am only a poor, simple country girl! The honour you suggest is too great.'

'No, you must, you must,' urged the crowd.

Well, I was just about to give in to them gracefully, when it happened. Eric shouldered his way through the crowd, and shoved me to one side. 'My good people, don't let this woman near your president. She is evil. She is a witch.'

'Oh, push off, Eric!' I said furiously.

'See how she snarls and spits. You have been basely deceived.'

The crowd showed signs of turning nasty. Which surprised me. They should have believed me, not him. Of course, I ought to have realised straight away that Eric had no business being in my dream. But one never knows what psychological quirks may bring back old enemies. Or old lovers.

Now, as the crowd began to howl and boo, I realised something was wrong. Someone else's mind was taking control of the sleep compiler.

Eric's mind.

I concentrated furiously, and one by one the people moved away. I was so angry, I made some of them slip over in the mud. Face downwards.

Eventually, only black-beard remained, and of course, Eric, who was smirking outrageously. But then, after all I had done to him, this was to be expected.

The black-bearded man turned to me, and announced portentously, 'You, witch, are under arrest.'

'Indeed?' I smiled benevolently at Eric. 'All right, my little tom cat, have your fun. Give me a few nightmares. But remember, in the morning, it'll be me in control again, and there'll be nothing you can do about it, you flea-bitten fur-bag!'

'Don't be too sure, mistress mine,' he replied mockingly. 'In *my* version of this dream, they *burn* witches.'

'Nothing that happens here can hurt me in reality,' I scoffed. I thought he was just trying to scare me. I'd read somewhere that the worst harm a sleep compiler could do was make you pregnant, and that was only if you were stupid enough to use it in the same room as an unsterilised man.

'Can't it? Why do you think this model's illegal?'

I shrugged my shoulders. Governments are notorious spoilsports.

'Illegal notices aren't just posted to give you and your addled-brain friends some extra thrills, you know. They're there for a reason. Like because a thing's dangerous. With this type of compiler, what happens here happens for real.'

I began to wonder if Eric was telling the truth. It was the type of detail Vicky *would* forget to mention.

'I'm not a witch,' I told black-beard winningly, just to be on the safe side.

'Then why,' he said self-importantly, 'are you being followed by your familiar?'

I looked down and realised that Eric had turned back into a cat. Of all the nerve! 'Because cats like me, okay?' No, that didn't look as if it was going to be enough. Eric was still in charge. Black-beard clamped his hand viciously on my arm and dragged me away.

They threw me into a cell. Normally I would have quite enjoyed that; there's often a scene or two of degradation in my fantasies. But I'd have been in the cell with a gorgeous princess or something, not Eric. And one of the guards would have taken pity on me and helped us escape. This time all I could get out of the guards was one measly cushion, and that was probably only a concession from Eric. I just couldn't understand why he had more control over events than me. After all he'd never had the upper hand before.

He, it was obvious, was having a great time. Playing the affectionate pet, the way he did when he wanted some food at home. Not that that was what he was after this time. He had just gorged himself nauseatingly on a big fat rat. Besides, I had no food to give him.

No, he was doing it for one reason only: to annoy me.

'You wouldn't really get me killed,' I told him, stroking his soft black fur.

He playfully nipped at my finger.

'But why? You're much happier as a cat, you know you are.'

His purrs thundered incomprehensibly through his body. I wished he would change back to a human and talk to me. But then, he'd probably only be unpleasant, which, when it came down to it, was why I had had him turned into a cat in the first place.

They came for me a few hours later. I was led away by two men in black hoods – Eric's imagination was definitely tending towards the macabre – to a mock-medieval courtroom. There I was forced to my knees in front of a man in a purple robe. I suppose he was meant to be a king or something since he was sitting in a fancy chair, but he didn't seem very concerned with the proceedings and ignored me to read what looked like one of those old horror comics Eric used to collect. A counsellor in a white wig stepped forward and let forth a torrent of picturesque and baffling sounds in High French. Then they let me speak. One of the men in the black hoods acted as an interpreter. Well, that is to say, he translated all my words into French, but he didn't translate any of theirs back to English. All the time, Eric sat at my feet, smugly washing himself.

Then it clicked at last. He could understand every word they said. And more to the point, it was his knowledge of French that was giving him the edge over me in controlling the machine.

After I'd worked that out, the trial seemed more of a joke than ever, and I couldn't even be bothered to try on the hysterics when they dragged me away to another cell. The last I saw of Eric, he had sprung up to sit in the judge's lap, and was being stroked and petted.

I had always wondered about Eric's fantasies.

They built the pyre within view of my little barred window. It looked just like those pyramid shaped mounds you get in the Joan of Arc films. (I had seen the whole series as a child. Joan only gets burned in one. In the rest she escapes in various disguises. Or was that the Scarlet Pimpernel?) I'd always wanted to be burned at the stake, but not for real.

They blindfolded me, and walked me out into the yard.

Someone took my arm. Eric. 'It's a lovely day for a burning,' he said pleasantly. 'What a pity you can't see it.'

'Blindfolds are for firing squads,' I told him acidly. Trust Eric to get his historical details wrong.

'A firing squad would be much too merciful. Do you know what your big mistake was, my dearest? It was writing in the death clause.'

I'd already figured that out. The thought that Eric would survive me, as a man, was definitely galling. The trouble is I'm just far too indulgent to my ex-lovers. You see, when I agreed the contract, I told the cat engineering people he could return to human form if I died before him. But it had never occurred to me that Eric would even find out about the death clause, let alone try to kill me because of it.

'It was your indifference to detail that let you down as usual,' Eric remarked. 'You paid to make me a cat, so I'm a cat. But only for as long as you say so. And once your pretty little mind ceases to work, my dear, I'll be a man again. Not that it's so bad being a cat – I learn to get my own way, don't I? How else did you think I got back into your room every night, my dear?'

'I wondered,' I said, though I was wondering more if I could possibly influence any of the guards to help me escape. 'But cats, they're such ingenious creatures, when all's said and done, and you're such a clever cat, Eric.'

'You ought to keep your room locked,' was all he replied. I most certainly would, once I got back. But Eric obviously didn't think I *would* get back.

He led me up on to the pyre, positioning me lovingly by the stake, and even tying the knots himself.

'Goodbye, my dear,' he declared melodramatically. 'I love you still, but I love revenge more!'

I heard the characteristic spitting noise of an igniter at work (probably he had paraffin cubes in there too, couldn't he at least do it properly?) and the wood began to crackle like a bad sound effect. I could still hope, at first, that he was only trying to frighten me, but then I felt the heat creeping up my legs. What was it I had wanted to know about being burned alive? Which part of the body caught first? Whether you passed out from the fumes or the burning? For some reason, I couldn't take much interest in these questions any more. My head was heavy, and I longed to lift my feet off the ground. I had a nasty feeling that Eric had not been lying and it was all going to be horribly, horribly real.

Then I heard Vicky's gorgeous husky voice, coming to me from somewhere near my right ear.

'I'm terribly sorry, darling, but I just *couldn't* sleep.'

I'd never loved Vicky so much in all my life. In fact I'd never loved her at all until then.

'Oh Vicky, darling, you turned it off,' I cried. 'You wonderful, clever girl!'

Eric was hissing at her from the far corner where he'd been hiding. I scrambled out of bed and began kissing and hugging Vicky. Then I fell down to the floor in pain. My feet were a violent, burning red.

After that night, I was careful to find the cat and lock him away in the decontam-chamber before I went to bed. It meant I never did discover what shape he became while I was sleeping – cat, human or a cross between the two – but I didn't really care. Just so long as he stayed out of my room.

Poor old Eric. But as I've always maintained, cats have a much better life than humans.

THE GROWING PLACE

SIMON OUNSLEY

SIMON OUNSLEY

Simon Ounsley is co-editor of *Interzone*, and was a runner-up in the Gollancz/*Sunday Times* SF writers' competition. His story, *Adam Found*, was reprinted in *Interzone* to great acclaim, and has since been translated into several languages. A civil engineer by profession, he writes and edits in his spare time.

'LAST NIGHT,' SAID Gorse, 'I dreamed that the train was running through a forest. Wild creatures were prowling by the line and I thought I saw human faces peering out of the undergrowth.'

'It's like air rushing into a vacuum,' Lambda replied, using the break in their game to apply lipstick. Heavy bangles clattered on the thin wrist. 'If you stare at a red wall for a long time, you will see the complementary colour green when you look away. It is only natural for your unconscious brain to populate this desert of ours with teeming life-forms.'

Gorse stared out of the train window at the wasteland of sand passing by them – a view without feature except for the dividing line of the horizon, a single event in an empty landscape.

'You think it is natural, then, to have such dreams?' Gorse turned towards Lambda, feeling, not for the first time, that one could swim down into those large brown eyes set in the pale face across the table. Forget the game. Forget even the journey. Simply swim down into some kind of oblivion.

'I remember one of my dorm-mates,' said Lambda. 'When I was thirteen. Prime was a joker, always messing around and finding ways for us to have fun. Very popular with everyone' – a smile – 'especially me.'

Lambda looked down at the game-pieces on the table,

then uncertainly back again, suddenly regretting, perhaps, having started the story.

'Please go on,' said Gorse.

'One day we learned that Prime was to be sent away. A shortage of labour in another part of the principality. They took away someone from every dorm. And Prime was to be our . . . sacrifice.'

'A sacrifice to common prosperity,' said Gorse, speaking dully, without emotion.

'That's right. We were proud, of course, that our dormitory was able to help. But I have to say that I missed Prime. I kept hearing that voice in the night, imagined that familiar laugh in the general hubbub of conversation. But Prime was no longer there of course.'

'Your mind was filling in the vacuum.'

Lambda hardly seemed to hear, just stared out of the window as though there was something to be seen there.

'I would hold conversations with the ghost. Tell it all my hopes and fears. All my longings.'

Gorse felt an inexplicable twinge of excitement. Longings! What a strange word . . .

'And what did you long for?'

Lambda said nothing for a while, then touched one of the gaming pieces, moving it to threaten Gorse's defences on the fifth tower.

'I really don't know . . . Pre-eminence at meta-ludo perhaps.'

Gorse saw that the move had been a mistake and that Lambda's own defences might be breached.

Occasionally, the train would stop by a small shack selling refreshments and the pilgrims were able to wander around for a while, stretching their legs.

None would go far from the train. They had not, after all, come to see the desert, and few wished to look at it for long. They had come to be carried through it in the baroque splendour of the train. They wandered round the train now in their fine clothes and their make-up, like moths in a great darkness, flapping their ornate wings in the light of a single flame.

'Do you think that our journey will change you?' Gorse asked, blowing on a cup of mulled wine as they walked.

'I didn't come seeking change,' said Lambda, 'so much as affirmation. Alone, it's easy to lose sight of a proper perspective on life. It can seem aimless and without meaning.'

'Ah, so you came seeking meaning?'

'I came to *rediscover* meaning. I came to remind myself of the pattern of life. Though perhaps it is equally true to say that I came from a sense of tradition and duty. Like the others on the train, I have spent my life working hard. Now, like them, I have earned enough money to come back and see where it all began. This journey is something one *does*, after all.'

'You make it sound like a bodily function.'

Lambda smiled. 'Perhaps it is – the third most important bodily function, the one between birth and death.'

'I keep seeing things out in the wilderness.'

Lambda turned to follow Gorse's gaze. 'I see nothing but a heat-haze. Are your dreams taking over the daytime too?'

'It's funny, but sometimes I feel like they always have done.'

'So why are *you* making the journey? To wake up?'

'I am making the journey because it is the only place I have to go. Because I have done everything I set out to do. Now I have to look for something else.'

Lambda began to laugh.

'You are going back to the beginning and starting again.'

'Perhaps it is time for another game of meta-ludo,' said Gorse, 'another entertainment.'

That night, they dined on chicken in a rich sauce, with fresh vegetables and a bottle of sharp white wine. The rich pilgrims filled their journey with such luxuries.

There were recitals by famous musicians in the concert car, previews of the latest films in the cinema, and all the splendour which the best designers and upholsterers could devise in the day and dormitory carriages. Gorse and Lambda sat on plush fabric as they played their games, fingering pieces made of carved wood set with jewels.

The tour operators had filled the train with every kind of sensory stimulation, to compensate, Lambda had speculated, for the featureless view from the windows.

'And are you enjoying your trip?' asked Lambda, as they relaxed after the meal, sipping liqueurs.

'I am enjoying the rest,' said Gorse. 'It has been a busy fifty years. There has been so much to do, and so little reason to stop doing it.'

'But you could have taken a holiday elsewhere if you simply wanted to rest.'

'I would never have set out on a holiday simply to rest. It would not be worth the bother. It would be like having to make complicated arrangements in order to sit down. But now I am here, now I am enjoying the rest . . . and I am also enjoying the company.'

Lambda smiled.

'It is nice of you to say that. Yes – it has been a happy circumstance, meeting you here. I had thought it might be a lonely journey, this . . . going back.'

Gorse stared down at the glass. What to say, now that the conversation had taken such a turn? How far was it possible to be honest?

'These last few days have been . . . some of the happiest of my life.'

Lambda did not seem offended by such boldness. 'I am pleased. You are impressed then, by the standard of my meta-ludo?'

'More than that. I am impressed by your conversation. By your style, your use of clothes and make-up . . .'

'Now you are going too far with your compliments,' said Lambda. 'I have always liked to think I had a good taste in clothes. But if you carry on like this and my head grows too big, I will not be able to get into them.'

'I am not trying to give you compliments,' said Gorse. 'I am trying to explain. I told you I came on this journey to look for something else, something new. Well, I am confused and unsure, but I think I have found something . . .'

'I have found something too. I have found that too much wine makes me sleepy. I really must go to bed.'

'I have offended you.'

'Don't be stupid.' Lambda stood up and reached over and squeezed Gorse's hand. 'I will see you tomorrow.'

There were dreams again that night.

Gorse wandered the corridors of a deserted train, staring out into a night full of forest, where animals shrieked and howled and strange shapes emerged from moonlit pools. Shadowy figures ran beside the train, shaking long spears. And out of the undergrowth came Lambda, naked, blowing kisses from bloated lips . . .

And there was another dream, a new one.

'The train arrived at the terminus,' Gorse explained, as Lambda sat and thought about the next move, 'and we all walked down to see the Growing Place.'

'You are trying to disturb my concentration.'

'No, please. You have to listen. It's important.'

'More important than meta-ludo? Now you *do* surprise me . . .'

'It wasn't there.'

'What wasn't there?'

'The Growing Place. There was just a swamp, and a few mangroves . . .'

Lambda began laughing. 'And this fantasy is supposed to be important?'

'But we all looked around at each other and we realised that it never had been there. And everyone looked sad and began to walk back to the train. In twos, holding hands. I looked round for you but you weren't there. And I suddenly realised that I was getting old and I was alone. And there was no one in the world who would ever speak to me again.'

'All right, I've stopped laughing. That's a strange and sad dream. But it's *only* a dream. You really shouldn't let it upset you.'

'But I woke up. And I was still sure that it was true.'

Later that day, Gorse began to drink, losing concentration and conceding many games of meta-ludo to Lambda. Eventually, they grew tired of the uneven games and Lambda started reading a book. Gorse moped a while then wandered off to attend a string quartet recital but fell asleep during the performance, disturbing the players with snores.

At dinner that night, Gorse was the object of many black glances. Lambda, fortunately, found the story amusing.

'And did you dream while you snored?'

'Not at all – it was wonderful.'

'Then in future you must stay awake at night, and sleep during the day in the concert car.'

'We arrive at the Growing Place tomorrow. Perhaps, after that, the dreams will stop anyway.'

'Ah, so you now believe that our destination exists after all?'

'I am giving it the benefit of the doubt. Perhaps it is the wine but I am filled with a certain optimism. And I prefer to think of the Growing Place as our point of departure.'

'So it was, once.'

'And could be again, perhaps. Our point of departure on a new beginning, a new life . . .'

'Perhaps we are not so far apart in our hopes for the future.'

'Oh no?'

'I hope for affirmation. A renewed belief and understanding. That is a new life, of a sort. Perhaps we can drink to this new life of ours.'

The glasses clinked across the table, and both drank deeply of their wine. But Gorse looked out of the window and saw a darkening landscape of forest.

'I shall drink too much tonight,' said Gorse quietly, too quietly for Lambda to hear. 'I shall drink to ward off my thoughts of Lambda. I shall drink to ward off the dreams.'

But the dreams came anyway. When it was morning and the train had reached the terminus, Gorse was still in the grip of their illusions. Lambda knocked on the dormitory door and tried to impart a sense of urgency but Gorse just sat inside and shouted out: 'There's no point – it won't be there. There is no Growing Place.'

'Look out of the window,' said Lambda. 'If there's no Growing Place, then look out of the window and explain what you see.'

So Gorse went across to the window and looked up and saw the ray which came out of the sky: a translucent red band teeming with particles which seemed to move, aimlessly but frenziedly, like a viral culture under a microscope, like people in a city, heading for the Growing Place in the valley below the railway.

'There you are,' said Lambda, 'the Ray Which Comes From God.'

They had seen photographs, of course, but those were no preparation for the splendour of the real thing.

'So,' said Gorse, peering up at the sky with a face like a child's. 'That is it. That is how we came out of the sky.'

Gorse and Lambda were the last of the stragglers from the train to descend to the Growing Place. When they arrived, their fellow travellers were standing in a group on the side of the valley, clustered together for mutual support, perhaps in case they should be overcome by the wonder of the place.

Gorse and Lambda stood a little apart, gazing up at the ray as it emerged from a point in the sky above, growing in amplitude as it descended to the valley floor and immersed their surroundings in a glow like a furnace.

The babies were growing in the mud on the bottom of the valley, out of the goodness of the soil and the Ray Which Comes From God. They were growing for as far away as the eye could see. 'How many?' Gorse wondered. 'Ten thousand babies? A hundred thousand?' They were at all stages of development. Some seemed like little more than pale slugs, rooting about in the brown mud. Others were waving their limbs around, some of them tugging at their cords and crying to be set free. The midwives moved among them with scissors, looking for those who were ripe for birth.

A few yards away from them, they saw a child that was ready. The midwife came through the mud and cut the cord, picking up the struggling child and wrapping it in a blanket.

'I'm taking it for washing,' the midwife explained to the onlookers. 'Then registration and its first dormitory.'

The remains of the cord were sticking out of the ground, like a stalk of wheat.

'I never realised . . .' said Gorse. 'I never realised it would be anything like this.'

Lambda was gazing about with open mouth, with eyes full of tears. 'It's wonderful . . . wonderful.'

But Gorse felt alone and afraid, dwarfed by the size of the Growing Place, scared for the embryos, crying as they grew, filling the valley with their sobbing. The midwives seemed to move among them like grim reapers, pouncing on ripeness and plucking it from the soil.

Where was the new beginning? Where was the 'something new'? There was nothing to be gained from this place, nothing but a sense of loneliness and misery. What had been the point of all the days of travel?

Gorse stared into Lambda's eyes, thinking of the bond

that had grown between them, having come so far together to see the Growing Place. From the answering stare, Lambda seemed to feel the same way. They moved together, as though through a great distance, and slowly, uncertainly, embraced each other, pressing hard, sharing the strengths of their differing emotions.

'This is the way ahead,' thought Gorse, feeling warmth displace the loneliness at last. 'This is the new beginning I looked for.' Their arms were locked around each other's bodies, their legs pressed together. Gorse wanted to be closer still, wanted to fall into Lambda, into some kind of oblivion.

'I want you,' said Gorse.

Lambda's embrace seemed to falter.

'Let's share each other,' said Gorse. 'This place has made me feel so alone.'

Lambda pulled away and stared into Gorse's eyes, trying to understand. 'We can go back to the train if you like. We're here all day. We can get a coffee and come back later.'

'That's not what I meant.'

Lambda was uncomprehending, head shaking in bewilderment. 'What *do* you mean?'

Gorse shrugged and slumped to the ground, skirt splashing in the mud, like an overgrown child ripe for plucking. 'I don't know.'

Gorse reached down uncertainly and felt beneath the skirt, searching for something warm, something with which to be close to Lambda. But there was nothing there of course: just the smooth firm flesh, the same as Lambda would have, the same as the babies, the same as everyone.

Lambda stood and stared in wonder at the ray, at the valley, at the crouching figure in the mud.

'This is a dream,' said Gorse. 'It isn't this way.'

'I'll see you back at the train,' said Lambda, and turned and walked away up the side of the valley.

Gorse bent down into the mud, caught between

dreams and reality, wanting something that did not exist in the world: a lonely figure kneeling in the soil of the great valley, bathed in the light of The Ray That Comes From God.

ACKNOWLEDGEMENTS

MORE SCIENCE FICTION AVAILABLE FROM NEW ENGLISH LIBRARY

ALAN DEAN FOSTER

☐	48601 X	Into the Out of	£3.50
☐	51571 0	Flinx in Flux	£3.99

Ed. JOHN CLUTE, DAVID PRINGLE & SIMON OUNSLEY

☐	42853 2	Interzone: The Second Anthology	£2.95

MICHAEL MOORCOCK

☐	05603 1	The War Hound and the World's Pain	£2.99
☐	50104 3	The Distant Suns	£2.99

JACK VANCE

☐	49733 X	Araminta Station	£3.50

All these books are available at your local bookshop or newsagent, or can be ordered direct from the publisher. Just tick the titles you want and fill in the form below.

Prices and availability subject to change without notice.

Hodder and Stoughton Paperbacks, P.O. Box 11, Falmouth, Cornwall.

Please send cheque or postal order, and allow the following for postage and packing:

U.K. – 55p for one book, plus 22p for the second book, and 14p for each additional book ordered up to a £1.75 maximum.

B.F.P.O. and EIRE – 55p for the first book, plus 22p for the second book, and 14p per copy for the next 7 books, 8p per book thereafter.

OTHER OVERSEAS CUSTOMERS – £1.00 for the first book, plus 25p per copy for each additional book.

Name ....

Address ....

....